SUNDAY
AT
SIX

BOOKS BY ELIZABETH CORBETT

SUNDAY AT SIX

A Novel

by

ELIZABETH CORBETT

HAWTHORN BOOKS,INC.,PUBLISHERS

NEW YORK

SUNDAY AT SIX

1 2 3 4 5 6 7 8 9 10

Design: Delia Tedoff

To Jason Smith
and
John Ross

CONTENTS

Book I

MORNING

❦ 1 ❦

DURING THOSE FIRST tender years Charlotte Emerson was, for so much of the time, a little girl alone among grownups. Her sister Agnes was already in her teens when Charlotte was born. At first a little resentful when she was shoved out of her position as an only child, Agnes soon became fond of the new baby; but a little sister occupied a very small position in the whirl of her madcap world. Paul Emerson was delighted to be a father again, and sharply on the defensive when people tried to commiserate with him because the newcomer wasn't a son. His lovely Inez was not the hovering type to begin with, and she saw no sense in allowing herself to become one of those mothers who are taken for granted.

The Emersons lived in the thriving Midwestern city of Saylesboro. Paul owned a large factory and also had other business interests. The country was prosperous and at peace; it was an age of expanding industrialism. A man like Paul Emerson could make money, spend money, save money, and enjoy all three processes.

The Emerson house stood quite apart from its neighbors. Not too far from downtown, it had the wide waters of one of the Great Lakes at its back, side streets to right and left, and across the avenue another house just as large and even more pretentious, though it did not have the advantage of a lake view.

Lovely young Inez Carleton hadn't married Paul Emerson for his money, of course. Still, she didn't find it any

3

drawback, and the mistress of an establishment such as his had a considerable responsibility. Inez sometimes sighed and shook her head, reported to Paul some difficulty with servants, complained about tradesmen, insisted that no man could ever understand what a terrific chore housekeeping was. Paul sympathized at first. Later on he only half listened. He never stooped to remark that she would have found it much worse if she had had to do the housework herself.

Inez did not have too much trouble with her servants. The Emersons paid top wages. The food and quarters were excellent, and the work not too hard. In a house the size of this, indeed, the servants spent much of their time waiting on one another. Besides, Mrs. Emerson had a nice little trick of consulting opinions instead of giving orders.

Almost always it was the nurse who took care of small Charlotte, but Mamma would come in sometimes to decide which frock the little girl should wear, or to rearrange things in the nursery, or to bestow a new toy or picture book. Almost always, too, it was the nurse who read Charlotte a fairy story at bedtime or taught her an age-old rhyme. Just often enough, Mamma would come in to play pat-a-cake with her or read aloud. The very rarity of these occasions made them a special treat.

Mamma read aloud very well. Mostly she stuck to the old standbys. Sometimes, however, she would make a change, or she would remark, "This used to be a favorite of Agnes's." That always made Charlotte feel closer to Big Sister than when Agnes herself tousled Charlotte's hair or showed her off to the contemporaries who might make a brief fuss over her or might think it was funny to tease the baby sister.

Charlotte was shown off to Mamma's women friends whenever they came to the house to drink tea or eat luncheon. Much more exciting, she was exhibited when Mamma and Papa set off together to one of their mysterious gaieties. If the party was right here in Papa and Mamma's own house, that made things very much better. The little girl stayed downstairs longer and heard more of that interchange which went on among the grown people.

She looked like such a little doll, they said. Almost as soon as she could walk and talk, Mamma taught her to curtsy to guests when they took her tiny soft hand in their big ones. She curtsied so prettily. She was so wide-eyed and serious, with the duties of hospitality thus early epitomized in her small person. She was there to be seen and admired. It never seemed to occur to the great gabies that she was taking in everything that went on.

She went over and over so many things when she was back in her pretty, quiet nursery. She tried them sometimes on her nurse, who either ignored them or told her nice little girls didn't say such things. That was all that was needed to complete Charlotte's private enjoyment. Nice little girls didn't say such things? But did she have to be a nice little girl? The way to pass for a nice little girl was just not to get found out.

The sayings were innocent enough in themselves. "Hello there." Then, with a change of voice, "Hello yourself." "You don't look a day older." "Where have you been keeping yourself lately?" "You know how those things go."

Charlotte developed a repertory. Presently she reached the stage where she had to act these things out. She would slide from her bed and repeat the drollery over and over.

If there was light enough in the room, she would act it out in front of the mirror. Once or twice the nurse caught her and demanded what she was doing.

"Nothing," Charlotte would reply innocently.

How could a little girl explain a thing like that to anybody? And why bother to try? You had to have something to keep to yourself.

At a big evening party she acquired something new—she heard a fascinating new word, and one she couldn't quite pronounce. It had to do with somebody's face, and the closest Charlotte could come to it was "foe-me-yoe." Imperfect though it was, she stowed it away for future reference. The saying was *familiar* to Charlotte long before she learned what the word was which had puzzled her.

The small person was making notes on this great sphere which she had entered so recently. She was inverting it to make a little world of her own.

In both worlds Christmas was the most exciting season of the year. In Saylesboro there was always plenty of snow by that time. Snow, which made everything so strangely beautiful, and left the air smelling so pure and sweet. Snow, which was such fun to play in. Charlotte would be taken for rides on her sled now. On Saturdays and Sundays she and Agnes would be taken for a ride with Papa and Mamma in the big sleigh which nobody but Papa was ever allowed to drive. Santa Claus's sleigh must be even bigger than this, because he had to pack all those presents in it. But of course Santa Claus had eight reindeer to pull his load; Papa had only a team of carriage horses, sometimes the bays, sometimes the grays, sometimes the big blacks with the flashing eyes.

On Christmas Eve Mamma would read aloud to her that wonderful poem about "The Night before Christmas." Charlotte knew it by heart, but somehow it always seemed as fresh as snow that had just fallen. Then she would hang up her stocking, and resolve to stay awake long enough to catch Santa Claus in the act of filling it. Last year she had failed to do so, but this time it was going to be different.

Christmas was the best. Little children all over Saylesboro and even way out beyond that shared it. So did the grown people. Wasn't it "Merry Christmas to *all*"?

But there was also something very special about your birthday. Presents then too, and a big beautiful cake with candles on it for the birthday child to blow out. Everybody kissing you the right number of times "and one to grow on," and the number of your new age counted on your fingers.

The early birthday parties had been strictly family occasions, and the little girl couldn't remember much about them: just a sparkling light which went out suddenly, and a sweet taste, and a sense of being very important. But the year that Charlotte turned four, Mamma decided that the time had come for her to give a real party.

The guests were sons and daughters of friends of Mamma's. Mamma had hesitated about asking boys; but she knew only four little girls of suitable age, and after all Charlotte might as well get used to associating with boys. Five of them were presently scheduled; that made the numbers come out even.

It turned out to be a brilliant August afternoon, hot but with a little breeze off the lake. Charlotte had a brand new white dress for the occasion, and in her hair a big blue bow to match her sash. Nursie stood by to help with the children's bonnets and caps; the second maid was there ready to take charge of the gifts as they were handed in.

The occasion went to Charlotte's head. When the third prospective donor was slow about coming across, she demanded, "Where's my present?" Mamma looked horrified, but the little girl's mother laughed and said, "Just like a child!" And to be sure it was a little boy who demanded, "When do we eat?" and another little boy who, without allowing time to light the candles, much less blow them out, inquired, "When do we cut the cake?"

For the great ceremony with the cake Papa and Agnes were on hand, too. Charlotte was instructed to close her eyes and make a wish before she blew out the candles. Sure enough, she blew them all out with the first breath. That meant that her wish would come true. In her excitement she forgot what the wish was. But perhaps that didn't make too much difference. It is always bad luck to tell what you have wished.

When the last guest left, Charlotte stood on the lawn looking wistfully after him. She did not realize that both her parents were watching her and Mamma's smiles were close to tears. It was Papa, however, who picked her up and whispered, "Never watch anybody out of sight, dear. That makes things seem just too sad."

He carried her into the house, and she sat on his knee while she told him all about the party. "The best party anybody ever had," she wound up.

"The best party until the next one," he said softly.

But Charlotte didn't want to think that far ahead. The next party, like next Christmas, was too awfully distant.

Next August was indeed a great distance away. But what Charlotte, with the inexperience of her years, had failed to reckon with was other people's parties. Mrs. Emerson had put nine mothers under a social obligation. People in Saylesboro did not remain indebted to the Emersons. It just wasn't done.

So now small Charlotte became a guest. She would remember to curtsy to the birthday child's mother, to wish

him or her a happy birthday, to present her carefully
wrapped package. It was often a large box of candy. Charlotte's father had a charge account at a leading confectioner's; and when you didn't know what a child's taste in
toys or picture books was, you could always count on his
greed.

There was another great change in Charlotte's life that
fall. Her mother took her to her first matinee.

For a minute or two the whole thing bewildered her. All
these people filing in and taking seats facing a great big
picture! She and her mother sat in a little enclosure at one
side. There were people a little below them, people on two
floors above them. A lot of men in an enclosure below the
big picture were making music together. Some of Mamma's friends were there, too. They spoke and waved; but in
this strange place and this queer light they didn't look like
themselves.

Then the big picture went out of sight, and people behind where it had been began to talk and move about.
Everybody around the Emersons watched and listened. In
a few minutes it came over Charlotte that this was a story
telling itself.

She sat entranced, living in the story. Nothing else mattered or even existed. She lost track of all the people who
were sitting on this side of where the big picture had been.
She forgot Mamma, forgot herself. Nothing else existed
except the fairyland beyond the footlights.

At the end of an hour—or a fortnight—or a century—the
big picture came down again and everybody clapped. Charlotte looked around at Mamma and let her breath go.

"Like it?" Mamma asked with her brightest smile. For
perhaps the first time since she had learned to speak, the
little girl was at a loss for words.

The music men played some more, but nobody paid much attention to them. People chatted to one another. A lot of them got up and moved around. One of Mamma's friends came up with a box of candy and treated Mamma and Charlotte. Charlotte could only smile her gratitude.

"Loves it, doesn't she?" Mamma's friend asked.

Mamma nodded. "Her first matinee. It takes me back."

"It takes us all back," the friend said softly.

Again the big picture rose. The story went on. After this installment there was a lot of clapping and bowing. Then again music and moving around down here where just people sat. Then one more hour of story, and it was all over. Everybody got up and left.

Charlotte was all for lingering. If she stayed here long enough, there might be more rapture to experience. But Mamma said No, it was all over. She put the little girl's wraps on and led her to where their carriage was waiting.

"There will be other matinees, darling," Mamma assured the little girl. There would be, of course. But there would never be another first show. It was like a first love, a first kiss, a first baby. That lovely strangeness had a charm of its own which nothing else could quite come up to.

There were indeed other matinees that fall and winter. Twice Mrs. Emerson tried taking along a woman friend and her little girl. But her duties as a hostess interfered with Charlotte's concentration on the play, and both times the little guest did some wriggling in her chair and stared at the audience instead of at the stage. Once when Mamma came down with a cold, Papa took the little girl sooner than see her disappointed. But again the experiment was not quite successful. Fathers were always a novelty and a treat. With him there beside her, Charlotte couldn't give her full attention to the show.

But that occasion reminded Mamma of something. "My father used to take me to the matinee sometimes. You don't remember him, dear. Agnes does." For an instant Mamma hesitated, and a shade of sadness crossed her face. Both Charlotte's grandparents were dead when she came along, and something very lovely was missing from her life.

"He was your father, just the way Papa is mine," the little girl prompted.

"Yes, and one day he took me to see a terribly exciting play. The man in it had had all sorts of trouble. He had been shut up in prison; we saw him there. But he planned his escape, and another prisoner told him where great wealth was hidden. It was on the island of Monte Cristo."

"And he got out of the prison and found the—great wealth?" Charlotte prompted.

"He did. He got out. You saw him swim. You saw him land. Then he stood there facing the audience, and he shouted to the wind and the waves, 'I am standing on the island of Monte Cristo! The world is mine!' "

Charlotte laughed and bounced in her chair. "Tell me that again! . . . Again! . . . Again!" Then she had it mastered. In her turn she shouted, "I am standing on the island of Monte Cristo! The world is mine!"

She repeated it over and over, until Mamma put up a restraining hand. Then Charlotte treated herself to a private performance when she was alone that night. Looking out at Lake Michigan, Charlotte pretended that she had swum here. In her own eyes she became the mysterious prisoner. The supreme moment had come: freedom, safety, great wealth. She shouted that the world was hers. Right then and there, it really was.

Of course there was a proper triumph in every good story, *Cinderella* and *Little Red Ridinghood* and *The Three*

Bears. But even to marry a prince or escape from a big, bad wolf or go to sleep in a bed exactly the right size was not quite so glorious as to tell the wind and the waves—and whatever audience might be listening—"The world is mine!"

Right here and now, the world was Charlotte Emerson's. Child among grownups, she lived surrounded by smiling faces. Her storybook realm was a land of wonder. At the matinee, other stories came to life and happened there right in front of her eyes. Santa Claus always remembered to come the night before Christmas. Again, the December after she was four years old, Charlotte had failed to catch him in the act. But just wait until she was five! This time she would surely make it.

❦   2   ❦

THAT SUMMER CHARLOTTE picked up a new expression. She heard Mamma's friends say it. In their crisp summer frocks they were seated in wicker chairs around the back lawn, where the only sounds were lake water plashing on the shore at the foot of the high bank and the occasional click of a horse's hoofs from the distant street. They sipped iced tea and nibbled at little frosted cakes. They gossiped in desultory fashion, and remembered sometimes to smile at the little girl watching them so gravely and sweetly. One thing they all agreed upon, "It isn't the heat, it's the humidity."

Charlotte waylaid Papa when he came home from the office and sprang that observation on him. He stared at her for an instant in silence, then burst out laughing. "Who on earth ever told you that, moppet?" he cried as he scooped her up in his arms and kissed her.

"Mamma's friends say that," answered Charlotte complacently.

Papa laughed again. "Far be it from me to contradict a lady, but I think the heat really has something to do with it."

"Contra-dict." Charlotte spaced the new word out carefully. Then she joined the halves together. "Contradict." She had that one nailed, and she knew what it meant.

"Come join me for a lemonade as soon as I've cleaned up," he offered. "Or have you already had yours?"

"And cake?" Charlotte asked. "I've already had a lemonade and one little cake, but—"

"But due to the heat *and the humidity* you could stand another one? I should hope so, indeed. A gentleman never drinks alone."

A lemonade with Papa was such fun. Charlotte loosened up now with some of those gems she had memorized earlier, and he caught on, and gave her the right answers.

"Hello there."

"Hello yourself."

"You don't look a day older."

"You took the words right out of my mouth."

This was the way the talk went back and forth at the matinee. "Actors," they were called. And what went up to reveal them to Mamma and Charlotte was the curtain. Charlotte had once thought of it as "the big picture." But of course, that was quite a long time ago.

Humid or not, the summer was going by awfully fast.

All the better that it was, in one way: It was bringing Charlotte's birthday closer. That magic August day when she would again be the hostess at a party. Be the most important person anywhere around: she, Charlotte Emerson, who would reach the mature age of five.

Preparations began several days before the party. Most of the guests would be the same as last year's. One little boy's family had moved away from Saylesboro; one little girl was off visiting relatives. But a small sister was now old enough to come along, and another girl's visiting cousin happened to be a little boy.

"It keeps things even, like the animals going into the Ark," Mamma explained to Papa. "I don't know that that makes much difference to them at that age. Still, that's the way it's going to be later on in her life, so Charlotte might as well get used to it."

Papa chuckled. "It's surprising how easy some things are to get used to."

Charlotte had a beautiful new dress. This year her sash and hair ribbon were of pale blue with a darker blue stripe, very grownup indeed. She would remember not to ask "Where's my present?" She hadn't known any better when she was only four. This time it would be quite different.

It was. Charlotte remembered to say "Thank you." Twice she managed to act a little surprised. "For me? Oh, thank you very much!" To the two strangers she said, "It's so nice that you could come." She remembered the wish she made just before she blew out the candles: "I wish that I may have another party next year." A nice simple wish, more than likely to come true; and if she chose, she could use it again in the future.

Toward the end of the party there was one brand-new ceremony. Papa had invented it, and he came home in time to watch it; but Mamma presided. She passed around balloons, a blue one to each boy, a pink to each girl. She coached the various mothers, who stood by to be sure that their offspring acted according to plan. Then she sang softly, and repeated,

> Take the word to the wide blue sky.
>   Tell it to wind and tide.
> This is Charlotte's birthday!
>   Spread the news far and wide.

The third time over, most of the mothers caught on and sang with her. So did some of the children, albeit haltingly. Then Mrs. Emerson whispered to Charlotte to release her balloon. The other mothers followed suit.

Off went the balloons on the wings of a land breeze. The new little girl began to cry at losing her balloon, but her mother picked her up and comforted her. The others were absorbed in watching the lovely spheres mount toward the summer sky and float farther and farther away. Before they were quite out of sight the restlessness of youth reasserted itself, but for a magic interval there the children had been breathless and spellbound.

When the time came for them to go home, each little guest was presented with two fresh balloons, a pink and a blue. Other balloons were taken to Charlotte's room, where the strings were attached to various articles of furniture. Thus something of the party remained for days; and by the time the last frail bubble had burst, the nights were beginning to be cool and autumn was on its way.

Although Charlotte of course knew nothing about it, her parents had had a decided difference of opinion about what was to be done with her that September. Mamma was all for starting her in kindergarten. "She hasn't any sisters or brothers near her own age. She needs to learn to associate with other children. Parties are all very well, but ordinary, everyday give-and-take is a lesson which can't be learned too early."

"She is learning that already. Much of it will come of itself," Papa protested. "Kindergartens are fine in their way—very good for children who haven't nice homes and people to take care of them. But give Charlotte one more term of being a regular child. Then in another year we can start her in at regular school."

"But my friends' children—" Inez began.

"Are your friends' concern," he snapped. "Charlotte happens to be my daughter."

Inez sulked for a few minutes. Then she came around very sweetly. She ought to be thankful that Paul took such an interest in his family. Some men seemed to feel that when they provided the shelter of their name and paid the bills they had done all that could be expected of them.

Mamma had enough other concerns to keep her busy anyhow, for that very week Agnes came to her with the news of her engagement. She was marrying Herbert Stanton, who had a good job in the First National Bank right here in Saylesboro. She wanted to be married in October. Then, when they came back from their honeymoon the young couple could look for a place of their own.

"So we're acquiring a boarder as well as a son-in-law," Paul Emerson grumbled. But of course he was actually doing nothing of the kind. He bought a small house on the other side of Saylesboro and gave it to Agnes as one of her wedding presents. Her mother would help her decorate and furnish it; and the Emerson charge accounts were always good.

So here was a big wedding to be staged in less than two months. Trousseau, attendants, during the last two weeks a round of prenuptial parties. The theatrical season opened without benefit of Mrs. Emerson that year, but twice Papa took Charlotte to the matinee, and the rest of the time he sent Nursie with her.

Charlotte was to be flower girl at the wedding, and very, very important she thought herself. She must have a special dress made for the occasion: a dress which harmonized with those of the grownup attendants. She saw all the wedding presents unpacked and put on display. She met the prospective bridegroom and learned to call him by his first name. Finally she went through the wedding rehearsal, which she didn't understand but remembered as one more interesting experience.

She was the coolest person present at the actual ceremony. She scattered rose petals in the path of the bride. Later she threw rice after the departing couple. All by herself that night she acted the whole thing out. "Do you take this woman to be your awful wedded wife?" She didn't see why the minister called Agnes "awful," but he did the same thing about Herbert, "awful wedded husband." And it was nice when he said to Herbert, "Now you may kiss the bride." Charlotte was the only person in the church who heard him say that. But he must have said it, for that was what Herbert did.

Agnes's room was empty now. Mamma was away now a good deal seeing about Agnes's new home. It was all very strange and exciting. So much so that Charlotte presently announced to Papa, "One of these days I'm going to get married to my awful wedded husband."

Just for an instant Papa looked mad. Then he asked, "What was that again? 'Awful wedded husband?' Maybe

you're right at that, darling. But the minister thought he
was saying 'lawful.' "

He picked Charlotte up then, and held her on his knee
for a long, long time. Twice he chuckled and muttered
"awful." Once she thought she heard him sob. Grown men
did not cry, of course. Papa couldn't have. But it was won-
derfully warm and happy sitting here just like this. Maybe
Charlotte would change her mind about that "lawful"
wedded husband. Maybe she would just stay here with
Papa.

It was nicer than ever here after things quieted down.
Mamma said that now she had helped fix up a new home
for her big girl, it was time she did something for her little
girl. She bought all new furniture for what had been Charlotte's nursery. Grownup furniture; and she allowed Charlotte to have a voice in picking out the new things. The
playroom was refurbished, too, though it still housed the
familiar treasures: an accumulation of dolls, a beautiful doll
house, all fitted and furnished to scale, two rocking horses,
one to be mounted astride, the other offering a little carriage seat between two steeds. There was a little tea table,
too, and a case filled with storybooks. A wonderful place
for a little girl on rainy days or after dark. A wonderful
place to act out scenes from what she saw at the matinee,
or make up plays in which she greeted imaginary guests at
a tea party and told them the face was familiar, and they
didn't look a day older, and do try the seed cookies, it's a
new re-ci-pea.

This year for the first time Charlotte gave presents as
well as received them. With colored crayons she drew a
picture of a house. A large house, of which you could see
three sides at the same time. It had a tree growing on either

side of it, and it was belching smoke from five chimneys. This was done under Mamma's direction, and was for Papa. A similar though less elaborate effort was made for Nursie. These were both laid away carefully to await the Great Day. Then while Mamma was out of the room and Nursie in charge, Charlotte drew a house for Mamma. It was to be a surprise to her, and to make sure that the surprise was a good one, Charlotte drew six chimneys this time.

On Christmas morning Papa was surprised and delighted with his gift. He kissed Charlotte on both cheeks and cried out, "You gave Santa Claus a helping hand, didn't you, little sweetheart?" Then he had to examine Mamma's gift and compare them; and when Mamma told him Nursie had one too, that had to be fetched for his inspection. The three of them remained on display together until after New Year's, when the holly and mistletoe came down and the Christmas tree was dismantled. Then he took them all and had them framed.

Agnes and that *lawful* husband of hers had been here for Christmas, as they were for Thanksgiving. But after that Agnes generally came alone. Several times she joined the party when Mamma was entertaining her women friends. Then the ladies said, "You're prettier than ever" and "How is the honeymoon going?" and "There's nothing like having a home of your own, is there?" Of course they didn't need to tell Agnes that her face was familiar; she already knew that it was.

Mamma again went to matinees with Charlotte. Once soon after the curtain went up the little girl realized that this was very much like something she had seen before. She continued to stare in some bewilderment. Then the

light broke in. This *was* something she had seen before.
They were doing it all over. She looked up into Mamma's
face, and Mamma smiled and nodded. So it was all to be
lived through a second time, and that was a different kind
of fun.

The other children's birthday parties went right on, too.
There were more games at the parties now, and the little
guests fell into the habit of singing "Happy Birthday to
You." Charlotte wondered what these children wished
when they blew out the candles. Sometimes they didn't all
go out at the first breath. But perhaps that wasn't really
such very bad luck. Perhaps if your wish didn't come true
you could always wish again.

> Wish again and wish again and wish again,
> And drop all your wishes in Lake Michigan.

What was that song Mamma and the other ladies had sung
at Charlotte's party when the balloons all went sailing up
into the sky? Maybe this year they would sing these words
that Charlotte had just made up. That is, if she could
remember them long enough to tell them to Mamma. "She
has a good memory," Charlotte had once overheard
Mamma tell one of her women friends. Mamma had told
only half the story; Charlotte also had a good forgettery.

This time, however, she did remember. Mamma said,
"That's fine, dear," and wrote it down.

"Not as good as yours," Charlotte protested loyally.

Mamma simply smiled. That was always nice, when she
smiled without answering.

The time came for Charlotte's own party. She would
reach the incredible age of six. She could remember two of
her own parties very well. Her lovely wish was there to be

used again. This was indeed an occasion to be looked forward to.

This year there was not only an abundant supply of balloons, there were also extra paper caps. They sang Mamma's song when they released the airy flock which was to "spread the news far and wide." When they had watched the pink and blue messengers fade into the distance there was an instant's silence. Then Mamma turned to receive a second supply of balloons and a round of paper caps. The new caps were tied to the new balloons; thus freighted, this second convoy was launched. Then Mamma again began to sing. This time, unbelievably, she was singing Charlotte's poem about "drop all your wishes in Lake Michigan."

Everybody caught on. Everybody laughed. Everybody sang. And sure enough, some of these craft foundered. Others went dragging away to nowhere in particular, and were still within sight when the audience tired of watching.

It was a fitting climax to the best party of all. A party that marked the end of something. Not of Charlotte's childhood, of course, but her little girlhood: those magic years when she lived in a realm of fantasy, when all that glittered was gold, when in a very real sense of the word the world *was* hers.

Infinite possibilities lay ahead, but this special richness was gone, and gone for good. In a very few weeks now, in time which might almost be counted in days, Charlotte would take her first step over the threshold of maturity. She was due to enter school in September.

3

CHARLOTTE WAS HIGHLY excited by the idea of school. It would mean going somewhere right along, and being with other children regularly instead of having to wait for parties. But at the last minute doubts assailed her. "How can I go to school, Mamma," she appealed, "when I don't know how to read and write?"

"That's the reason why you're going," Mamma explained. "They will teach you how to read and write, and lots of other things. That's what schools are for."

"That's what schools are for," Charlotte repeated slowly. After a slight pause she added, "Is everything for something?"

Mamma looked as if she wanted to laugh. But her voice was quite serious when she replied, "I'm sure I couldn't say. If you find out, tell me."

That was a question which had puzzled wiser heads than Inez Emerson's. Charlotte might be a long time learning the answer.

Mamma escorted Charlotte to school that morning, but she left before the session opened. The other mothers left, too. Charlotte was alone with her teacher and her fellow pupils. One little boy had been at Charlotte's birthday parties and she at his, but the rest of the children were strangers to her.

The teacher's name was Miss Fox. She was small for a

grownup, and had a round snub-nosed face which somehow reminded Charlotte of the pug dog that one of Mamma's friends often brought with her when she came calling.
She smiled at the class and began, "It's a beautiful day, isn't
it? We're beginning a year which I am sure we shall all
enjoy very much. The first thing for us to do, of course, is
get acquainted. So I am asking each of you in turn to rise
and face your classmates and give your name."

The first pupil gave her name, "Alice Adair." Miss Fox
said, "Thank you, Alice. It's nice to have you with us."
Alice sat down again, and Miss Fox nodded to the little boy
in the next seat. When Charlotte's turn came, she not only
smiled at her classmates, she made them a little curtsy.
Some of the children tittered, but Miss Fox said, "Thank
you, Charlotte, that is very nice."

When the last pupil had been introduced, Miss Fox said,
"Now we are all friends, we will have our first lesson." She
turned to the blackboard and wrote two letters, a large and
a small one. "This is 'A.' 'A' is the first letter of the alphabet. It is also the first letter of the word 'alphabet.' You will
all pronounce it aloud. . . . That is fine. . . . Alice Adair, your
name begins with this letter. Will you come to the blackboard and write it, please."

It went on thus for an enchanted period. Charlotte wrote
the 'C.' Not long after 'D' it was time for recess, when all
the pupils were free to move around and talk and go for
drinks of water.. Then they went through the whole rig-
marole again, writing the small letters this time. When she
was called for at the dinner hour, Charlotte almost hated
to leave. But it was great to get home and report. Then she
still had the afternoon ahead of her, and all the rest of the
week after that.

Now the weeks all began to fall into a definite pattern.

Previously Charlotte had noted Sunday because then Papa was at home and it was always a festival when he was there, and often an expedition. These past few years Wednesday had been matinee day. Now Mamma took Charlotte to the matinee on Saturday, when she took her at all. Agnes was sometimes there, with another young wife like herself. She would smile and wave to her mother and Charlotte. But she obviously considered her little sister of small account.

Friday afternoon always brought with it a lovely sense of release. School was out!—and nothing else compared to that sensation. Monday morning seemed a very long distance away. There was always just a little sinking of the heart late Sunday afternoon. Some things were too good to last.

Charlotte learned fast and easily. When a slower pupil hesitated over a sound or a word, it was all she could do to keep from shouting it aloud. By Thanksgiving she could read anything that Miss Fox wrote on the blackboard. Her *First Reader* she finished before the class was a third of the way through it.

Recess was different—and puzzling. Instead of sharing their games as they did at parties, the girls and boys had separate playgrounds. Passing to and from theirs, or breaking out of line for a moment, her masculine classmates would hurl taunts at her. At home she was never called by anything less than her full name. But now shouts rang in her ears,

Lottie!
Dotty!
Go way back and squatty!

The standard retort was easily learned,

> Sticks and stones
> Will break my bones,
> But names will never hurt me.

But Charlotte could do better than that. She soon learned to shout back,

> When he calls me a nasty name,
> Dirty little boy is the one to blame.

Pretty soon she would be able to write that down. Mamma had noted her rhyme about dropping wishes in Lake Michigan. But Charlotte was in no hurry to have her hear this one.

It was a little girl, however, who dealt the worst blow. Right there in the magic month of December, she informed Charlotte that there wasn't any Santa Claus, and it was "baby" to believe in him.

Charlotte was aghast. She rushed home and flung herself on Mamma with this ghastly heresy.

Mrs. Emerson drew a long breath. She had known that this moment must come, and that she must face it. Very quietly she said, "Don't pay any attention to what horrid people say, darling. Somebody is always trying to take the joy out of life."

"But Mamma, isn't there—is there—?"

"Santa Claus is love," Mamma said firmly. "It's the same thing."

Charlotte gazed open-mouthed, taking the whole thing in. She plumbed the depth of her disappointment; then she came up with a pearl. "There is a Santa Claus, or why would so many children believe in him? We just haven't caught him yet."

She remembered that when she drew her Christmas pictures. Each chimney now had a fat Santa Claus in a red tunic and cap going down it. This was quite a job for the young artist, and this year she drew four pictures instead of three. The new one was for Miss Fox, of course; and Miss Fox's pictured house had seven chimneys on it.

The Christmas holidays this year were the best yet. Charlotte once more hung up her stocking. The old excitement and suspense were lacking, but she didn't want Papa to think that she had any doubts. Many of her gifts were books, and now she could read them for herself. Read them aloud to her dolls, too. Read them to Papa and Mamma. The wealth of the ages was now hers for the taking. No Phi Beta Kappa receiving his Ph. D. could have had a prouder sense of achievement.

That summer Papa awarded himself a six-week vacation. He took Mamma and Charlotte on a long trip to the West: Yellowstone Park, California, Arizona, even a glimpse of Mexico. "Small Fry is old enough now to observe and remember," he said. "It's her first real vacation, too. There's no reason why she should have to spend it in her own back yard."

So many strange people. So much moving about. So many wonderful sights. It reminded Charlotte of all those matinees she had seen through these past years; only the curtain never came down for the end of an act, and this show wasn't being put on by actors, it was really happening to Papa and Mamma and Charlotte. It was marvelous. It was stunning. It was breathtaking.

It was also bewildering. It became confusing. And it was

very fatiguing. By the time the long trip was half over, Paul Emerson was beginning to doubt whether he should have undertaken so much in the case of such a young child. In another week he wished there were some graceful way for him to backtrack. Presently he was driven to remark privately to Inez, "It's a good thing you're not the type of wife who says, 'I told you so.' "

"But I didn't," she reminded him.

She was the one of the three who enjoyed the trip the most. She liked having Paul away from his everlasting business. She liked having her child with her all day and every day. She admired the way that Paul arranged the manifold details of the trip, such as seeing that all of them always had plenty of clean clothes. A good husband was always a handy thing to have around the house. On a trip like this, he was practically indispensable.

"Maybe it isn't too bad, at that," Paul Emerson concluded. "Maybe it's better for a child to get a good honest stomachache from too much candy than to have to stand out in the street gazing in at the window of the candy store and wishing and longing and never getting."

"Don't!" Inez cried. "Please don't talk about things like that."

"Right, it's no way to talk when we're on our vacation. The vacation that I wanted to be the best one ever."

"It's all of that," she assured him. "It is something that Charlotte will remember all the rest of her life."

Then in next to no time it was ending. The three of them were again in a Pullman stateroom, with friendly brown men ministering to them. The landscape was again flashing past the train windows. It looked as if it were the fields and houses and people that were moving, but of course it was the train that moved, with Charlotte and Papa and Mamma on it. And the three of them were headed back for Saylesboro.

Charlotte began to hum to herself. Presently she turned from the window and caught Papa's eye. He was watching her instead of the moving world outside. She smiled and began to sing aloud, "The wheels of the train keep moving. They are singing when they move. They are singing, singing, si-i-nging, 'We are all of us going home.' "

When she repeated it, Mamma sang with her. The next time over, Papa joined them. He nodded at Mamma, and she nodded back. At that moment Paul Emerson felt the deep, warm glow that comes so seldom even in the happiest life.

The big house overlooking Lake Michigan looked a little strange at first, and it was queer to think that now Charlotte would go to sleep every night in the same bed, the bed to which she had been so attached before she started on this trip. Agnes had met them at the station, and made a great fuss over them. Nursie and Cook had been waiting on the front steps, and Charlotte clung to a hand of each when she went into the big front hall which somehow smelled different from any place that she had traveled to. Smelled largely of flowers, to be sure; there were vases of them here and in the rooms to right and left, visible through open doors. It was home. It was all wonderful. It was all just a little strange.

They got back in plenty of time for Charlotte's birthday party, of course. This time they repeated the balloon ceremony and the songs, but with one change: instead of paper caps to attach to the balloons which were to take their chance of flying away or falling into the lake, the guests used paper horns.

Charlotte was growing up very fast now. She was a seasoned traveler; she could tell other children about the many places she had been and the many sights she had seen; and if she sometimes confused fact and fantasy—well, she was not the first traveler who had ever done so. She was a seasoned student, too; she would be going back to school instead of just beginning it. Life was very, very exciting, and the days were going by much faster than they used to. Or was it here the way that it had been on the train? Was it Charlotte that was doing the moving?

There was another wedding this October. This time it was Nursie who was married. Papa gave her her wedding. It wasn't as large as Agnes's wedding had been. It wasn't quite as exciting, either, because by now Charlotte was used to being a member of the wedding party. She didn't scatter any rose petals in the bride's path this time; she walked side by side with a sister of Nursie's who was half a head taller than Charlotte. Nursie's name wasn't Nursie at all, of course; the minister called her Anna when he spoke to her during the ceremony. Yes, and it *was* "lawful" he said. How could Charlotte ever have been so young and silly as to make a mistake about that? He didn't tell Frederick that he might kiss the bride, but Frederick did it anyhow.

And afterward when the newlyweds were going away together, Papa said to Frederick, "You better be good to this little girl, young man, or you will have to answer to me."

Young Frederick looked a little taken aback, but Nursie, now Anna and Mrs. Something-or-other, laughed and blushed and said, "Oh Mr. Emerson, you're being just too good to me!"

It was queer at first getting along without Nursie-Anna. She had always been there, just the way that Papa and Mamma had been, and Lake Michigan. But Charlotte was

a big girl now, and very busy with school. She could do a
lot for herself, too, and there were plenty of servants
around the house. As Charlotte heard Mamma tell her
women friends, "My girls leave me only to get married."
They all said, "How nice!" Other girls had left from time
to time, Charlotte remembered now. But Papa hadn't given
any of the rest of them a wedding, and that was too bad.
Weddings were fun.

Traveling, too, was great fun, especially after you got
back home and caught up on your sleep and had time to
think things over. There were times this fall when Charlotte felt as if she had ranged the way the best of her balloons did. She had seen herself in so many different
mirrors, too, that she sometimes wondered whether she
didn't look vastly different herself. But when she gazed
attentively into the mirror before which she had so often
acted things out, it was still very much the same Charlotte
who looked back at her. High wide forehead, over which
a curl or two was generally pulled. Big blue eyes set wide
apart. Eyes just the color of Papa's; Mamma's were a sunny
brown. Small straight nose, wide firm mouth, with the
upper lip just a little short in the middle. Very fair color-
ing. A tendency to smile whenever she caught anybody's
eye, even that of the little girl the other side of the mirror.

Alice in the storybook had walked right through the
mirror. Charlotte wouldn't have done that even if she
could. Not unless she could take Mamma and Papa with
her. Or Nursie-now-Anna. Or maybe one of those nice
brown men who had all smiled so pleasantly at her when
she was on her long trip. There didn't seem to be any of
them here in Saylesboro. Did they spend all their lives
riding on trains or waiting on table in those big rooms
where so many people ate together?

Weddings were fun. Traveling was fun. And parties. And matinees. Seeing all the children in school was great, too, and learning new things every day. Only, school was just not the same as it had been last year. It wasn't just that the novelty had worn off; the fact that you could remember last year's lilacs didn't spoil this year's fragrance, and ice cream for Sunday dinner tasted just as good as it had last Sunday and would again another week. The difficulty lay with her new teacher.

Miss Jones was an angular woman of fifty, with small, pale eyes and a thin, tight mouth. She was hard, precise, immobile, except in the presence of the principal or of visiting parents. In front of the principal she taught with enthusiasm and smiled at her pupils. To the parents she was gushing. In a sense she was a good teacher; but if an unknown rich uncle in Australia had died suddenly and left her a million dollars, she would never have picked up another piece of chalk or taught again the simple processes of elementary arithmetic.

Monday now meant going back to Miss Jones. But after Nursie-Anna's wedding there was Thanksgiving to look ahead to, and after Thanksgiving Charlotte began her private preparations for Christmas. She no longer expected Santa Claus to come down the chimney. This year she didn't draw many pictures of him coming down many different chimneys. But she did draw several pictures of houses seen from three angles and smoking away defiantly, and above the front door of each, on a rectangle which might have been a banner, she lettered painstakingly "SANTA CLAUS IS LOVE." She took one to Miss Fox, of course, and Miss Fox thanked her and kissed her.

That really meant a lot. Just a little, Charlotte regretted the loss of her old childlike faith. But if Santa Claus was love, that meant he could be with us all the year around.

This year, instead of hanging up her stocking, Charlotte helped Papa and Mamma trim the tree. Then the three of them settled down in Charlotte's room, and Mamma read aloud about a man who said Christmas was "humbug." Three spirits came to show him that it was not. Christmas meant love even in the grownup world, meant it even to horrid old men like the one in the story.

It was a very cheerful Charlotte who went back to school after the holidays. Monday might be "blue Monday," the way some people said it was. But then the other days could have their own colors too, following one another in regular order. After blue Monday green Tuesday, yellow Wednesday, orange Thursday, red Friday. She must remember to tell that to Alice Adair at recess. When she got home that afternoon she would take her crayons and letter the whole thing out.

She did just that, all of it. Then on green Tuesday she was back in school, one day nearer to the end of the week, with a possible matinee on Saturday and maybe a sleigh ride on Sunday. Blue Monday was over, anyhow, and next Monday awfully far ahead.

She was still in that beautiful mood during the afternoon study period. She got her work out of the way rapidly; then she sat back in her seat and looked off into the distance. Some time later—a minute, five minutes, ten, who could tell?—she laughed aloud.

The sound startled her. She dropped her eyes instantly, and pretended to busy herself with her desk work. But she was too late. Miss Jones had heard her, and Miss Jones jumped her. "Charlotte Emerson, what are you laughing at?"

"N-n-nothing," Charlotte faltered. She could not have

explained that entrancing mood, even if she had not been startled into forgetfulness.

"Nothing?" Miss Jones echoed acidly. "Dear, dear! Here is a little girl who laughs at nothing. Very well then, Charlotte. You may stay after school and write fifty times, 'I laugh at nothing.' "

That penalty brought a titter from some of the other pupils. Miss Jones had no need to ask them what they were laughing at. She had gained her point, and made a little girl ridiculous.

So when school was dismissed, Charlotte remained behind. She got out pencil and paper. Slowly and with infinite care she began to write, "I laugh at nothing." Directly underneath it, "I laugh at nothing." And so on down the sheet, then onto a second sheet. She paused every now and then to count up. She would complete her assignment, of course, but it would be just too bad if she wrote those unlucky four words even one extra time.

She finished presently, and laid the sheets on Miss Jones's desk. Miss Jones nodded but did not look up from the arithmetic papers she was correcting. Charlotte put on her wraps and dashed out to where the coachman was waiting for her, with his horse shivering in the cold. "I got kept after school, James," she said. "I'm sorry about the horse."

So now she was on her way home. Kept after school, for the first time in her life. Punished for being happy, and for telling the truth. Wormy old Jones! She grudged a little girl a moment's laughter.

Mamma happened to be at home that afternoon, and alone. She glanced at the clock when Charlotte came tumbling in. The whole story took only a minute to tell.

"Take off your wraps and wash up, darling," Mamma

said. "You're here. That's what is important."

With her own hands she made Charlotte a cup of choco-late: she, Mrs. Paul Emerson, who seldom went into the kitchen except to consult Cook and give orders. She sat with Charlotte while the little girl drank her chocolate and ate two cookies. Then they went into the sitting room where Mamma had been at her embroidery when Charlotte came home. Mamma seated herself in a rocking chair and took the little girl on her lap and began to rock her and caress her. Mamma, whose skin always smelled faintly like flowers. Mamma, who when a little girl fell down and hurt herself, would kiss the place to make it well.

Presently she said softly, "There's a very good reason why you laugh, darling. You're made that way." Charlotte threw back her head in relief and release. Now they laughed together.

In her college days Charlotte used to tell the episode of her clash with Miss Jones purely as a funny story. A funny story on herself. But gradually she realized that it wasn't so funny, at that. The time came when she was sorry for the frustrated older woman who reacted to gaiety by squelching it.

❦ 4 ❦

CHARLOTTE WAS OLD enough now to share in the gen-eral excitement of momentous events. If she didn't quite understand what the hullabaloo was about, that made it all the more fun.

It began with a headline in the Saylesboro *Morning Senti-nel*, "MAINE BLOWN UP." A United States battleship, on a friendly visit in the principal harbor of a large neighboring island belonging to a great European power, had been the victim of a mysterious, wanton attack.

Americans were at first stunned, then outraged, then resentful. President McKinley, himself a veteran of the Civil War, was reluctant to take a definitive step in the matter, but he really had no choice. The outraged young giant of the West was forced to take up arms against the Spanish Empire. Late April of 1898 saw the beginning of hostilities.

Then there were flags flying, bands playing, young men rushing off to enlist. New songs were being played and sung, "Goodbye, Dolly Gray" and "The Lone Grave," "The Trench at Santiago," and "There'll Be a Hot Time in the Old Town Tonight." A general began to send back dispatches signed "Shafter, Major General commanding." He was a huge mountain of a man in his blue uniform. Mamma, looking at a picture of him in a magazine, said, "Isn't he a cute little sylph?" What could she mean by that?

On the other side of the world Commodore George Dewey said, "You may fire when you are ready, Gridley." Captain Gridley did so. The Battle of Manila Bay was won without the loss of a single American life, and for months thereafter American baby boys were almost automatically christened "George Dewey." A great empire crumbled; Spain sank to the rank of a fifth-rate power. For the United States of America a new, strange, dazzling era was beginning.

While all this was going on, Agnes and her lawful husband moved to Milwaukee. A year later they moved again, this time to Chicago. It was there that Agnes's little baby

was born. It was a girl, and they named her Inez after
Mamma. So now Mamma had not only a granddaughter
but a namesake, and Charlotte, though still a little girl
herself, was an aunt. That gave her something to brag to
her schoolmates about. She took full advantage of it.

Her third-grade teacher was Miss Wilson. She was nice,
but sort of plain and quiet. Then came Mrs. Myers, a
widow who had a little boy now entering school. Miss
Randolph, in fifth, was very pretty; it was a treat just to sit
there in the classroom and look at her. Miss Synder, in
sixth, was a smiling soul, who didn't mind restlessness in
the classroom. Charlotte could easily imagine that in her
own childhood *she* had laughed at nothing. Charlotte liked
them all. But not one of them quite came up to Miss Fox,
with her cute pug dog face and her way of liking all the
children and making them like one another.

There was always a dog or two around the Emerson
stable. Charlotte knew them and sometimes played with
them. But when she was in the fourth grade, Papa gave her
a dog of her own. A fox terrier puppy whom she named
Stub in honor of his shortened tail. She taught him a lot of
tricks: to sit up, to beg, to shake hands, to bark once for
"yes" and twice for "no." He always wagged all over when
she came home from school. He slept in his own bed in
Charlotte's playroom, and if she slept late on a Saturday
morning, he would come scratching at the door for her to
get up.

That next year Charlotte went to dancing school. That
was fun, too, but at the suggestion that she go back another
fall Charlotte shook her head. That would give her one
more schedule to live up to. As it was she had little enough
time to play with Stub, and to draw crayon pictures, and
to read. She had left the world of children's books now and

embarked on the great sea of world literature. First J. Fenimore Cooper's tales of Indian life and fighting and the wise white man who knew all the lore of the woods. Then three or four of the exciting romances of Sir Walter Scott, and after that Charles Dickens.

"The real reason I'd like to be young again," Papa told her, "is to get a first reading of *Ivanhoe* or *A Tale of Two Cities.*"

Perhaps that was what Mamma's friends meant when they droned, "Your school days are the happiest days of your life." But Charlotte had amended that to read, "Your school days are the daisiest days of your life." Another of their favorite oldies now ran, "It isn't the humidity, it's the heat."

After that one lengthy and exhausting tour, Papa arranged for shorter vacations. The three Emersons now revisited in turn all the various scenes which they had once telescoped together, but now they took them one at a time. They went slower and rested more. They took little side trips. But the very fact that she had been here before now added to Charlotte's enjoyment. Just going was more fun too, now that she was older and had seen more.

"I don't think anybody wants to be young again," she told Papa. "Things are more fun the second time over."

"Best of all is when you see them again through young eyes," Papa said quietly. Just for a minute he looked a little strange and sad. Then he smiled brightly and added, "But we'll have to have some new firsts again one of these days. If you don't have a first, you can't have a second and a third."

The things that Papa said made sense. Charlotte remembered them and thought them over afterward. They weren't like that "Hello there," "Hello yourself," stuff that

Charlotte used to mimic when she was a little girl. Papa really meant what he said. So many people talked just to be saying something.

Then all of a sudden it was over. That eight years which had seemed endless when she looked ahead at it. The eight years which began with Charlotte as a little girl and ended with her as a big one: an inch taller now than Mamma. Embarrassingly grown up in some ways; she didn't know quite what to make of it.

Her schoolmates scattered for the summer. Papa had Charlotte's diploma framed to hang on the wall of what had so long been her playroom—but they must call it her sitting room now. Charlotte had plenty of time that first leisured week to play with Stub. Once she took him for a walk past the now closed school. Queer to think that it was all over. A little sad, maybe, but very exciting. Charlotte would have to sit down in the back garden to think it over; sit and look out over the wide expanse of Lake Michigan stretching out to meet the distant sky.

Some things looked so far away; but the time might come when a person would see and hear them. So much could happen. So much did happen. Meanwhile it was pleasant just to sit here in the fine weather of early summer, and remember, and wonder.

She hadn't too much time, however, for reminiscence or for conjecture. Papa decided that this year the vacation trip should be entirely different. "We'll go far and fast," he promised. "We'll cross our northern border this time. Border, not frontier. We maintain no frontier against Canada."

They took three weeks for this trip. They saw much beautiful country and two great cities which were very much like the cities back in what Canadians called "the States." But instead of going on toward the Pacific coast, they turned east and went into a very strange land, where even the railroad crossing signs were in French. Quebec was a picturesque city set in a beautiful province, but very odd, very foreign. So many churches and roadside shrines, so many black-robed priests and nuns everywhere about. It was all fascinating and just a little frightening. Was Europe like this, Charlotte wondered. Wondered, but didn't ask. She was too busy taking in.

The three of them left Saylesboro again in August. Papa took rooms for them in a big hotel in Chicago. He stayed in Saylesboro during the week, but joined the ladies for Saturday and Sunday. Then they went to visit Agnes and her family in their house on the South Side. Small Inez was great fun to play with, and she soon learned to know and like Aunt Charlotte. Sometimes during the week Mamma and Charlotte went out to Agnes's. Sometimes they went on expeditions: to a huge art gallery, to a great museum, to a department store which was like another museum. Once they rode on a great ship called "the whaleback" to Milwaukee and back, and ate on the boat. Traveling was wonderful, on a short trip as on a long one, and it was great to have Mamma to herself like this, with no relatives to bother and none of her friends "my dear"-ing around.

They had to get home for Charlotte's birthday, of course. It turned out to be a rainy day; for the first time, her party was driven indoors. The guests were too big now to play games with balloons, but there were paper capes as well as paper caps and horns and beautiful place cards hand-lettered in blue for the boys and in pink for the girls. When Charlotte blew out the candles this time, she whispered to herself, "I wish tonight would last forever." She was tired of that old self-fulfilling gag; this time she dared Fate and wished for the impossible.

There had been another of those behind-the-scenes disputes between Papa and Mamma as to how and where Charlotte's education was to be continued. "I think I'd like to send Charlotte to boarding school, preferably one in the East," Inez said. "Let her associate just with girls for a few years. She has reached the age now when she's liable to go boy crazy. You remember how Agnes was in high school. Nothing but chasing around and raising Cain. Flunking right and left. It took her five years to finish a four-year course, and her report cards were a disgrace."

"There's no justice in punishing Charlotte for Agnes's sins," Paul snapped. "Agnes has turned out all right, too. Kids in their teens are all sort of half crazy, and if you ask my opinion, that's all right too. You're young only once."

"You just don't want to have Charlotte out of your sight," Mrs. Emerson twitted.

"All right then, if you say so. Make the most of it." Mr. Emerson set his lips tight. He seldom wore that look at home. When he wore it in the office, everybody jumped.

So Charlotte entered a strange new world. She who had been among the first now took her place at the tail of the procession.

To begin with, there was no homeroom teacher like Miss Fox, presiding over a place where a girl could sit down and get acquainted. All the students had desks in a huge impersonal assembly room, with the seating arranged alphabetically. For each subject the student had to go to a different classroom. They were addressed as "Miss" and "Mister." The sound of a bell signaled their goings and comings. Charlotte felt negligible, lost in a crowd, homesick for the days when, friendly or not, the teacher was always the same and always *there*. This wasn't fun. It wasn't even tolerable. Miss Emerson didn't see how she was going to endure year after year of this loneliness and monotony.

She was too proud to complain to Papa. She didn't know how she could explain the situation to Mamma. She whispered some of it to Stub, who didn't understand but did wag his tail at her and put up his head to be patted. Charlotte lived now for Friday afternoon, and it seemed barely a breathing space from then until Monday morning.

Then gradually she became interested in her work. English was always fun, of course, and her Latin teacher was good-looking and trim and crisp-spoken. Latin came alive on her hands. It was hard, yes; but this was the way people had once written and spoken and even thought. Algebra was hard in a different way, but it was nice when the thing finally came out for you. Long division had once been hard for her too, Charlotte remembered. But that was such ages ago, it might almost have happened to someone else.

By Thanksgiving she was pretty well straightened around. She had a lot to be thankful for this year. Yes, and some of it was her own doing. A nice thought. Charlotte wrote it out in crayons and put it in a desk drawer in what had now become her study. The crayon drawings framed in her childhood still hung there, but now she gave people store-bought Christmas presents. She charged them on Papa's account, of course, but she did go to the trouble of selecting and wrapping them.

The Christmas holidays were only too short. They always were. But then in February came an extra vacation. At the end of the first semester, students who had an average of 85 or better were exempt from examinations. Charlotte scored 87 in Latin, 90 in Algebra, and in English a proud 93. All this wonderful winter week to herself—and no homework. Charlotte now liked high school. Indeed she did. But she liked it best from a distance.

As a sophomore she would be required to carry four subjects. Three of them followed naturally: Sophomore English, Caesar, Geometry. For the fourth Charlotte elected French. She was going to be a linguist, maybe, when and if. She would go back to Quebec and jabber at the natives in their own jargon. Or maybe just content herself with reading French books. There must be an awful lot of them. What a joy to be Charlotte Emerson, with more and more ability to read, and all those years ahead of her in which to read and keep on reading! Dear little Miss Fox and the alphabet! It all went back to that.

By the time she reached her junior year, East Division High School had sunk its tentacles very deep into Charlotte's personal life. Now when they went to the Saturday matinee, Mamma often bought three seats, and they took a high-school friend of Charlotte's along with them. Three times during the winter Charlotte gave a large luncheon party for the other girls. Several of them repaid her hospitality. Really the year was not long enough. Or was it just that there weren't Saturdays enough? Boys often walked her home from high school; carried her books, talked about teachers and their oddities, came in to play with Stub and drink lemonade or eat candy.

Passing fancies, but very real while they lasted. They made Charlotte's heart beat faster. Her ready laughter rang out at the slightest quip. When she posed before the long mirror in her bedroom, she laughed just to hear how she sounded. She struck various poses and tossed her head and glanced provocatively over her shoulder. And those after-school lads! Sometimes it was one boy, sometimes another, sometimes two of them together. That was awful fun, when there were two of them together, each trying to edge the other one out.

Her class work suffered slightly. She had to take one examination the first semester and two the second. But she passed them both with flying colors, and found that she rather enjoyed pitting her wits against the examiner's. Then when Papa took her to Quebec in the summer, she asked several questions of French-speaking natives, and they understood and answered; and she read some of the petitions posted in the little French churches. Such droll petitions many of them were, asking a supernatural agency to help Jacques get through fourth-grade arithmetic, or make Suzanne's bad leg better. Still, they did show how many people needed help.

For her senior year Charlotte was appointed a monitor. That meant that she had a back seat in the assembly room, took the attendance, and had charge of the report cards of everybody in her row when the day came for getting the monthly marks. It also meant that she could talk to anybody she pleased during a study hour, and could leave the assembly room without asking permission at the desk. A reward for faithful service. Yes, and a stimulus; Charlotte would work harder than ever this year.

She would! She would have, only—oh well, she worked hard enough, at that!

That year she began to go to dances. She had three beautiful party frocks, ankle length, with lovely full skirts which could be made to billow out around her when her partner gave her a quick reverse. Her patent leather pumps had high heels, and from the lightness they lent to her motions they might have been Mercury's feathered sandals. For school she now wore her hair braided, with the braid turned up and fastened by a second bow at the crown of her head; but on dance nights it was piled high, fastened with shell pins such as grownup ladies wore. The dances were well chaperoned and ended at midnight. But while they lasted they were sheer enchantment, a rapture such as Charlotte had not known since she was a tiny girl at a birthday party and watched the balloons sail away into the beautiful blue unknown.

While she danced with him, Charlotte and her partner experienced a mystical union. Each youth in turn was a prince to her, but only while they whirled and dipped and slid. A dance and its encore—and that was that. Charlotte's idea of a heavenly evening was to have every dance a waltz, to dance each one with a different partner, and to have him give her a double reverse every other time.

She had two different swains that winter, both of them boys who had walked her home from school—was it only a year ago? In the spring a third youth cut in. He had the attraction of novelty, and, yes, he was a little bit better dancer than the others. When May was turning into June, he brought her home from a dance one night, and not only came in but walked through the house with her and out into the back garden.

They stood there drinking in the night's enchantment. Then they turned to each other; he put his arms around her and with one hand lifted her face toward his. Very softly and gently he kissed her; kissed her a second time, then allowed her to withdraw a little, but still stood looking down at her. Charlotte had a strange sense both of surprise and of fulfillment.

Then he spoke—or rather whispered—"You will wait for me. You *will* wait for me, won't you, sweetheart?"

With a crash, Charlotte came down to earth. Did he mean he wanted her to spend the rest of her life with him? To be tied to him day and night, when there was no more dancing and Lake Michigan was out of sight and the music had long since ceased to sound? She put out both hands and pushed him away.

He seized her again. This time he kissed her roughly. Charlotte jerked away from him, and slapped his face sharply.

He let her go then. Charlotte turned and dashed into the house. He followed her and began a stumbling apology. Behind the open door of the sitting room Papa and Mamma were waiting up for her. Papa got to his feet, took a quick glance at the two of them, then hoped that the young man had had a pleasant evening and showed him out.

"Sit down and get your breath back," Mamma invited. "Would you like a lemonade? Or maybe a soda pop?"

"I'd like a long drink of ice water," Charlotte answered. "I'll get it for myself."

While she was out of the room Inez lifted her eyebrows at Paul. He smiled and shook his head.

"Think they've had a quarrel?" she asked.

"All the better if they have. I'd hate to see her, at her age, getting any serious ideas."

"At her age!" Inez was suddenly wistful and a little sad. She was looking, not at the wall of her charming room, but down the vista of her own past. After a moment's pause she sighed and said, "At her age, I suppose she's in love with love itself."

"That's just fine," said Paul. "That's something she will grow out of. And before too long, I hope."

"Paul dear, you know what happens. She'll grow away from us. You don't really want to see that happen."

"You're telling me?" he snapped. "She plans to start in at the university this very next fall. She will be away from here most of the time for four years, and home will never look the same to her again."

"She will be in good surroundings for four years, and doing congenial work. Besides, that's next fall. We still have this coming summer which she can spend with us."

"Indeed we have. We must make it a very special summer." Paul's brow cleared. He was smiling when Charlotte came back into the room.

❧ 5 ❧

PAUL EMERSON TOOK a four-week vacation that summer. He and his wife and Charlotte spent the time in New York City.

To Charlotte, the seasoned traveler, this was the best trip yet. Each day was different, but every night they could return to the homelike comfort of their hotel suite. They had breakfast here in their sitting room, but they lunched all over town and never dined twice in the same place. They visited the Statue of Liberty, and climbed up inside it, and tried to imagine what the first sight of its majestic bulk must have meant to thousands of poor immigrants. They rode up and down town on the doubledecker Fifth Avenue bus, with its open-air seats on top. They took a big boat around Manhattan Island, and another which carried them up the Hudson River, with a stopover at West Point. They visited museums and art galleries until their heads swam. They saw shops of unimaginable richness. They went to theaters and to a roof garden. Papa bought

Charlotte a string of small perfectly matched pearls. For Mamma he chose a ring, a large opal surrounded by diamonds. Yes, some people thought that opals brought bad luck, but Paul couldn't see Tiffany's selling, or telling, fortunes.

Home again in Saylesboro, Charlotte hardly had time to get her breath back before she was off again. This time not for a trip; this time to stay and study. She would live away from home. She would have to make important decisions for herself. A scant four years from now, she would face a fully adult future. Bachelor's degree in hand, Charlotte Emerson would take her place in the adult world.

She had elected to go to her own state university. Her high school was accredited there, so college entrance examinations were a hurdle she need not face. The campus was extremely beautiful, and Charlotte was accustomed to beauty in her surroundings. Finally, the University of Wisconsin was coeducational, with more than three men to every girl. When it came to choosing a college, perhaps that was as good a reason as any.

In undergraduate life a large part was played by Greek letter societies, both men's and women's. Charlotte Emerson was clearly a desirable addition to any group; she chose Gamma Delta. Pledging was fun, initiation very solemn and impressive—almost like a wedding, but lasting longer and with more persons involved.

All girls. That was the catch. When she went into the chapter house to live, Charlotte found it was a real catch. Nobody but girls at the table: girls and the chaperone, a gray-haired woman who earned her keep by living there in the house and making sure that everything was kept respectable. As if it wouldn't be, with all the sisters feeling

entitled to poke their noses into other people's business!
Being expected to answer the telephone right along, just
because she was a freshman. Having to share a bedroom
with another girl. They had separate beds and dressers, to
be sure, but Charlotte wasn't used to having somebody
everlastingly *there*. Worst of all, on week nights after dinner, dancing with other girls. That wasn't Charlotte Emerson's idea of what dancing was for.

But the academic side of life was wonderful. There was
no tiresome assembly room to make you feel that you were
serving out a jail sentence; you simply showed up when
you were due to get to work. In the classroom, you didn't
have to stand when you recited. Many courses proceeded
by means of lectures, and attendance was taken only at the
weekly quiz sections. In the evening, studying in the great
reading room at the library was fairly a social function in
itself. If sometimes a sister could be observed making a
quiet track into the periodical room—well, maybe she had
reached the point where she could no longer concentrate,
and a little diversion was in order.

Weekends were fun. A caller would presently walk his
girl downtown to an ice cream parlor; or several couples
would get together in the big Gamma Delta living room
and exchange badinage and eat candy. If no fraternity
party was available, there were dancing clubs to be patronized, the Knockers or the Doodlers or the Idle Hour. There
was intercollegiate football in the fall, with a preliminary
mass meeting to work up enthusiasm. Basketball was even
more fun to watch, and Wisconsin did better at it. Just
before Christmas vacation began, the Gamma Delta girls
had their Christmas tree, with a cheap present for every-
one and a verse supposed to satirize her peculiarities. Charlotte's ran,

> Lottie has all the virtues
> Of which the poet sings,
> But she is just a little bit too prone
> To turn up her nose at things.

That really hit home. Charlotte flushed and bit her lip. Maybe it wasn't altogether too bad that the sisters took an interest in her affairs. Maybe it was true that Charlotte was a little too accustomed to adoring parents and to youths who told her how pretty she was and how well she danced.

The Thanksgiving holiday had been so brief that it was over before she knew it. But at Christmas came a real vacation. Time for a good visit with Papa and Mamma, for a round of Saylesboro parties, for sorting out impressions of those three packed months as an undergraduate. They had been interesting, exciting, stimulating, but by no means flawless. On the train going back to Madison, Charlotte was just a little bit homesick.

She had barely finished her unpacking, however, and had hardly become accustomed to all that feminine chatter at the dinner table, when something very pleasant happened. Charlotte received an invitation to attend the University of Wisconsin Junior Prom.

No one called it "an invitation," of course. It was a "Prom bid." It would never have done to say "professor" or "library" in full. Time was just too valuable.

Here was something to look forward to. Something to write home about. Something that the other sisters would notice and admire.

Her acceptance of his bid gave Nat Briscoe a mortgage on Charlotte's time for the next six weeks. That was fair enough, and fun enough. Six weeks of a nice fellow, seen always in the radiance of what was to come.

The Prom itself was like a trip to fairyland: the lights, the music, her gorgeous new gown, her corsage getting just a little crushed as the evening wore on, and smelling all the sweeter for the crushing. Familiar faces looking strange in the crowd. Man after man, but always back to Nat at intervals. Back to Nat there at the very end, when it seemed as if it couldn't end and had never had a beginning; seemed as if she had always been dancing here in this great room with the pulsing music and the soft lights, and would go on dancing here until time itself should cease.

There were other festivities that weekend, too: all enjoyable enough, but none of them possessing the enchantment of the Great Night itself. The first balloons had floated off into the unimaginable distance; these others were a little bit handicapped.

Then classes resumed, and the familiar round of life at the chapter house, and each weekend pretty well looking out for itself as it came along. Nat Briscoe came calling, and took her out on two or three minor dates. Then when he phoned, Charlotte pleaded a previous engagement. She learned that she would be expected to take him to the Gamma Delta Spring Formal. That was fine. He was a nice fellow. Their dance steps agreed perfectly. Charlotte really liked him. But enough was enough.

So here it was late June again, and Charlotte back home in the big house on Lake Michigan, and Papa blessedly here at the dinner table. Charlotte wasn't here every night herself; not by any means. She now belonged to the young set in Saylesboro, just as surely as if she had stayed right here and made her debut. But some of her old friends were already married. Others made a point of getting away for the summer. A few Charlotte simply ducked; vacation was too precious to be wasted. She did go to see Nursie-Anna, who now had a small son, with another baby on the way. That young man hadn't had to account to Papa for the way he treated "this little girl."

This year Papa took only a two-week vacation, and the three Emersons spent the time pretty close to home. They visited the Dells of the Wisconsin, a region of rare natural beauty, and nearby Devil's Lake, a place so strange as to justify its name. The more Charlotte saw, the more she marveled and remembered.

Charlotte and Mamma made two shopping expeditions to Chicago. They did not see Agnes, who was off at a summer resort and sent them occasional picture postcards. She came to Saylesboro for a visit late in August. She had grown fat and fretful. She complained a great deal about how hard it was to keep servants, and how men didn't appreciate what a job housekeeping was. "They think as long as they pay the bills, a woman ought to be satisfied." She was snappish with little Inez. The child liked to be with Charlotte, who put aside her own concerns to try to make her niece happy.

If that's what marriage is like, give me single blessedness, Charlotte grumbled to herself. To be sure, Papa and Mamma were married. But in their case it was different. In their case, everything was different.

Then in September Stub died. Poor darling little Stub, the only dog Charlotte had ever owned. She hadn't had much time to be with him in recent years, but she mourned his passing. They buried him in the back garden, and Charlotte bought a little balloon to put in his grave, and another to set floating in his honor.

So now here was Charlotte back in the chapter house, a full-fledged sophomore, if you please. With another generation of freshmen to answer the telephone for her. With something of a record to live up to, and something of a reputation to live down. She had been to Prom last year; too bad if she had to sit it out this time. And she had shown that she didn't consider all the girls' doings so fascinating. Had shown it all too plainly. What if she was Charlotte Emerson, daughter of Emerson Manufacturing? Here in Madison she was just one of the sisters.

The problem of after-dinner dancing she tackled first. Sometimes she left early for the library and the evening's studying. Other times she invented new quirks just to puzzle her partner, or doubled or halved the beat of the music. On odd evenings she simply danced straight through. The sisters never knew which one was coming. Neither, for that matter, did Charlotte.

Nat Briscoe came briefly back into the picture. With a little encouragement he would have repeated last year's performance. But twice in a row would be too much of a good thing. Charlotte could take a flying trip back to Saylesboro if she turned out to be at loose ends the weekend of Prom.

She didn't have to. Jeff King came along. He was just as nice as Nat Briscoe, and he had the added attraction of novelty.

So there they were again, making their way through another evening of enchantment. If once or twice Charlotte found herself recalling the other—well, perhaps that was to be expected, but it was just a little sad. This might be the penalty of growing older, that she would have fewer and fewer of those fabulous firsts.

Early in the spring Jefferson King came up with another idea. "Let's you and me get engaged, Charlotte. You wear my pin. We can have such wonderful times together when we're engaged."

When a girl wore a man's fraternity pin, it was a trophy. Just like those scalps an Indian chief might dangle at his belt! An engaged couple had a recognized right to do a considerable amount of love-making. "An engagement for spooning purposes only," some cynic had dubbed such an arrangement. Doubtless it was convenient. It was enjoyable, if that was your idea of having fun. But it did tie a girl down. No man would try to date a girl who was wearing another man's pin.

Charlotte smiled and shook her head. "I really can't take your pin. But thank you for asking me."

Jeff flushed with anger—the age-old anger of the rejected male. "Have you anything against me personally? Or is there someone else?"

"No, and no. I like you, or I shouldn't be talking to you this minute. But I'm not ready to tie myself down."

"Later, perhaps?"

Charlotte did not answer. "Later" was a short word when you wrote it out on paper, but spoken it had tremendous implications.

Jeff took an early and dignified departure. The next weekend he did not phone her. Charlotte bore up bravely under the deprivation. She would sooner miss him once in a while than have him constantly under foot.

He came back into the picture soon enough. Charlotte invited him to the Gamma Delta Spring Formal. Jeff danced better than ever that evening, and his double reverse was really tricky. Charlotte hated to see the evening end, hated to part from him. But when he spoke of coming to visit her in Saylesboro that summer, she told him that she was going to be away most of the summer. Papa always took her on a long vacation trip, and she also planned to visit her married sister in Chicago.

As it turned out she wasn't away all that much. But while she was at home, she wanted time to herself. That was a luxury which college life did not afford her, and she had some important decisions to make. All these years she had been Charlotte Emerson, daughter of Emerson Manufacturing and inhabitant of the big house overlooking Lake Michigan. At home and when she traveled, she had been waited on hand and foot. It was grand and glorious, and she enjoyed it. But there were other ways of living. She would have had to get along somehow if she had been born plain Jane Smith. Couldn't she, just once in a way, go out and be taken at her own unvarnished value?

That fall, when she embarked on her junior year, Charlotte decided to take the required courses in pedagogy which would qualify her for her teacher's certificate. If she completed a year's satisfactory teaching anywhere in the state, her certificate would be countersigned. She would be a full-fledged schoolmarm, qualified to earn her own living. She would have shown everybody that she was capable of standing on her own two feet, even when they were not shod with dancing slippers and moving in rhythm.

She was majoring in English, with a minor in Romance languages. Funny how much there was still to learn in English, though she had spoken the language all her life, and in French, though she had been able to make herself understood in the Province of Quebec. All the better if there was. That would give her more patience with her pupils when she embarked on her teaching career.

Papa was proud of her decision to teach. She had a long life ahead of her and might do many different things. "You might even come into the business one of these days," he said. Never a hint that if she had been a boy, that was what *he* normally would have done.

A person makes an important decision, and the heavens fail to fall. Here was Charlotte Emerson looking ahead to classroom chalk and attendance records, but undergraduate life, and in particular the doings at the Gamma Delta chapter house, went along much as before. Charlotte studied and went to parties and got excited about football games. She went to Prom with still a different man. She had to keep up her record, to be consistent in inconsistency. Milton Young was quite the nicest one yet. Or at least he was as nice as any of the others. A really neat bunch of scalps now dangled at Charlotte's belt.

She bargained with Papa this summer. If she spent most of her time right here at home, could he afford her a big trip next year? Would her graduation gift be a tour of Europe?

"You're a shrewd bargainer, Small One," Papa chuckled. "I think after all we'd better put you to work in a bank."

So Charlotte finished her senior year. She went to Prom this time with Jack Steenis. They made a neat quartet, those Prom partners of hers. She was recognized now as a popular girl. Word had also got around that she was hard-hearted. All the better if she was, of course. She could afford to be.

The week after she graduated she cinched her job for next fall. She would go to Belair, Wisconsin, a town only two stations from Madison. There she was to teach English and history in the small high school. Doubtless, with a little wire-pulling, she could have managed to secure a position right there in Saylesboro. But that was exactly what she didn't want. She was going out to learn as well as to teach.

Papa sent Charlotte and her mother on a conducted tour of Europe. It would last eight weeks, and would take them to England, France, and Italy. He went with them to New York, saw them aboard their liner, waved to them from the dock. That was often the destiny of the American male, Charlotte realized later; to finance the trip, to see the womenfolk off, and to get his satisfaction out of their happiness.

The trip was wonderful. It was a dream come true, but better than any dream that Charlotte could remember having. It was the finest thing that had ever happened to her in a lifetime of fine things. It was breathtaking while it unrolled; it would always be hers to remember. It ended only too soon. On the return voyage Charlotte settled down to sort out her impressions, and to enjoy that lovely last experience of a sea voyage.

Then it happened. A man spoke to the cruise director and afterward introduced himself to the ladies. He was an American, somewhat older than Charlotte but much younger than Mamma. He was in business in Euclid, Ohio. He had been to the Continent on a business trip. Would they take pity on his loneliness and allow him to escort them to some shipboard functions?

Charlotte had a queer catch of the breath when he spoke to her; the color rose swiftly to her cheeks. But of course her agitation didn't mean anything. This was just a natural reaction to a fellow American after seeing so many foreigners. Still, he was rather nice. Mamma seemed to like him. It was pleasant to have an agreeable escort. And yes, he danced well, and he complimented her on her dancing.

His name was William Andrews. "But it's Bill to friends, of course." He was engaged in the manufacture of automobiles.

Well, ships were good enough for Charlotte. Ships, and a shipboard acquaintance. Very pleasant, and highly transitory. Quickly coming and quickly going. Not to be taken seriously. But fine while they lasted. The crowning touch

to a wonderful summer. Nothing to be startled or upset
about. Something to be taken in one's stride. And of course
Charlotte Emerson was taking this in her stride.

❦ 6 ❦

BELAIR, WISCONSIN, was geographically not far from
Madison. In living conditions, it was very far removed.
Vastly different, too, was Miss Emerson, neophyte teacher,
from Gamma Delta Charlotte, who had Prommed it with
Nat and Jeff and Milt and Jack, hollered herself hoarse at
football games, went canoeing on early summer evenings,
enjoyed those long sessions of study in the great reading
room with its rows of green-shaded lamps shining down on
bent heads and intent faces. She wasn't a fish out of water,
exactly. More like an early amphibian painfully learning to
live on dry land.

The high school was small. In a way, that was an advantage; she would soon get to know most of the students by
sight if not by name, even those who were not in her
classes. It was also poor; the building was shabby and not
any too clean. She was a stranger come among natives; she
could not guess how she looked to them in her simple but
sophisticated clothes and her rather elaborate grooming. A
stranger is always suspect; he is an alien, a foreigner.

She was lucky enough to secure a room with a middle-
aged couple who lived in a small house on the outskirts. It
was the only room finished off on the second floor. In the

middle of it was a large "drum," through which heat was supposed to come up from the big stove downstairs. The washstand contained a full set of bedroom crockery, the like of which Charlotte had never seen before. It made cleanliness laborious. But the room possessed one great advantage: she had it to herself.

Charlotte had one lengthy session with the principal. His name was Eric Swenson. He was a graduate of a small college in Minnesota, and this was his third year here. Obviously he thought quite highly of himself. Well, his principalship was success of a sort. A big frog in a small pond can create a splash which sounds very loud in his own ears.

That afternoon they had a faculty meeting. There were two other teachers present, a middle-aged Miss Nerman, who lived here in Belair with her parents though her experience might have entitled her to a better job, and a shy, awkward newcomer who wore thick-lensed spectacles slightly askew. She was introduced as Miss Kaminski. Embarrassed perhaps by her foreign-sounding name, Miss Kaminski giggled and remarked to Charlotte. "Any relation to Ralph Waldo Emerson?"

Charlotte started to say, "Ralph Waldo? Seems to me I've heard the name somewhere." She checked herself in time, and replied, "I never cared much for Emerson's essays, but I've found some of his poems very much to the point." Misplaced facetiousness could cause a very bad first impression.

The schedule was organized and Miss Emerson and Miss Kaminski shown to their respective classrooms. Charlotte sat down at the desk where she was to preside during all these months to come. She drew a long breath, and for a moment experienced a sense of unreality. Exactly what had she let herself in for? And why on earth had she let herself in for it?

Then school began in earnest. The students made out their programs and were assigned to classes. Charlotte taught two classes in freshman English, two in sophomore. In the afternoon she had one class in American history and one in general history. That last was a poser; it meant covering too much space in too little time. But after all, the students must learn something.

Freshman English papers were appalling at first. Then Charlotte discovered that she had set her standards too high. She must take things as they came. If a person could begin further back—! But her business was to go on from here.

It was all so new and strange. Sometimes Charlotte could scarcely believe that it was happening. Other times, when she sat in the evening in her lonely room, or stretched out, tired but wide awake, in her slightly lumpy bed, it was her other world that seemed unreal. Especially the wonderful summer just past. Most especially that Bill Andrews. A shipboard acquaintance. She would never see or hear from him again. But their meeting had been thrilling. The excitement of it was wonderful to recall, here in the dullness and the loneliness.

She wrote home, of course: short, cheerful letters. Mamma answered at more length, and gave her various items of news. But as yet Charlotte had no plans for visiting home. As for Madison, that was now merely a place where she would change trains on her way back to Saylesboro.

Then in the middle of the week a package arrived for her. A package from Euclid, Ohio, in fact. From W. G. Andrews. It was a five-pound box of chocolates.

He hadn't forgotten. He was keeping himself in the picture, sending her something which in ordinary decency she must acknowledge. Or—the inevitable catch when hope sprang too high—was this just a gracious way of bowing out of the picture?

Charlotte stood treat to her landlord and his wife, to the other members of the faculty, to students who came in after school with questions about their work. Then she sat down to write Bill her thanks. She didn't stop with a brief note; she went on to tell him that she found the little town strange and her job interesting. She wound up with, "I hope the world is treating you well. How goes it in the business of making gasoline stoves on wheels?"

That night when she undressed, Charlotte found herself singing. Humming one of those waltzes which had once whirled her away into a land of enchantment. It was pleasant to be here singing to herself. Her wide experience gave her an insight into narrow problems. (Or at least it should do so.) She knew she was going to like Belair very much.

Mamma's next letter reported that she too had had a box of candy from "nice Bill Andrews. It was courteous of him to remember the old lady." Better not attach too much importance to a trifle like that. It might be that Bill wished to stand in well with the parent. Just as well, it might be merely a casual gesture. He must have bought a good many boxes of candy in his time.

Bill answered Charlotte's letter promptly. He used office stationery, but his reply was carefully written out in longhand. She appreciated his going to all that trouble; it was complimentary that when he communicated with her he did not desire to do so through a stenographer. But there were advantages to a dictated letter; these scribbles were not easy to read. Bill realized that himself. Twice he scratched out a line and rewrote it; twice he printed out an important word.

But what he had to say was worth deciphering. Business was good, thank you. There would be improvements in next year's models. It was interesting to be in a business which was developing so rapidly. The weather was cooling off very pleasantly; he always enjoyed the approach of fall. His birthday was in October, too. "But let's not say which birthday. Women aren't the only ones who are sensitive on the subject of age. Oh, you're too young to have that make any difference to you!"

Before Charlotte got around to answering this letter another box of candy arrived, this time from a different confectioner. Mr. Andrews must like to spend his money. She wondered whether he had favored Mamma this time too.

In her free hours Charlotte explored the little town. To her eyes it did not look quite real. The men dawdled over their yard work, the women over their marketing. Everybody seemed to have time to stop and talk to everybody else.

What they talked about was something of a mystery to Charlotte. Family affairs, probably, and minding the neighbors' business for them. There was one small weekly newspaper, and no public library.

That lack of a plentiful supply of reading matter bothered Charlotte. Doubtless Robinson Crusoe on his desert island had somehow managed without it. But this wasn't a wilderness. This was modern America, the land of the common man and the public school.

In her own small way Charlotte could do something about that. She went home for a weekend early in October. Papa was so glad to see her that he almost cried. Mamma said, "Paul, anybody would think to see you that Charlotte had just got back from exile in Siberia." But Mamma was just disguising her own emotion by blaming it on him.

In honor of the occasion they each had a cocktail before dinner. Ever since she graduated from the university, Charlotte had been allowed an occasional cocktail. She and Mamma chose Manhattans; Papa had himself one martini. They dined on porterhouse steaks an inch thick. They found plenty to talk about; there is so much that does not get into letters. Then at her late bedtime Charlotte had a hot bath in her own tub. She nearly scoured her skin off, and after her vigorous scrubbing she refilled the tub, and lay there in the clear water and basked.

Charlotte and Mamma went to the matinee Saturday. Afterward Papa met them and took them out to dinner. This was just like the old times, only better. Anything is better when it comes as a novelty.

That evening she told her parents of her project. The three of them spent a delightful hour selecting and arguing and reminiscing. When Charlotte returned to Belair on Sunday, she carried with her a suitcase full of recent novels.

She began with her sophomore English classes on Monday. "I'm sure that you all have books at home and enjoy reading them. But there is extra pleasure in reading a new book. I now have some which I brought here just to lend to you. The five students who have the highest marks this week will each be entitled to borrow a book on Friday. You may keep them until you have finished them, then return them to me. Do you all understand?"

The idea caught on. There were some delays, of course, and some disappointments. But by the time the books had been exchanged twice, the lucky five began to talk about them to Charlotte, then to one another. In another two weeks it had become stylish to read.

"Your students come into your room and talk to you after school," Miss Kaminski complained.

"That's because I teach English and they like to read," Charlotte said easily. But she felt a warm glow in her heart. She was making them like to read. That was one of the greatest gifts that could ever be bestowed on a person, and it would last all his life.

Then she softened a little. "How about walking downtown with me this afternoon, if you've nothing better to do? I'll treat you to an ice cream soda, and we can both relax."

Miss Kaminski flushed, hesitated, started to refuse. Then she said in a very small voice, "Thank you, I'm sure that will be very nice."

They had their sodas in the town's ice cream parlor. When Charlotte offered refills Miss Kaminski said, "That will be nice. But you must let me pay this time."

"I can't," Charlotte said. "This is Thursday, and your money isn't good on Thursdays."

"Why are you like this?" Miss Kaminski demanded in a shrill tone. "Why are you always lovely to me, when I'm sometimes horrid to you?"

"You're not horrid," Charlotte said quickly. "You're shy, and that makes you say things you don't mean."

Miss Kaminski's voice grew even edgier. "You're always so terribly kind. But that's easy for you. You're pretty, and you're rich. You've never had to wear spectacles that made you look like an owl. You've never had to wear clothes that were cheap to begin with, and belonged to your older sister, and were shabby by the time you got them. You've never—oh, what am I saying?"

"Nothing that isn't true," Charlotte assured her. "Go ahead and say some more, if it will make you feel better."

Miss Kaminski shook her head. "I'm not going to open my mouth again except to eat that other soda. Will you please go ahead and order it for us?" And she smiled a little.

There must be many such people in the world, worthy souls, honest, conscientious, hard-working, but destined to a completely drab existence. Charlotte felt slightly guilty for having been born with every advantage. She couldn't reshape the lives of all the less fortunate. But she could do something to help an individual. She would find out Miss Kaminski's size and buy her a brand-new blouse for Christmas. Meanwhile she would take her one of the Saylesboro books to read in her off hours.

Charlotte wrote to Bill Andrews about her book project, of course. Having such a good subject made a letter very easy to write. She would have managed to fill a page or two in any case, just for the pleasure of hearing from him. Bill answered:

Would that I had had a few teachers like you in my unregenerate youth, kind lady! In that case I might have turned into a nice, kindly, absent-minded professor who flourished in the groves of Academe, instead of the sponsor for so much noise and stench. I never hated learning, really; it was just that I didn't like to have it forced upon me. Now you have invented a system of teaching by rewards instead of penalties. Maybe you will write a textbook one of these days. Then your name will go up in the Teachers' Hall of Fame alongside Socrates's. (Is that the right way to spell the possessive?)

He did more than write; he sent her a sizable package of brand-new books. So now Charlotte could read before she lent. When you are willing to help other people, maybe somebody will come along and help you. Charlotte could hold that saying in reserve for the textbook she was not going to write.

She did manage to get to Madison for the big football game. But she returned to Belair that very evening. Among the undergraduates she felt curiously ancient and remote. As for the alumnae sisters, they would be there again next year—most of them.

Charlotte went home for the Thanksgiving recess, of course. Home was one of the things she had to be thankful for. Only one of the things, at that, though a home like hers would in itself have been sufficient cause for the festival.

It was nine o'clock Wednesday evening when she reached Saylesboro. Papa and Mamma both met her at the station. On their way home through the familiar streets, Mamma informed her, "This is the second train we've met tonight. Guess who was on the first."

Charlotte gasped audibly, guessed, was afraid to voice her guess. It just wasn't—it couldn't be! She said lightly, "Santa Claus, I suppose, getting here ahead of time."

Papa chuckled. "Right, of course. But he has shaved his whiskers, and his sleigh has a motor."

"Not Bill Andrews?" Charlotte insisted.

"Well, that's the name he goes under."

"He wrote to us a week ago," Mamma explained. "He asked whether we would 'take pity on a poor forlorn bachelor' and invite him for Thanksgiving dinner. He said he wouldn't inflict himself on us farther than that; he'd stay at an hotel."

"An" hotel. That was right. "An" historical, but "a" history. The schoolteacher in Charlotte's bosom gave a single parting salute. She wouldn't be heard from again for four days.

"It seems a long way for him to come just to get a slice of turkey," Charlotte said softly. Nobody else said anything.

Thanksgiving day was itself something to be thankful for. Then on Friday Papa showed Bill Andrews over Emerson Manufacturing. That evening Bill had the three Emersons as his dinner guests at his hotel. His good night this time was good-bye, but before he left he had accepted their invitation to spend Christmas with them. He had been a shipboard acquaintance, then the "stranger within thy gates"; now he was established as a family friend.

Charlotte still knew little about him. His parents were dead; he was a graduate of Yale; he had a married sister living in Denver. As if all that really mattered! She knew him as she knew her own good right hand, as she knew the air she breathed, as she knew the vast beautiful expanse of Lake Michigan. Somewhere he had always been waiting for her. Through all these past years, while she had eaten and slept and studied and danced, Charlotte had been waiting for him.

Back in Belair once more, she was too busy to be lonesome—or almost too busy. Winter was beginning in earnest; more than once Charlotte had to wade through snow drifts on her way to school. In her general history class, the Roman Empire was headed for ruin, and on the horizon loomed the Dark Ages, that epoch of medievalism when the mass of the population was totally illiterate and, worse still perhaps, in the words of a former professor of Charlotte's, spent "a thousand years without soap." Correcting papers was monotonous and sometimes exasperating; too many pupils kept making the same mistakes over and over. But her plans for teaching the bright ones to love reading really were succeeding. The mail was something to look forward to. Close to her heart was the lovely consciousness that somewhere Bill was thinking of her, and knew that she must be thinking of him.

He was coming to her at Christmas; and by "he" Charlotte did not mean Santa Claus. But Charlotte did not forget Santa Claus. She gave Miss Kaminski that beautiful new blouse, and she read the immortal story about Scrooge aloud to her freshman English classes, one installment at a time.

Charlotte reached home in time to help with the Christmas decorations. Mamma added an extra touch this year. In the middle of three different doorways she fastened a sprig of mistletoe. Agnes's husband sniffed when he saw it. He was a balding old bore. Agnes was fatter than ever, and sillier. Had those two ever been in love with each other in their dull and shallow way? Could love of any sort let two people down so badly?

The mistletoe was for Bill Andrews' benefit, of course. He took full advantage of it. The first time that he ever approached Charlotte under it, she saw him coming and escaped. But the second time he caught her fairly. He kissed her three times, quickly, lightly. Then he held her away from him and whispered, "You know?"

"I know," Charlotte whispered back. This time she kissed him, and their embrace was long and solemn.

The two of them had a week of unbelievable happiness. Back in Belair after New Year's, Charlotte almost regretted her decision to teach. The town seemed so far away and the job so dreary. But she never even considered welshing. She would finish out her year just to show everybody—herself included.

Bill wrote to her even oftener now, and his missives were frankly love letters. But hadn't they always been that, in a sense? He had never allowed a third person to intervene in their composition.

He suggested once that he come to visit her in Belair. Charlotte vetoed that idea. It would make a long hard trip for him, and it would inevitably set tongues wagging.

She saw him again at Easter, of course. All too briefly, but to some purpose. Bill asked Papa's consent to their engagement. He also wished to know Charlotte's ring size.

"Plenty of time for that later," Charlotte said airily. In a sense she was eager for the Great Event which would make them one; in another way she almost dreaded it. This present bliss was filled with longing, but the light of that Paradise ahead was too intense and dazzling.

In May Charlotte paid Madison a visit. The short train trip was a pleasure in itself; the country was at its loveliest, in the tender green of late spring, with great patches of wild blue iris in blossom at the sides of the railroad track. The sight of her old haunts brought back a past already grown incredible and persons once close who had altogether vanished from her ken. There was a tradition that one of the ushers at a wedding was always a disappointed suitor of the bride. How touching was the idea that Charlotte might have been preceded up the aisle by a quartet of them!

Then the school year drew to its close. Charlotte marked her final set of examination papers. She didn't flunk anybody; maybe the borderline cases would do better under another regime. She handed in her resignation.

Her teacher's certificate had been countersigned. She was actually worth her salt. She had paid her current expenses in Belair, and had actually managed to save a little money. She was no longer just Paul Emerson's daughter.

Papa thought all the more of her for that very reason; in his paternal pride he magnified any little achievement. She had really shown him something.

It gave her a pointer for the future, too. She would take good care not to be just Bill Andrews' wife.

Book II

HIGH NOON

❧ 1 ❧

ACTUALLY IT HAD all been settled in that brief interval under the mistletoe when Charlotte and Bill kissed each other and exchanged four words. They were truly married from that time on. But there were certain formalities to be gone through now, matters of law and of custom.

The law was easy enough to comply with. A marriage license could be quickly obtained, and at trivial cost. After that, any magistrate or parson could officiate. But custom was harder to satisfy, as Charlotte soon found out. She said, "I want to be married very simply and quietly." But Papa's feelings were hurt. In an injured tone he announced that he had done more than that for her nurse. And Mamma shook her head in deep discouragement. Going off to teach school in a country town had been bad enough, but this latest caprice passed all bounds. What would people say? Everybody would think that Charlotte was getting queer.

She couldn't hurt their feelings, of course. It was bad enough for them to know that they no longer came first with her. Charlotte smiled and said, "You want me to show what a big fish I've hooked? Very well then, I'll put Bill Andrews on exhibition."

She didn't realize what she was letting herself in for. Perhaps it was just as well that she didn't. Perhaps if we could tell in advance what is going to happen to us, cowardice would get the better of us all.

First her engagement was publicly announced. There

was a formal paragraph in the newspapers, accompanied by a photograph of Charlotte in one of her Prom gowns. Bill had obtained her ring size now, and had presented Charlotte with a solitaire diamond in a beautifully chased setting. Everybody was cordial and congratulatory; most of all, perhaps, Mamma's women friends. Mamma beamed and preened herself; you might think that she had done the whole thing. Papa shook his head and said wryly, "I can't quite realize this. It seems as if it was only yesterday that we were starting you in at school and I was trying to get used to the idea."

Only yesterday? Why, it was in the very distant past. Everything was prehistoric if it dated back to the days before Charlotte had met Bill Andrews.

But she ought to be ashamed to feel this way: she, who had always been especially near and dear to Papa. She laid her hand on his and said softly, "You've always been a wonderful father to me. Don't think I don't appreciate it."

He tried to sound offhand. "Forget it. It's been a pleasure." But neither of them would ever forget it, or forget this moment of acknowledgment.

The first fun was over now, the thrill of an announced engagement dying down to a steady pulsation. Charlotte had been designated as a prospective bride, but the complicated business of marrying off an Emerson daughter still lay ahead.

An orgy of shopping got under way. Mamma had always been extravagant where her children were concerned, but this time she really let herself go. Household linens first, relic of the days when our great-grandmothers spun and wove and cut and stitched. Bill Andrews presumably had not been sleeping on a bare mattress or using paper napkins, but Charlotte must not go to him empty-handed.

Charlotte had some choice in this matter and a real power of veto, but it was primarily Mamma's undertaking.

Next, the date for the wedding had to be set. On that subject Charlotte consulted Bill. After all, he too was getting married, though to judge by some of the goings on, you would think that the groom was just an incidental figure in the setup.

Their joint decision was for mid-September. By that time the heat of summer would have abated, but the garden would not yet have lost its summer verdancy. The garden would play a very important part in the wedding arrangements. For, yes, Charlotte would be married at home, in this stately mansion so well suited to be the site of weddings and formal dinners and ladies' luncheons and children's parties. High noon, when people had had plenty of time to get ready but the fullness of the afternoon still lay ahead of them.

The guests lists took much compiling. An omission would be pretty deadly. There was Bill's list to be included, too. He sent it, all neatly typed, with a longhand note, "Most of these people won't come, so under the circumstances an invitation is practically a bid for a present. But that's all right. It's about time I got some return for the dozens—nay, hundreds—of silver sandwich plates that I have come across with."

Charlotte's trousseau was elaborate, although she already had clothes enough to last her for the next five years. Her wedding gown took two fittings, and the veil too had to be made to order. For her "going away" outfit she had a sage green suit with all the accessories. She would have preferred blue, but to choose it would be just like hanging on herself a big sign: "I AM A BRIDE."

The bridesmaids had to have their gowns prescribed and

paid for, and since two of them were sisters in Gamma Delta and former roommates, that involved mailing patterns and lengths of silk out of town. The bride's only niece had to be included among the bridesmaids, though she was still a little short of adult stature and very gawky. The bride's only sister must be matron of honor, though she was too fat to be decorative and looked old enough to be her own mother. The women guests would notice those things. Most women had gimlet eyes.

"I declare," Charlotte grumbled to Papa, "if I had known it was going to be all this much trouble, I would have asked Bill Andrews to put a ladder up to my bedroom window so I could elope with him."

"And I," he replied, "would have helped you onto the ladder with a hundred-dollar bill pinned to your lapel."

The night before Charlotte was married, Mamma gave her a short, embarrassed, and rather incoherent talk about what lay ahead of her. It reminded Charlotte of that other talk when she was entering her teens. Only then the daughter as well as the mother was embarrassed, and the girl was puzzled instead of enlightened. Now she was sorry for her mother, and faintly amused. Charlotte had never seen any storks hovering over Saylesboro, though the population continued to increase at a normal rate.

Then at length the Great Day dawned. Dawned very fair, and just warm enough. The instant she was out of bed, Charlotte went looking for her mother. "It's such lovely weather," she said, "I think I'll go out and get married."

"Do just that," Mamma laughed. "Do, and make it the happiest day of your life."

On the stroke of noon a trio of stringed instruments struck into the voluntary, Mendelssohn's "Spring Song." At the first note of the Wedding March the bridal party started down the great front staircase. A minute later Papa gave Charlotte his arm and they waited their turn. He had given her just one look there as she was putting her hand on his coat sleeve, but that look told everything.

Charlotte had sometimes heard wives say that they couldn't remember much of their own weddings; to them, the whole thing was just a blur. She had decided that with her it wasn't going to be like that. Sure enough, it wasn't. Every detail was clear to her. Yet at the same time there was an air of unreality over everything. It was like a beautiful dream: a dream from which she wished never to wake.

Then in a matter of minutes it was all over. The ring was on her finger. The minister had shaken hands with her and called her "Mrs. Andrews." Bill had kissed her right there in front of everybody, renewing the pledge he had made her under the mistletoe. The trio struck into the strains of the second wedding march. Charlotte, on her husband's arm now, moved across the hall and took up her position in the receiving line next to her father and mother.

Then the party really got under way. The wedding presents were on display in the sitting room. A refreshment tent had been set up in the back yard, and champagne punch was being ladled out. An elaborate buffet meal was served. A wedding breakfast wouldn't be any good unless it gave at least a few of the guests indigestion.

The party drew to an end. Charlotte went upstairs to change. On the landing she turned to toss her bouquet to the waiting bridesmaids. One of the Gamma Delta sisters caught it; then, sensing the wistfulness beside her, she turned and presented it to Small Niece.

They were all waiting when Charlotte came down in her going-away outfit. On the landing she paused and feigned surprise. Then she and Bill made their escape in a shower of rice. Some of the guests pursued them to the station. They were greeted by smiles from fellow passengers when they boarded the train.

Seated and in motion, they turned to look at each other. "Well, we're here, Mrs. Andrews," Bill said.

"We are here, Mr. Andrews," Charlotte echoed dutifully. "But just where are we?"

They had agreed to spend their first few days at a lakefront hotel in Chicago, where Bill had reserved a suite. There they would make plans for the rest of their allotted two weeks. They settled and did some unpacking, went down to the dining room for a meal, came back and faced each other. Here, in the place which was blessedly if briefly theirs.

Almost timidly they turned to face each other. Bill said softly, "I know where we are now, Mrs. Andrews. We are in our bridal suite, beginning our life-long honeymoon."

Charlotte nodded. "Far be it from me to contradict you, Mr. Andrews. Haven't I just promised to obey?"

He took pains not to watch her while she was preparing for bed, but when she was ready, he picked her up and lifted her in. Stretched out beside her, he looked at her for some time in silence. Then he turned out the light.

Charlotte finally went to sleep from sheer weariness. The next thing she knew the room was filled with the faint light of dawn. Bill was lying there looking at her. "Now I know," he whispered. "I know how Adam felt when he woke in Paradise, and found himself with a rib missing, and there on the turf beside him lay the most beautiful thing that God had ever created."

Charlotte smiled and lifted a hand to stroke his hair, but she forebore answering. She did not want to make a habit of capping his sayings. Anyhow, silence was sweet right now. But she thought sleepily that Eve must have felt completely bewildered, not knowing how she got there or what it was all about. The real thrill was when the wished-for actually came to pass, when with full awareness on your part your dream came true. Charlotte felt more like a little girl who has actually succeeded in catching Santa Claus.

She woke the next time in broad daylight. Again Bill was lying there watching her. This time he whispered, "You're still here." And Charlotte, herself thrilled and amazed and slightly incredulous, whispered back, "Still here—and likely to remain so."

Bill ordered breakfast sent up to them. In the blessed privacy of their sitting room, she poured his morning coffee for the first time. He took his black, with two lumps of sugar; Charlotte had cream. There were slices of melon like no other melon that Charlotte had ever tasted. This was followed by a cheese omelet unbelievably delicious. It was noon when they finished eating, two o'clock when, immaculate in the outfits which had lately sustained such a bombardment of rice, they emerged into a sun-drenched world.

There were countless changes after a woman was married, some of them great, some relatively small, but none without its own significance. So many things now became "ours." Even many of those which remained "yours" or "mine" were affected. Charlotte had had time to learn how to take care of her engagement ring; she always removed it when she washed her hands for fear its prongs might catch the soap. Once a day she washed it all by itself and dried it very carefully. Her wedding ring she had vowed never to remove; but on that very first day of her married life, while she was having a cool rinse after her hot bath, it slipped from her finger. That wasn't a catastrophe, of

course; it wasn't even an omen. But Charlotte gave a gasp
of dismay. She didn't really get her breath back until it was
safe on her finger again, with her engagement ring to guard
it. A wedding ring was only a symbol, but it *was* a symbol.

Charlotte and Bill strolled slowly down Michigan Avenue. To their left lay the glorious expanse of the lake, the
same lake that had lent its magic to Charlotte's childhood
parties, the same lake that had yesterday been the background for her wedding. Yet it was not the same, because
Charlotte and Bill were looking at it together. It never
would be the same again to either of them.

They strolled, and looked in at shop windows, and then
they strolled some more. Presently he took her into a
florist's, where he bought a corsage for her and a flower to
stick in his own buttonhole. "Our first purchases as Mr.
and Mrs. Andrews," he reminded her.

"Our first little extravagance," she agreed. One of our
first "ours." For no particular reason, Charlotte's mind
slipped away for a moment to poor little Miss Kaminski,
who could not afford to buy those lovely little superfluities
herself and had no one to indulge her in them. She had been
touchingly grateful for that small gift at Christmas. Charlotte must be sure to remember her again this year.

On their return to the hotel they sat in the lobby for a
while and watched the people coming and going. So many
people, busied about their own concerns. So many people,
strangers to Charlotte and Bill, yet each the center of his
own universe. Charlotte and Bill had breakfasted so late
that they preferred to omit luncheon and save their appetites for an early dinner. What fun it was to have their
choice of restaurants! Chicago afforded a wide selection.
They decided to eat that night at a popular place where
they had both been before, but always with other people.

Tonight they would go together. That made all the difference.

When they changed for dinner, Charlotte allowed Bill to hook her into her dress. That was an intimate proceeding, and he made the most of it; he bared and kissed her shoulder. Charlotte flushed a little, then laughed with sheer delight. This fellow had imagination. He put something into his love-making besides sheer physical vigor.

They dined in a leisurely fashion, and afterward went for a long ride in a horse-drawn hack. Plenty of motor cars were to be seen about the streets; many more of them, Charlotte realized, than there had been two years before. Bill Andrews was in an up-and-coming business. But Bill wasn't out tonight to do business, or even to think about business. He wanted privacy, leisure, the sense of being quietly in motion even when he wasn't going much of anywhere.

He soon put his arm around her, and Charlotte rested her head on his shoulder. He kissed her sometimes, and murmured soft words of endearment. But for the most part they simply sat there in the deep satisfaction of being together in the quiet: they who had been only yesterday the center of all that attention. Only yesterday? It now seemed as if all that excitement and publicity was very far in the past: not as far back as the discovery of America, of course, but say about the time of the Civil War.

The streets were beginning to empty, and the city was settling itself for the midnight lull, when Bill at length gave the word to go back to the hotel. "Back." They had been away together for all these enchanted hours. They were returning together. Together, just the two of them.

It was two mornings later, when she was pouring their breakfast coffee for the third time, that Charlotte and Bill arrived at their decision. They would not attempt to go anywhere else, as they had originally planned to do. The rest of this brief, bright interlude they would spend right here in Chicago. Charlotte long-distanced her parents, and Bill got in touch with his business associates.

Now the young people were committed to a set program for the first time since they had entered this hotel. The great experiment was succeeding; the great adventure was shaping up. Charlotte and Bill had just this much more in common.

They continued to dine at a different restaurant every night. They went to the theater twice; the new season was just opening up, and it promised to be a grand and glorious one. Bill bought six new books. Three he inscribed to Charlotte; the others, he explained, were for her to give him. "That's a lovely arrangement," Charlotte said. "It assures you of getting something you really want to read."

"There's a long winter coming," Bill reminded her. "Right here and now I don't believe it; but in its own good time it will catch up with us."

"Worrying won't warm the winter," Charlotte mocked. "Do you like alliteration? Perhaps I shouldn't have asked that. You might regret that you married a schoolteacher."

"I'd marry the President of Vassar, if she happened to be Charlotte Emerson," he assured her.

At the picture of herself in that august position, Charlotte burst out laughing. Bill, joining in her mirth, remarked, "I love to hear you laugh."

She remembered something that she thought of from time to time but hadn't yet got around to telling him: about the day when she was kept after school and made to write fifty times, "I laugh at nothing."

Bill looked puzzled and a little indignant. "Did that old

hag actually resent your childish gaiety? Or did she simply have to show you who was the teacher? Anyhow, she supplied you with a good story. Thank you for telling me."

Once more they dined at a different restaurant. A second time they went for a ride in a horse-drawn hack. Charlotte loved Bill better every day. She had all her life ahead of her in which to go on loving him. "All my life, and eternity after that," she whispered to herself.

Just the same, their honeymoon was all too brief. Charlotte hated to see it end. The two of them would leave their private little paradise. They would go to live in the city where Bill was established and important, but which Charlotte had never even visited. Bill's life would again center on his business. Charlotte would see him only nights and weekends. However much she loved Bill, she might have a hard time getting used to being Mrs. William Andrews.

❦ 2 ❦

THEY PLANNED TO live in Bill's bachelor apartment until Charlotte found one larger and more to her taste. "In a few more years I expect to build or buy," Bill explained, "when we know better what we want, when the needs of a growing family—"

"When you become so wealthy and important that you can no longer be satisfied with being a tenant," Charlotte cut in. "Or when I get to talking too much about the mar-

velous mansion I used to live in as a girl back in Saylesboro."

Bill grinned. "Well yes, at some later date."

They arrived in Euclid late in the afternoon. Charlotte's
first impression was that it was much like Saylesboro, but
not quite so sightly. At Bill's apartment his housekeeper
was waiting for them: a gaunt woman in her fifties, a
widow. She took a good eyeful of Charlotte, but her man-
ner was pleasant enough. It was evident that she liked her
employer.

As soon as they had removed what Victorian novels
called "the stains of travel," Bill showed Charlotte around
the apartment. Everything was in excellent taste, beautifully kept, and just a shade impersonal.

They dined on steak, and spent most of the evening unpacking and settling in. Bill shifted some of his traps to the
guest-room closet. The guest-room dresser had been moved
into the master bedroom for her use. "Buy a new one if you
don't like this," Bill suggested. "Change anything you want
to, you know. It's your home."

That was good to hear; but she wasn't going to make any
changes until she had looked around a bit and thought
things over. Perhaps not any changes at all until they
secured their next place. She had plenty of time.

A strange room, a strange bed. Of course Charlotte had
slept in a good many such. She was here fresh from a hotel
bedroom. But that had been different. Traveling was traveling, and in Madison and Belair she had always had the
Emerson house in Saylesboro as her point of departure and
return. Now she was here to stay. This wasn't the least bit
like prison, of course; yet she was in Euclid to serve out a
life sentence.

Just before he got into bed beside her, Bill wound and set

his alarm clock. He grinned at Charlotte. "My nose is back on the grindstone. But you sleep as long as you want to. Mrs. Khaut will be glad to get your breakfast whenever you're ready for it."

"I'll get up in time to pour your coffee," Charlotte said crisply. "It's a poor wife who can't do that much for her husband."

She poured his coffee, pecked at her own breakfast, kissed him good-bye at the door. He would be back about six, he told her. If anything came up, she could always get in touch with him at his office.

Charlotte went to the front windows and stood there until she had grown moderately familiar with the prospect. Then she sought Mrs. Khaut and consulted her about to-night's dinner and plans for the rest of the week. "I'll have only a very light luncheon," she said. "Soup and a salad, or a cup of tea and a sandwich. Just go on doing as you have done for Mr. Andrews. I can see that you've taken beautiful care of him." It was just as well to use a few honeyed words here at the start. An old retainer would naturally be resentful of a new lady of the house.

She sat down and wrote a long letter to Mamma and Papa. There was so much to tell them, and nothing but good. Then she wrote to Agnes. She had not seen her sister while she was in Chicago, and didn't even know whether she was back in the city. This letter was much shorter and cooler, though Charlotte did say that she feared she might find it hard to get used to keeping house. That afternoon she went for a long walk. She was getting through the day very well. And so soon now he was coming back to her. Back to her in his own home, which was now home to her, too.

On her return she let herself in with her own latchkey.

That was surely an act of taking possession. She put away
her wraps in her bedroom—*their* bedroom. Then she went
into the living room and turned on a table lamp. How
friendly and sheltered it looked at this hour, with the windows turning into mirrors against the gathering dusk!

Alongside the lamp on the oblong mahogany table the
current issues of five national magazines were carefully
arranged. Here was reading suited to an interval like this,
when a person needed something to amuse her but didn't
want to get involved in a book which she would soon have
to put down.

Charlotte picked up a magazine which she used to read
regularly back in Saylesboro. Selection was itself a pleasure, but this wasn't like making a choice from a tray of
French pastries. Here she could eventually have the whole
thing, one treat after another.

By the time she had turned ten pages, she was so absorbed in her reading that she had lost track of everything
else. It was thus that her new husband caught her when he
returned from his first day back at business.

He had caught her off guard, the young lady who had so
long stood him off. He loved her spirit, of course; he would
never have tied himself down to a woman who allowed him
to do her thinking for her. But this quietude was a novelty
and a delight.

She must have sensed his eyes upon her, for after a few
moments she glanced up. Her first reaction was bewilderment; then her face lighted up as a woman's face does for
one man, and for him only.

"I didn't hear you come in," she began, then caught
herself. "But you don't generally come in tooting a horn or
ringing a cowbell, do you?"

He shook his head. "You look so pretty with the lamplight shining down on your wonderful hair. I was giving myself a little time to enjoy it."

She rose and came around the table. "How did things go at the plant today, dear?"

"Slowly. I was still in a little bit of a daze, but the people in the office understood and indulged me."

"They do say all the world loves a lover," she said, only half mockingly. She went into his arms, but held him off for an instant's inspection at close range.

"All the world enjoys some things by proxy. A good thing for all of us that it does. Makes everybody much happier."

They kissed quietly, lingeringly. He rubbed his cheek against hers. She could feel the beard under the skin, and it thrilled her. "Mrs. Andrews, here and waiting for me," he whispered.

"Mr. Andrews, coming home to me," she whispered back.

He released her presently, and drew a long breath. "This is the first time I have ever come home to you after a day at the plant. The occasion really requires a celebration."

Charlotte laughed. "If you want a drink, any old excuse will do."

"It isn't an excuse. It's a reason."

"Have it your own way. Schoolteacher Charlotte is in no mood to give a language lesson."

"Your cocktail is a Manhattan, I believe?"

"Not unless that's what you're having. I wouldn't put you to the trouble of making different drinks."

"It might be better if I joined you. Seems that for this special evening it should be ladies' choice."

He went toward the kitchen. Charlotte picked up the magazine which she had been reading and dog-eared a page. She had been very much interested in that story, and would doubtless finish it some other time. Right now she could not have told anyone what it was all about.

Bill came back with a tray bearing a small plate of crackers, a cocktail shaker, and two glasses with a maraschino cherry in each. "Mrs. Khaut beamed at me when she saw me mixing," he reported. "She asked whether I wanted her to hold back dinner."

"We don't have to run things through on a strict schedule," Charlotte pointed out. "You left that behind you at the plant."

"And you in dear old Belair. Looking back on my own school days, I think that was the thing I principally resented. I didn't really object to learning; often I was even interested. But I hated doing everything on the stroke of a bell, and being lectured about tardiness as if it were a sin against the Holy Ghost."

He poured the drinks and they lifted them to each other. "Here's to another first for us," she toasted.

"Here's to it. And may it have plenty of successors."

Charlotte sipped, licked her lips, sipped again. "I married a very good bartender," she reported.

"It's an accomplishment, and a resource," he acknowledged. "If I ever go broke in the gas buggy business, I can always get a job in a saloon."

"And I can go back to the chalk and the grammar lessons. Wait a minute, though! I believe there is a prejudice against married teachers; and a teacher with a bartender husband would be completely out of luck."

"Let's cross that bridge when we come to it. Tonight I don't feel like thinking about the bridges that I may have to cross in the future. We have already crossed the greatest bridge of them all: the bridge into Holy Matrimony."

Charlotte nodded. She was afraid to say aloud how happy she was tonight, here with him. She was almost afraid to think it.

It was wonderful, the sense of leisure that she enjoyed during the next few weeks. Charlotte postponed apartment-hunting until she knew a little better what she wanted. No sense anyhow in looking ahead when the present was so absorbing.

She spent very little time with the newspapers. Local doings were not yet of any interest to her, and there was altogether too much about the threatened outbreak of war in Europe. It couldn't be true. Anything so disastrous and appalling simply couldn't happen.

But she had a wonderful time with magazines. She had barely finished those on hand when next month's issues began to arrive. The Emersons had had most of these same magazines at home in Saylesboro, and Mamma had subscribed to three "women's magazines," too, but Charlotte had never read any of them exhaustively.

She went for long walks, sometimes downtown, sometimes farther out. Bill had said that he and she would some day buy or build; but that was almost as difficult for her to imagine as Bill in the role of bartender. She would believe it when she saw it.

On rainy afternoons, or when the walking urge was not so strong, Charlotte explored the apartment, partly to plan the changes she would make when they moved into their new place, partly for the light her researches might shed on Bill. He was fantastically close to her in most ways, but there were still sides of him that she did not know.

On one point she was driven to ask for information. What use had he for a guest room, he who in Saylesboro had insisted on staying at an hotel?

"I kept my distance because I wanted to make a good impression," he explained. "Break the Emersons in by degrees. But I've always liked to have a few fellows here sometimes for a Saturday-night party. That way they could stay as late as they liked, then sleep right here with no difficulties about transportation or chance of an accident. Sleep as late as they liked, too." He paused, pondered for a moment, then decided on further confidence. "And sometimes couples have stayed here, couples who were sticking it out in their respective marriages on account of their children, though they were very much in love with each other."

Charlotte started to say, "You could still have them come here." She checked herself in time. Because of course he couldn't. Couldn't bring them in here with his pure young bride, who might make the other woman feel ashamed of herself. They would be driven to hotel registrations under a false name. Oh, the pity of it! The unfairness, that some lovers should have to snatch a little happiness in secret, while others had full measure as their everyday lot in life.

She looked away, and they sat in silence for a moment. Then Bill began in a vastly different tone, "It's only just now that I've discovered the best reason of all for that guest room. If you ever get mad and want to leave me, you can go in there to sleep. That way I won't worry about you, and I'll know where to find you when I seek a truce. I mean a reconciliation."

"You would come after me?"

"Yes, I would."

"Then what would be the sense in my leaving?"

"Just to show your power."

Silly talk that, when the telltale shine was scarcely off Charlotte's wedding ring and some of her new frocks hadn't been worn even once. But it was nice to have somebody with whom she could be silly.

When Bill decided that he wanted to show Charlotte around the plant, he asked her what day would be convenient for her. "Tomorrow, if that's all right with you," Charlotte said crisply. "I don't have so many engagements that I must postpone something so important." Actually she didn't want to have time to start to worry about it. She realized that she would not only see but be seen.

Her visit was not an ordeal, however. It was fascinating to watch men and machines turning out other machines, much as they did at her father's plant. If the machines were different and the product strange, that was all the better. It was a big world, and a lot of different things played their part in it. The finished product was fascinating.

Back in his office Bill motioned Charlotte to a chair, and asked, "Well, what did you think of it all?"

"It's fascinating. It's amazing. It's even more wonderful than I had imagined it would be. It's the coming thing. And you—" She drew a long breath and looked up at him. "Bill, you're the coming man."

He was also a different man here at the plant. He was a real executive, somebody she might see in a bank, for instance, aloof, a little stern, noticing everything. Three times, however, he had said a word of commendation, and it had been more warmly and gratefully received. It looked as if he could bring out the best in his employees.

Bill seated himself and smiled at her. Again he was his old familiar self. "Keep your fingers crossed. When you go looking for our new apartment, bear in mind that we need one with a garage either in the basement of the building or nearby. This coming summer, I intend to begin taking you for rides in a brand new Andrews."

"Surely you've driven one of your own cars lots of times before?"

He grinned. "My own car is here right now. It's just that I wanted to give you a little chance to get used to things."

They had been married almost two months now, and he was still keeping things from her. It gave her that much more to look forward to.

They went back to Saylesboro for Thanksgiving, of course. The Emerson mansion was as hospitable as ever, the lake view as entrancing. But it seemed a little strange to occupy one of the guest rooms with Bill Andrews, and Charlotte's old domain looked lonesome and almost bleak. So much of her past lay buried here. She had not realized how far she had grown away from young Charlotte Emerson.

Bill invited the Emersons to come and visit the Andrewses in Euclid. Inez smiled and said, "Later on, of course. But in-laws are not to be encouraged this early in the game. They might make it a habit."

Paul Emerson agreed. "No doubt with all our wisdom we could run your lives better for you than you are running them for yourselves. But you wouldn't be one bit grateful for our advice," he said with a smile.

The turkey festival was over in no time at all. Back in Euclid, Charlotte began to get ready for what one of her sisters in Gamma Delta had termed "the great annual gift swap." She could see the point of the jest, but to her that was the less important part of the festival. This was the season of St. Nick and Scrooge.

With the New Year Charlotte made one change in their domestic arrangements. On Mrs. Khaut's day off, Bill had been taking her out to dinner. Now Charlotte arranged to get dinner for Bill. He loved her going to that trouble for him. He insisted on wiping the dishes, too. "I'm just as much married as you are. It's a good thing for me to be reminded of that fact."

She began meeting his friends, too, and the two of them were asked out to dinner. "I've lost my standing as a desirable bachelor," he explained. "I'm no longer expected to fill in whenever the hostess wants to make things come out even. I couldn't always plead business or a previous engagement, and I lost too much of my beauty sleep."

"It must have been a very great hardship," Charlotte agreed dryly. "But there was always the chance that you would meet the one girl."

"Is that so, Mrs. Andrews? Let me remind you that you're not fresh out of kindergarten yourself."

"I never went to kindergarten," Charlotte asserted. "Remind me to tell you some time about all the different men I went to Junior Proms with. It's very uninteresting."

"Just don't bother. You had to put in the time somehow while you were waiting for me."

Charlotte snapped her fingers. "I have it! When your gas buggy goes up in smoke, you and I can go into vaudeville together. A husband-and-wife team exchanging witty repartee. I think an audience could stand twenty minutes of us, especially if we put in a few dance steps to relieve the monotony."

"Um-hum. The long-suffering public has every reason to wish me success in business."

This was the first Christmas of their married life, but the second time they had returned to Saylesboro for a holiday. It was three months since their wedding day—but yes, it was the anniversary of a very special Christmas. Mamma had remembered that, too. She put sprigs of mistletoe in the same doorways, and again Bill kissed Charlotte under it. But this time he was repeating not only the mistletoe kiss but the nuptial kiss. She was more and more his as time went on.

"Happy New Year" was no empty phrase this time. Nineteen fourteen offered a clean sheet, and it was all wonderful and promising. Right here at the start, Charlotte's plans and prospects were always at the back of her mind, ready for her to turn to whenever she could spare the time from the marvelous present.

In January she did indeed retreat to the guest room, but not because she was angry with Bill. She came down with an attack of influenza, and didn't wish to pass it on to Bill. She ran a high fever for several days, and was thoroughly sick and miserable.

Mrs. Khaut ministered to her with hot lemonade and chicken broth. Bill brought her flowers, studied her flushed face anxiously, and told her items of news that he thought might cheer her up. Charlotte whispered her thanks, downed the steaming liquids, tried to smile at Bill. But in her state of misery nothing and nobody really helped; she might as well have been alone in the Sahara Desert.

Then one night she went suddenly sound asleep. She stirred just once, to move to the other side of the bed. After a solid fourteen hours she awoke in the blessed light of early afternoon, her fever gone, her head clear. She was ravenously hungry, and once more glad to be alive. She had a long, wonderful bath, and returned that night to her own bed.

She hadn't been half grateful enough for her usual good health. She had better take a little time off and count her blessings. It was altogether too easy to take things for granted.

Though it was not quite so cold in Euclid as it was in Saylesboro and Madison, March came in like a lion and, as usual, went out like a lion. But with April came days of spring promise. With the advent of spring, young Mrs. Andrews started house-hunting.

It was a discouraging job in some ways. Charlotte saw many places which might do if you made them, but that wasn't what she was after. She sought a place which would come up to certain specifications. A place which would be an improvement over Bill's present digs. A place where she could create a home for the two of them.

Eventually she found an apartment in a building a little farther from the center of town than where they were now living. The rooms were large and light, and on the lot right next door was a brand-new garage erected for the tenants' use. She talked terms with the agent, and reported to Bill. He inspected it the next day and approved her choice. He signed a two-year lease with a renewal clause.

The worst of her troubles was over, but the work was only just beginning. First she had to select the colors that she wanted for the walls, supervise the painters, see to it that the floors were properly waxed. Then came the gigantic task of deciding which of Bill's old furnishings they would take with them, which they would replace. Eventually she decided to retain the living-room furniture and scrap most of the rest. Her trousseau linens were shipped to her from Saylesboro, and her wedding presents. Charlotte made a quick trip there to select some of her own favorite belongings from the rooms which had so long been hers. The new place would be a home of her own creating: hers in a very special sense.

Moving day came, with its attendant chaos. It was an ordeal. But settling in was satisfying when she reached the end. It was going to be the end, too. Bill had said that one of these days he expected to buy or build. Well, Mr. Bill Andrews had another think coming. Charlotte intended to have her funeral from this building.

Charlotte bought new rugs and curtains, of course. When she suggested that Bill go with her to pick them out, he smiled and said, "I know that I can trust your taste." Trust her taste, and pay the bills—that was what the American husband was for.

But it was great to have him coming home every day to admire the new improvements. Coming home in his new car, the car that was as much his own creation as this home was hers. She hadn't married him because he was a highly successful businessman in a new and expanding line, any more than he had married her because she was Paul Emerson's daughter and had always been very popular with men. Still, it all helped. Those things did count. You could not have too many factors in your favor when you made your casual day-by-day reckoning.

❦ 3 ❦

SUMMER WAS THE traditional season for vacations. Not only schoolchildren and teachers had the traditional two months off; many families maintained summer homes in the country, where the women and children lived during July and August. Those who could not manage that, patronized resort hotels, where there was boating and bathing and fishing. Privileged souls like the Emersons traveled.

The newlyweds planned to be different. This home of theirs was still a great novelty and a never-ending source of wonder. They could spend their time here, so blessedly together. They would go for short spins in *the* car on fine summer evenings, for longer drives on Sundays. In August they would give Mrs. Khaut two weeks off, and Charlotte would have a real go at being a working housewife.

"When Mrs. Khaut gets back, we'll have Mamma and Papa here for a visit," Charlotte planned blissfully. "They will want to see our new home. Mamma has kept hands off long enough; she can't stay away forever. They will be interested in your plant, too—Papa especially. I'd like to go there again myself, some time when you feel like being bothered."

Lovely plans. The bliss of planning together. Lovely hours by herself. Getting acquainted with her new neighborhood. Looking over her new home with fondness and pride. Making small changes, and often changing them back, in the indulgence of her house pride. Best of all, knowing that at the close of day he would return to her, would share with her the joys of reunion, would bring her some brief account of what went on in his particular world.

Then in July it happened. It was dreadful, it was uncalled for, it was incredible; but it happened. An obscure archduke was assassinated in a place nobody had ever heard of. Ultimatum followed ultimatum, until the conflicting powers had gone too far to withdraw. War broke out on the continent of Europe. For a few hours the question was, What will England do? England joined her Allies. Europe became one vast battleground.

"Universal catastrophe!" Charlotte whispered, appalled.

"Noah survived the Flood," Bill reminded her.

"I'm thinking of the countless thousands who perished."

"Deploring won't do any good."

It wouldn't, of course. But such things were difficult to understand, and Charlotte was almost ashamed to be happy herself in a world which was the scene of such widespread disaster. But he was right, of course. There was too little happiness in this world anyhow, and it wouldn't help the French or the Belgians a bit if she made Bill Andrews' life a burden to him.

The Red Cross opened a workroom downtown. Charlotte put in three afternoons a week there fashioning surgical dressings. Monotonous labor. Was this how the unskilled workers in a factory put in their time? Stultifying, she found it. Then she learned to knit, under the tuition of a lively old lady who had learned the craft from her own grandmother. This was better; Charlotte could see that she was really making something. She enjoyed visiting with the other women, too, though she listened more than she talked. They reminded her a little too strongly of Mamma's friends.

Mamma and Papa came to Euclid for their promised visit. They were there on Bill and Charlotte's wedding anniversary. They saw all the sights. They highly approved of the apartment. "It's perfect. Just like a doll house," Papa said. Mamma suggested a few minor changes. On the Great Day itself, the four of them had dinner at a restaurant. With champagne, of course; nothing else was suitable for occasions of high festivity.

The evening after the Emersons' departure, Charlotte and Bill talked over the visit together. "Your parents are such nice people," he informed her. "Your father appreciated all the fine points about my plant. It's so good that he's a manufacturer himself."

"If he had been a lawyer—" Charlotte suggested.

"We'd still have found a lot to talk about, but it would have been different."

Bill was smoking his customary after-dinner cigarette. Reaching for a second, he said, "You've never learned to smoke, Charlotte?"

"Light one for me," she suggested. "This is as good a time as any to begin."

Actually she had sometimes smoked with the Gamma Delta sisters in a spirit of escapade, but she had never made it a habit. Now she savored her cigarette, watched the smoke rise in beautiful thin spirals, caught Bill's eye, and nodded. This was one more thing that they could enjoy together.

It became a nightly rite. A small pleasure, but real enough in its own way. Charlotte always cleaned out the ashtray before she went to bed. Stale ashes were nothing to leave overnight.

She was well into her Red Cross work by Thanksgiving. Yes, and thankful that she could do something to help out. Belgium had been overrun and France invaded. Christmas was quieter than usual, and New Year's really subdued. You could only hope that no one else would get involved in this widespread conflict. "No one else" meaning—yes indeed, *meaning*.

Nineteen fifteen brought many different things to different people. To Charlotte it brought the dearest of all, and the strangest. In January she discovered that their union was to be fruitful, or as people so baldly put it nowadays, she was pregnant.

She and Bill kept the precious news to themselves for a time. It was just too wonderful to share. They told each other that they wished to spare the Emersons worry, and until the Emersons were notified, nobody else very well

could be. As if the principal reaction of the expectant
grandparents would be worry! As if they wouldn't be, in
their own way, just as deeply delighted as the young couple
themselves, and far more complacent! But the excited par-
ents-to-be needed time to get used to the idea.

Not that the fact of parenthood was in itself any great
novelty. On the contrary, it was quite the commonest thing
in the world. People were having babies every day of the
year and every hour of the day, having them all over the
world, not just here in the land of good old Uncle Sam.
The lower animals multiplied. Insects proliferated. Repro-
duction went on and on and on, in this endless continuity
where we all played our little part. But this was the first
time that the prospect of parenthood had confronted William Andrews, Esquire, and Charlotte his wife.

They had loved. They had realized together the depth
and the height and the rapture of love's natural climax.
Now out of their love was to come another human being
like themselves, theirs uniquely and very deeply, yet a separate and independent creature. Any baby in the making
was a marvel, and this marvel was theirs, joining them as
even Bill and Charlotte had never been joined before.

The first person to be let in on their secret was a stranger
to Charlotte, though Bill knew him fairly well. He was Dr.
Henry Chrisler, who was called in when they had an accident at the plant. Charlotte demurred about consulting
him. She knew what was in the wind. She felt all right.
What was the sense in going to a doctor about it?

"You might just as well meet him now as later," Bill
urged. Then, as quick color flared in Charlotte's cheeks, he
hugged her and cried out, "Oh, my dear, it's nothing to feel
that way about! It's a matter of pride and joy!"

He was right, of course. Queen Victoria had been dead
for quite a while, and Victorian prudery was as out of date

as hoopskirts and bustles. Mamma's shame over certain
natural phenomena had caused Charlotte embarrassment
and bewilderment. She would do better than that with her
daughter when the time came.

Her daughter? Well yes, that might be what this fuss was
all about. A daughter, or a son. Either would be equally
welcome, but it would be sort of nice to have the first one
a son.

"You'll go with me to the doctor's office, dear, won't
you?" she asked. "Or would it be asking too much to have
him come here?"

Dr. Chrisler came there, of course. He looked Charlotte
over rather casually, asked a few questions, then beamed
and said, "Yes, you can go ahead and get ready for your
party. Fall is a nice time for a baby to be born. Gives the
little stranger a chance for a few breaths of fresh air before
it gets so cold he has to be shut up indoors."

"And will he really be adjusted to things before his first
Christmas?" Charlotte asked.

"He!" Bill echoed, and both men laughed.

But Charlotte said stoutly, "I don't think it's nice to call
any baby 'it,' even this early in the game."

"You're very keen on this baby, aren't you?" Dr. Chrisler
asked.

"Women aren't always, I know," Charlotte said. "But
when I think what most of them have to face across the
breakfast table every morning, I'm not surprised. Besides,
a first child is a little miracle. It's different, of course, when
you get to the state of the old woman in the nursery rhyme,
the one who lived in a shoe—"

" '—and had so many children she didn't know what to
do,' " Dr. Chrisler finished for her. "Yes, that's quite different."

Charlotte knew almost as well as he did that many

women loathed pregnancy and dreaded childbirth. But such women should stay unwed, even if it put them to the necessity of working for a living. For them, marriage was nothing but a form of slavery.

Later when the two of them discussed the sex of their coming child, Charlotte said, "It's always nice when the first one is a boy."

"A big, husky male out of your feminine fragility. Yes, I can see how that idea attracts you," Bill conceded. "Personally I should like a little girl. A little girl just as feminine as they come, of course. Beautiful like you, of course, but with a distinct facial resemblance to me—if you can imagine those two things united."

"We will take what we get," Charlotte reminded him. "Still, it's nice to dream."

"To dream together," Bill echoed softly. "And this is a dream which must come true, in its own time and form."

Charlotte let Mamma have the Great News then. She wrote a short, carefully worded letter which she let Bill read:

Dearest Mamma and Papa:
    I have real news for you this time. Startling news. Be sure you sit down before you read it. By next Thanksgiving you will have an extra bundle of joy to be thankful for. A grandchild, a small Andrews. I am feeling very well, and am of course overjoyed by my prospects. Did you feel this way over me under the same circumstances? I suppose you must have, though it's a little hard for me to realize. I've put you to a lot of trouble over the years, but perhaps your grandchild will make up for it.

Your ever loving
Charlotte

P.S. Girls seem to run in our family, but you can't always tell about things like that. It will be nice if the new baby is a boy, though of course he won't be an Emerson. Your grandchild, anyhow. Now you can't say I never did anything for you.

Handing the letter back, Bill said, "I'd like to see your mother's face when she gets this."

Charlotte grinned. "She'll think she did it all. To be sure, she is indirectly responsible. But that was really pretty far back. Right here and now, our little future belongs to you and me."

Oh, the blessedness of that "our"! And the transience! Right now the baby belonged to them, but when the allotted months were past, he would begin a life of his own. Theirs still, of course, and unspeakably close and dear to them, but a human being in his own right. That was the way things went.

Charlotte was not mistaken about Mamma's reaction to the situation. The moment she heard the news, Mrs. Emerson forgot all about her scruples against being a visiting mother-in-law. She invited herself to come for a visit. She came, and she stayed. She took Charlotte into the glorious company of the elect. She treated Bill as an outsider. Oh, not too blatantly, of course! But she did give him to understand that he had done his part at the beginning, and he'd better stand aside now and leave women's business to women.

During one of their sessions Mamma asked Charlotte, "Have you told Agnes yet?" Charlotte hadn't. She and her sister were close relatives. The closest, in fact; when you came right down to it, only siblings were of all the same blood. But they differed widely in temperament as well as in age. Perhaps, too, Agnes had resented being ousted from her cherished position of only child.

"I haven't yet," Charlotte said. "I thought there was plenty of time." Then she had a bright idea. "I think I'll invite her for a visit while you're here. That is, of course, if you don't mind her rooming with you."

So that guest room of theirs was put to a use which was quite a change from Bill's bachelor days. Visiting in-laws were not written into the marriage vows. By the time the young husband ran up against them, it was too late to do anything about it.

Agnes showed considerable interest in Charlotte this time, though their slant on things differed too widely to permit any real intimacy to develop. Men were brutes, Agnes would insist, but she never wearied of telling how popular her Inez was with boys. Agnes's face lighted up when she talked about her daughter and her daughter's whirl of gaiety at home. She seemed to Charlotte rather touching at those moments. Young romance meant everything to women of Agnes's type; when their own days of glory were over, they could relive them in the lives of their daughters.

Agnes went home after five days. The next week she sent Charlotte a charming little knitted hood and mittens. Mamma promised Charlotte a carriage robe to match them. Presently she, too, took herself off. Her parting words were "You will come home to have your baby, of course."

Yes, Mrs. Emerson really did think she was doing it all. But this was Charlotte's baby, not Mrs. Emerson's. Though the big house overlooking the lake was very dear to Charlotte's heart, home was right here in this apartment which she herself had selected and arranged. Mrs. Emerson was thinking how she would like to boss such a party. All very fine for her, to be sure. Charlotte felt a little stifled.

"I mustn't think too much about the war," she told Bill on one of those evenings when they were so blessedly alone. "It might mark the baby."

"It's your baby, and it's Europe's war," Bill reminded her. "President Wilson has pledged himself to keep us out of it."

"We-e-ell, yes. I wouldn't say he's done it with his eye on next year's election. But he's in a position where he has to say something. We don't necessarily have to agree with him."

As time passed lots of people didn't agree with him. "Preparedness parades" were the order of the day. Changes were going on in Bill's factory; fewer pleasure cars were going into production, and more vehicles which might be put to military uses. Charlotte lived in her rich present and in her own expectations. Nothing must be allowed to take this from her. Nothing!

Nine months was a long time when you looked ahead at it. Almost as long as a school year. But school years had a trick of getting past you almost before you knew it, and these "expectant" months went even faster. After all, time wasn't lived through by the year. A day was a nice little comprehensible unit, and the days soon added up.

Charlotte's baby was born in a hospital. That was the way things were done nowadays. It was much safer and surer, and if it was a little impersonal, a little rule-bound, that made it all the pleasanter afterward, when the newly arrived was back home and the proud parents could have him all to themselves.

For it was "him" in the Andrewses' case: a beautifully formed eight-pound boy. A fine son to carry on the family name. A miraculous first-born, so that Bill and Charlotte, who had been a couple, were now a family.

They were soon involved in an argument over the new-comer. Charlotte had wanted to name him for his father. A natural step, and one which usually pleased a man very much. Mr. Andrews was pleased, but he dissented. "I don't care for all this business of Senior and Junior. It makes me feel like somebody who has just come out of the Ark. Bill and Willie is just as bad, or Big Bill and Little Bill. Let's show a little originality, and at the same time keep it all right in the family. *I* want to name him after *you.*"

"Bill Andrews, are you out of your mind?"

"I suppose I am, in a way. But it's such a pleasant form of insanity."

"Bill, you think more of me than you do of your own ego."

"Well, that's no cause for divorce, even in a state which has fairly liberal laws."

The baby was accordingly named Charles.

Charlotte experienced all the ecstasy of motherhood. She had known plenty of happiness in her life, happiness of many kinds, shared with different people or enjoyed all by herself. Infinite happiness sometimes, as when she had watched the balloons disappearing into the beautiful dim distance at her birthday party. But this was unique bliss, at once selfless and selfish. This was what it was all about. This was what life was meant for.

So must other mothers have felt, but that was difficult for Charlotte to realize. So must Mother Eve have felt when she produced her first-born. Her first-born, whom she named Cain. Dreadful to think what lay ahead of him. But no need to think of that right now. No need ever to think too far ahead, or to frighten yourself with the thought of what might happen. A baby is the most hopeful thing in the world. And here was Charlotte with hers. Her little son and namesake. The crowning proof of Bill's love for her. Yes, and a brand-new life starting off into the future. Bill's child. Charlotte's child. But his very own self, bless him!

🌷 4 🌷

Woodrow Wilson, running for a second term as President of the United States, saw to it that the voters were constantly reminded, "He kept us out of war." He reminded Charlotte of that legendary king who bade the tide stop coming in. With this important difference: Canute did it as a rebuke to his fawning courtiers, but Woodrow apparently believed what his advisers were telling him. It worked, anyhow. Enough voters were convinced, and the Democrats remained in power.

Yet after that it took only five months for us to be drawn into the conflict, which instantly became a crusade. A War to Make the World Safe for Democracy. Everything in capital letters, everything at fever pitch. American General Pershing, arriving on French soil, declared dramatically, "Lafayette, we are here!" All these years afterward, America was repaying its debt for the aid received during the Revolution. Few were ungracious—or foolhardy—enough to remember the advice of the general under whom Lafayette had served. It was George Washington who adjured this country to "avoid entangling alliances."

Bill Andrews' plant was now manufacturing only war

vehicles, including those caissons which in the stirring song were "rolling along." Up in Saylesboro Paul Emerson was making munitions. Both the gentlemen were making money, too. But they had to do so in order to keep up the good work, and they had both been doing very nicely, thank you, in peacetime.

Up in Saylesboro Mamma and her friends were busier than ever with their war work. They faced domestic complications, too; many servants were quitting household drudgery and earning big money in munitions plants. This, too, at a time of shortages and food rationing, when no patriotic American family would eat anything unless they were perfectly sure that our dear Allies couldn't use it. Send the good wheat flour and the choice American beef to France and England. Eat cornbread and barley bread. Make "mock meat loaf," with ground peanuts and minced green peppers serving to kill appetite, even if it couldn't satisfy it. Mrs. Khaut sniffed at the recipes Charlotte handed her, but she went ahead and struggled with them. She couldn't very well do anything else. Not only was she a faithful servant; these days anyone with a German name was suspect. It was all a part of "doing your bit": lovely phrase borrowed from our English cousins, and either inspiring or mock-modest, depending on how you looked at it.

Charlotte knitted and made surgical dressings and marched in Liberty Loan parades. But she had a personal undertaking which demanded time and attention. She had her hands full caring for young Charley, who grew and flourished and was cuter and sweeter and more interesting every day. This first little home of young Mrs. Andrews' was just not big enough for her fine little family, and she suspected that one of these days Charley would no longer be an only child.

This was no time to build, of course, even if they had really wanted to do so. Plenty of time to see about that later on. They must get this war over first, and feel free to draw a deep breath and look around them.

So Charlotte went house-hunting. Her remarkable child crept early, and so managed to get into mischief. Then he walked early, and so got into a great deal more mischief. Charlotte took him along sometimes on her house-hunting expeditions. She had a little harness made for him and hung onto the reins, so that he couldn't get too far afield or run into too much danger. This was all great fun for him, and by the time he was old enough to view things with some degree of realism, there would be a much better view for him to watch.

The wartime boom had narrowed the market, but there were still some old houses for sale, and almost as many new ones. All at skyrocketed prices, of course; that was what you had to expect nowadays. When a few of them were reported to him, Bill grinned and shrugged. "There's a very old joke on that subject. It should be told in German dialect, of course. But since everything German is taboo nowadays, I'll simply tell it in English. 'What do we care for egzpenzes? We got lots of them.'"

"Then we'd better buy a good sizable place while we're about it. It will pay off in case we ever want to sell."

She chose a roomy house about twenty years old. Much smaller at that than the old Emerson mansion where she grew up. She missed the lake view too, and the lovely sound of waves lapping on the shore. But there was a fine large yard with a stout iron fence around it. Plenty of room for little Charles to play. A good garage, which had once been a stable; living quarters over it, too, so that if the Andrews family ever reached the place where they wanted to put on airs and sport a chauffeur, they would be able to do so.

They bought the house, had the main rooms repainted, moved in their possessions, and drew a long breath because there was no one in the same building with them. Charlotte made a flying trip to Saylesboro and had the furniture of her old rooms packed and sent to her. One more link with her maiden past broken; or, rather, a segment of that past brought where she could weave it into her present-day life.

Then came the inevitable reaction. Charlotte, barely settled for a long stay in her full-sized house, sighed deeply. "Oh, Bill, I'd give anything if we could get into the old gas buggy and go wheezing up to Madison for the big football game of the season!"

"All in good time, young lady," he admonished her. "We still have that to look forward to."

"I suppose so. In another year, two at the outside—"

That wasn't the way it worked out. The victory so long delayed came with startling suddenness. There was a preliminary false report, but disappointing as that was, the end was really in sight. On a blessed day in November the armistice became a fact—a fact which would be commemorated by its institution as a national holiday. The Central Powers laid down their arms, and the Kaiser, who had envisioned himself as dominating the entire civilized world, fled ignominiously to Holland.

All over this bright and beautiful America, the natives of every city, town, and hamlet went chasing off downtown. All those who could lay hands on American flags did so. Everybody laid hands on some sort of noisemaker. Ice wagons and grocery carts were pressed into use to stage impromptu parades.

The Andrewses took Mrs. Khaut with them. Her emotions were perhaps somewhat mixed; it is not easy to make a complete break with one's origins. But she did enjoy little Charles's pleasure. Bill was luckily able to buy balloons from a vendor who sold out in no time at all. Charlotte tied two to the little boy's wrist. Each of the grown people carried one. Two Charlotte released. She watched them float away from the exultant crowd, floating off to peace and remoteness, lose themselves in the distance. In this so wonderful present, they had gone to join all the loveliest of Charlotte's past.

The Andrews family settled down then to readjust. Bill had a lot of reconversion to do at the plant. Domestic help again became available, and Charlotte was able to hire a second maid to take part of the load off Mrs. Khaut's shoulders and her own. The Andrewses again had baking-powder biscuit for Sunday breakfast, and meat loaves made with meat. Charlotte used up her odds and ends of knitting wool to make a large and beautiful afghan. Commemorative, of course, but useful too. And it was such a pleasure to be knitting for one's own selfish ends.

She would soon be knitting a much smaller afghan, of wool bought for the purpose, and in carefully selected colors. Her second child would be a war baby, but lucky to arrive when the actual conflict was over. A world at peace. A family eager to welcome the newcomer. A fine substantial house, which would have accommodated a much larger family than the Andrewses. This was a proper setting for the little stranger's arrival.

After a brief experience with a neighborhood handyman, Bill installed a resident houseman. He had comfortable quarters in the basement and ate with the other servants. Early in the new year Charlotte hired a nurse girl. Doubtless Charlotte could have been happy with Bill in a cottage and doing her own housework. But her present arrangements were much more comfortable and less fatiguing. Money could not buy happiness, according to the wiseacres. Nevertheless, money was a very handy thing to have.

When Charlotte and Bill discussed the sex of their coming child, Charlotte was all for its being another boy. "He would make such a fine chum for Charley."

Bill held out for a girl. "When people already have a son, it's better to have the second one a daughter. Then not so many stupid comparisons can be made."

It was an argument that settled nothing, of course, but it gave them a chance to talk about their coming child. Mamma was not so enthusiastic this time, and Agnes stayed away and sent no contributions. Oh well, if they chose to look at it that way, they could do so and welcome! A second baby was not such a novelty as the first one had been, but it was entitled to just as much love. Perhaps the process should not be repeated too many times; this was a case in which Charlotte thought thirteen would definitely be bad luck. But surely a mother should have love enough to spread out over the first five or six at least; and from purely prudential considerations, it did not pay to put all a person's eggs into one basket.

The second baby was another boy. Chance had made Charlotte the victor on that issue. The real argument she won simply by coming out flat-footed. "I'm going to name this one William, and this time you can't stop me. Oh, I know it was sweet of you to name Charles after me! But now it's your turn to be complimented. William it is, even if I have to call the baby Willie."

"Willie sounds silly," Bill said. But it was a weak retort; actually he was delighted that she was carrying her point.

William Junior had put in his appearance on the twenty-first of June; his advent coincided with the arrival of summer. Not that that meant anything, of course, but he would be able to be outside a great deal during those first important months. Charlotte had fitted up a pretty nursery for him, and had allowed Charley to witness the preparations; she told him it was for his little brother.

"Where he?" he demanded.

"He hasn't come yet. I'm getting ready for him," Charlotte explained. Charley did not pursue the subject further. In the world of fantasy where he lived, anything might come up at any time. So long as Mommy was here, or Daddy, or Nursie, everything was beautifully all right.

Charlotte's preparations for Willie's arrival were both cheap and simple compared to what Bill was doing that late spring and early summer. July first would see the onset of national Prohibition: Prohibition by Constitutional Amendment, if you please. The bluenoses had somehow managed to acquire tremendous financial backing, and had decided that their fellow citizens were going to be abstemious, whether they liked it or not. In fact, the less they liked it, the more good it would do them.

"I wish those so-and-so's would look after their own morals and let me look after mine," Bill grumbled. "Our ancestors came to this country so that they could have a little freedom."

Charlotte laughed. "My ancestors don't mean so much to me now that I am an ancestor myself. But I do think it's a rotten trick to play on the returning soldiers, to take their beer away from them."

So Bill set about preparing for the long official drought. The house had a small wine cellar. He had a larger and stronger room partitioned off in the basement. He stocked up those two, with wine, whiskey, brandy. The very idea of New Year's Eve without champagne! Then he appropriated the one second-floor bedroom which they had not yet got around to furnish.

"But Bill," Charlotte remarked, "We can't drink all this up in thirty years."

"You'd be surprised how much people can drink when they are told that they mustn't."

"Besides, people may come to their senses one of these days and get that amendment repealed."

"Don't hold your breath while you wait for people to come to their senses," Bill warned grimly. "If they had any sense, they wouldn't have let this thing happen in the first place."

It was a thing that couldn't happen; yet it had happened. Just like the Great War. Thinking of that holocaust, Charlotte decided that Prohibition couldn't be so bad after all. Not, at least, when you had your own cellar full and your friends likewise were busy stocking up.

Soon the baby was brought home from the hospital. Charlotte, fearful of anything like sibling jealousy, emphasized, "He's *your* little brother." To which Charley generally responded, "Want to kiss him." He gave the baby some of his own most cherished toys, then later took them back and played with them himself. Charlotte, looking up at the blue summer sky, thought of the wonderful summer when she had seen at its best a Europe which was now a shambles, and on her return had picked up a shipboard acquaintance. What if they had had different sailings and had never met each other! She shivered a little at the very idea. But she was "what-iffing" just to make herself realize how happy she was.

The baby was the sweetest thing anywhere around. Not quite such a miracle as little Charles had been, perhaps. But why make comparisons? He was a prince in his own right. Soft, warm, cuddly, with just enough fuzz on his head to show where the hair would grow some day. Adorable little feet, which looked as if they never would be capable of taking him anywhere. Little hands which would grasp your finger as if he knew you. That wonderful baby smell, brand-new human flesh faintly tinged with talcum powder. Charlotte wasn't going to call him Willie, of course; that was a sissy name even for a child in his cradle. He could be Will while his father remained Bill. That was a perfectly valid distinction, but with a very discernible difference. It was nice that Charlotte didn't have to struggle with a name like George. "Georgie" suggested nothing but that old nursery rhyme about the porgie pudding and pie who was scared of other boys.

The nursery rhymes all came into play again now. Charlotte knew the old favorites by heart, of course, but she bought a big picture book of them, too, so that Charley could see the characters come to life. Dear Goosey Goosey Gander and the King of Hearts and Jack and Jill; they were as much a part of a child's world as Daddy and Mommy; and in dealing with them Mommy renewed her own childhood. Wasn't that a part of the fun of having children, that they made us once more dwellers in the realm of enchantment? What a wonderful person Mother Goose was! Just as wonderful in her way as Santa Claus was in his, and they both showed that the principal pleasure of old people is to make children happy.

Charley was old enough now to hear about Santa Claus

and to hang up his stocking. He hung a tiny sock on little Will's crib, too. That way, he felt that he was doing something for his baby brother. The joy of giving couldn't begin too early.

Bill was frightfully busy at the plant these days. They were converting back to civilian cars, vastly improved cars at that. Dealers were hopefully stocking up on the new cars. Come spring, Bill Andrews would have one of the new buses himself. Even though the old bus was good on fine days for more than a spin around the block.

Bill generally took Charley in the front seat with him when they went for a Sunday afternoon drive. For short periods he would hold the little boy on his lap and allow him to pretend that he was driving. Charlotte sat in the back seat and held the baby. Very early he showed that he loved the sense of motion, and he would bounce on her knee in an accompanying rhythm of his own. Being still at the age of two naps a day, he often went to sleep in his mother's arms. Then the fun was all Charlotte's. Nowadays babies were not supposed to be held except for strictly utilitarian purposes. As if the "authorities" really knew what went on in those tiny heads! They didn't know what went on in their own. The closest thing to a baby was surely his own mother, and even after the birth pangs were over, he remained very much a part of herself.

Other Sunday afternoons the four of them went for a stroll. Bill would proudly push the baby carriage. Charley toddled along with his hand in Charlotte's, except when he broke loose to make friends with a passing dog or to get a better look at another child. Often enough a little girl; he seemed to notice the difference already. When he got tired and began to lag, Bill would relinquish the baby carriage to Charlotte and pick up his elder son. Very much the head of the family was big Bill Andrews on these occasions. The family itself was the all-around finest in Euclid, or in the State of Ohio, or presumably in the entire country. And since this country was the finest in the world, Mr. William Andrews Senior was really sitting pretty.

Charley sat in his high chair now for meals in the family dining room. He did fairly well at feeding himself, though sometimes Mommy or Nursie had to step in and speed things up, and he often got as much on the outside as he did on the inside. When his performance struck him as particularly meritorious, he called attention to it. "Charley is a good boy today. He ate up all his mashed potato and his carrots." "Charley cleaned—up—his—plate. Now he wants ice cream." Sometimes he caught Daddy's eye and his own twinkled. Was the rascal putting on an act? Or was it just that he loved Daddy so much, and wanted to stand in his good graces?

Charlotte began to play childish games with him. Pat-a-cake was a favorite. Or she would pretend she was a stranger, and ask his name and his parents' names, and where he lived, and whether he had any brothers and sisters. Or they would pile up their hands alternately, and the hand on the bottom would always be drawn out and become the hand on top. Or she would fetch pencil and paper and draw a very amateurish picture for him, and then hand him the pencil and let him try to copy her drawing.

She and Bill often had a drink together now; with all that good liquor on hand, the temptation was always with them. They usually smoked an after-dinner cigarette, too. Bill would light them both with one match. Sometimes he put both cigarettes into his own mouth and lit them there. That was a pretty gesture, a courting gesture. It gave Charlotte an additional reason to love him. This was a splendid way to feel. Too often a creeping boredom invaded marriage. People got used to each other, and that was that. Charlotte had never quite got used to Bill. She would wake sometimes in the night, and find him lying quietly beside her, drawing the deep slow breaths of heavy sleep. This was just too good to be true. But it *was* true. Charlotte and Bill hadn't exactly invented marriage, but they had discovered it for themselves. Scarcely believing it even now, Charlotte would reach out a hand to touch him and verify his presence; and Bill, without ever waking, would stretch out an arm and draw her close to him.

❦ 5 ❦

CHARLOTTE HAD MADE friends in the neighborhood now. First there had been a speaking acquaintance with the ladies to the right and the left of her and the one across the street. Then a couple who made friends with the children on a Sunday-afternoon walk accepted an invitation to walk along with the Andrewses, came in with them to see their house, and stayed for a drink. At Bill's suggestion officials at the plant were invited to come and bring their wives to a Sunday buffet supper. That led to return hospitality. At those parties Charlotte met other people. Bill Andrews was a person of importance in Euclid; but also, people liked Charlotte for herself. She ran into some of her old Red Cross acquaintances, too. It was great to feel herself settling in. She expected to live right here in Euclid for a long, long time.

Late in the winter Mamma came for a visit, and Papa joined her for a week. Mamma and he had a wonderful time with the children. "It's nice they are so close together," Mamma said a little wistfully. "Nice that they are boys, too. I should have liked a son."

Agnes and Charlotte had never been at all intimate, but Charlotte did feel sorry for Agnes, married to that awful Herbert Stanton from whom she stayed away as much as possible, and mother of an only daughter. Charlotte was a little sorry for any woman who hadn't the ineffable bliss of being married to Bill Andrews. Oh, not for Mamma, of course! Papa was, in his different way, just as much of a paragon as Bill Andrews.

In the spring Agnes came across with her great news. The Stantons were announcing their daughter's engagement; she planned to be a June bride. "She says it's all because she caught your wedding bouquet," Agnes wound up.

"Young Inez didn't catch your wedding bouquet. It was handed to her," Bill pointed out.

"What's the difference? It made the child happy."

"Just the idea of getting married?"

"Of course. A woman is technically successful when she has managed to catch herself a husband."

Bill chuckled. "A meal ticket, you mean?"

"Well, yes, if you want to put it that way."

"Then all these women in their bridal white really have only one eye on the groom, and the other on the main chance?"

"It's nice to be the center of a big show. I grant you that."

"Charlotte, sometimes I think you just like to talk."

"That could be, of course. But I never heard that you were widely known as 'Silent Bill.'"

Bill was silent for hours, to be sure, when the two of them were alone of an evening. They would sit and read, each absorbed in his own book. Yet each was conscious of the presence of the other. That sort of communion was one of the best parts of a happy marriage.

In June Charlotte and Bill went to Chicago for young Inez's wedding. They were gone just two days, but when they returned little Charley threw himself on his mother as if he could eat her up. "I had quite a time with him after you left," the nurse confided. "I couldn't make him believe you were coming back."

The fear of desertion was an elemental fear. Charlotte did not realize that Charley would feel it. The purpose of her absence and its brief duration were so clear in her own mind that she thought she had made them plain to him. But you never could tell what was going through their funny little heads.

That night Charlotte put Charley to bed herself, and although he was accustomed to going to sleep with nobody in attendance, she sat by his bedside until long after he had dozed off. Poor little mite, so dependent on a mother's love and care! She wasn't going to leave him again for a long, long time. Soon enough he would grow away from her. But she wasn't going to think about that tonight. She would dwell on the bliss of having him with her, her miraculous first-born, hers in a way that he could never be anybody else's.

In July Charlotte took the two children and their nurse up to Saylesboro to spend a month. Bill spent the second two weeks with them. "This is as good as a second honeymoon," he told Charlotte. "That house was just too quiet without you, and waking at night in my lonely bed—gosh, girl, how I missed you!"

"It's nice to be missed," Charlotte said demurely. "I was afraid it might be a case of 'When the cat's away, the mice will play.'"

"See here, young woman, don't you go calling my wife a cat!"

They laughed together then, as they so often did. That night in bed they lay with their arms around each other. It was a long time before either of them dozed off.

Charlotte hunted up dear little Miss Fox and showed off the children to her. "I only hope they have as lovely a first teacher as you," she said. "Perhaps that's too much to hope. But there are a lot of good teachers. Not quite enough, unfortunately."

Miss Fox's bright little face darkened for an instant. "I've actually heard teachers say that they were in the profession only because it was a genteel job with a long summer vacation. I don't like to think about them." Then, after a brief pause, she smiled again. "You were always such a good pupil, Charlotte. And I do appreciate your coming to see me and bringing along your lovely children."

Then the four of them were back in Euclid again, and Charlotte could begin outfitting the boys for fall. Little Will had clung to his grandmother at the last moment, and on Inez Emerson's face was the sweetest expression that Charlotte had ever seen there. Grandchildren were the reward of a well-spent life. Not the only reward, of course. But it did give a person something to look forward to.

Looking forward was wonderful. It was even more wonderful when it involved a certain amount of looking back. "I am standing on the island of Monte Cristo! The world is mine!" There was Edmond Dantès looking forward to everything his heart desired, but his heart would not have desired so much if it had not been for the bitter wrongs he had suffered. Charlotte thought about him every now and then, when things were especially going her way. She looked forward to telling the little boys about him, and she looked backward every time to the beautiful days when she had first made his acquaintance.

Everybody should have a home, of course. Practically everybody did, though not all homes were as happy as one would wish them to be. But in addition to that, it was desirable that people should have a home away from home. That was what Charlotte and her children had. The big house overlooking the lake in Saylesboro was now Charley and little Will's home away from home. Oddly enough, it was Charlotte's, too. The big house where she had grown up would always be very dear to her, but right here in Euclid was her true home, the house which she had herself selected and fixed up, the house in which her children had been installed as newborn babies, the home which was Charlotte's own cherished creation.

When she did her fall shopping for the boys, she took them one at a time, and it was "Charge and send." The evening after the purchases arrived, the proud new owner would have a style show for Daddy. This was the procedure for all the more prosaic items, but when it came to the important matter of overcoats and best suits, all four of the Andrewses went together on a Saturday afternoon. That way, there was no chance of Charlotte's not buying the best and the most expensive clothes in the store. Will thought he was the most important person in Euclid, and Charley, from the standpoint of his greater maturity, gave his opinion on what was suitable for Baby Brother. Today they charged, but they took the packages with them. Then Daddy rounded off the afternoon by treating them all to ice cream. It took the edge off their appetites, of course, but it proved that the expedition really was a party.

When the new clothes were put to use, the old ones were given away. No hand-me-downs for little Will. The English system of primogeniture was out of place and out of date; young Mrs. Andrews did not propose to have any vestiges of it hanging around her place.

Her own clothes she selected with just as much care as she had in the days when they had to run the gauntlet under the eyes of "the girls" in Gamma Delta and undergo inspection at the Prom. But they ran along different lines now. She had to hold up her end, of course, when she and Bill entertained or were entertained, but her choicest effects were reserved for quiet dinners at home, when she had her one all-important man to look pretty for. Did he always notice? Doubtless she would have looked good to him if she had worn sackcloth and sandals. But Charlotte wasn't running any chances. She was good friends with the bathroom scale, too; a fat woman just was not the same when it came to intimate relationships.

This year they had their turkey at home. A beautiful big turkey, with a drumstick for each boy. Then Will was stashed away for his afternoon nap. Charlotte long-distanced her parents in Saylesboro. Charles frolicked around outside, with Daddy to keep an eye on him. Mr. Parker from across the street joined them; he was just walking off his dinner.

Presently he got Bill aside long enough to say, "I like to make the rounds in the neighborhood Christmas Eve. I have a Santa Claus suit, and I dole out small toys. Would it be all right with you if I visited your house then?"

"It would be wonderful," Bill said. "I'm sure it's very good of you to take all that trouble."

"Trouble it isn't. I enjoy doing it." His expression showed that he did. An instant later his face clouded. "I must say, though, that I sometimes get a little miffed at the parents. They will call up and say, 'Don't forget us Christmas Eve, Mr. Parker; the children are counting on it. We won't be here to receive you; we're going to a cocktail party. But the maid will let you in.'"

"The ungrateful so-and-so's!" Bill sympathized. "There are plenty of other nights in the year to go out and get drunk. People who have children young enough to believe in Santa Claus ought to be satisfied to stay home with them on Christmas Eve."

The cocktail party was one of the unforeseen results of Prohibition. By invitation, but always with the possibility of gate-crashers, a married couple would provide plenty of strong cocktails at the fag end of the afternoon; with them would be served a variety of thirst producers. They were large, noisy parties, which soon reached the point where the guests laughed hard at nothing. Later some of the men would get very affectionate with other men's wives, or a woman might even make the overtures. Insobriety was becoming the fashion; not to drink was to set oneself down as a prig and a spoilsport. It was natural enough in a way. The bluenoses wanted to run other people's lives for them; rebellious Americans didn't see it that way. Doubtless there had been other such rebels long before America was discovered. To forbid anything was to call attention to it. If the apple had not been forbidden fruit, Mother Eve might have gone placidly on eating oranges.

So Santa Claus came to the Andrews home just as the little boys were preparing to hang up their stockings. Will simply stared wide-eyed, but Charley was beside himself with excitement. This was a dream come true: this on top of everything else. He took this first, best toy to bed with him. To a parental eye it might look as if the toy had come from the ten-cent store, but to a true believer it had come straight from the North Pole. Enjoying the children's pleasure was very great happiness indeed.

But being a parent had its dark moments. If one of the boys caught a cold, he was sure to pass it on to his brother. Vaccination and immunity shots against various contagions were something of an ordeal: easier with Will, of course, because Charlotte had been through it all with Charley, but still a strain. And the day Charley fell out of a tree and broke his arm, his mother felt as if the end of the world had come, though actually it was a very ordinary mishap.

Once the first shock was over, Charley rather enjoyed his injury. Since it was his right arm that had had to be put into a cast, he needed to be fed his meals, "just like when I was a baby." He could manage an apple or a banana very well, however, and he strutted in front of his little brother and the neighborhood urchins. Then when the cast came off, there was the novel experience of reeducating the weakened muscles. Little brother Will, aping him, pretended that he too had an injured arm, and favored it; but he couldn't always remember which arm it was, so it kept shifting.

He wasn't always an admiring and imitative little brother. Only too soon the two reached the stage where they got into fights. Charlotte was constantly being called on to step in and stop a brawl. Then it was always, "He hit me first." Generally, indeed, it was Charley who hit first, but Will teased until Big Brother lost his temper and struck out.

Charlotte remembered some of the Victorian maxims on that subject:

> Let dogs delight
> To bark and bite;
> But little children, never.

As if barking were always a form of combat, and children's mode of combat were biting! Or again, "Birds in their little nest agree." As of course they didn't; the others were always trying to push the weakest one out. Still, competition was healthful—without the desire to excel, we would still be wandering through primitive jungles.

Every year on their respective birthdays the boys were measured against a door jamb in their rainy-day playroom, and a pencil mark left to record each age, with an identifying initial. Charley was reasonably honest about the procedure, but Will, always touchy about being the younger and smaller of the two, would try to hunch a little by getting off his heels. These marks Charlotte carefully recorded, and renewed after the room was repainted.

Yes, they were growing. Will was still at the stage where he changed from day to day. Charles was coming along fast, too. He was still devoted to Mother Goose, but he was now avid for fairy stories. Also, Charlotte had bought them a dog. They played with him a lot. He barked a good deal, but it was purely in the excitement of the game. He did not bite anybody. He was a fox terrier, and in honor of her own long-dead pet Charlotte named him Stub. The boys were supposed to feed him and keep his water dish full. The houseman bathed him. But he was primarily Charlotte's responsibility. Well, that was what she was here for; to see

that everybody on the place, pets included, was properly
looked after.

In June Will celebrated his second birthday. The whole
lovely summer stretched ahead of the young family; it was
time they made some plans.

"Are you planning to go back to Saylesboro for a visit?"
Bill asked.

"I don't want to make things too routine. Of course, that
is our home away from home—mine and the children's,
anyhow. But don't you think they are old enough now to
travel? I'd like them to see something of the country while
it's still a wonderland to them."

"Just what part of the country do you have in mind? Oh,
don't look so innocent, Queen Charlotte! You never make
random suggestions."

"Your sister lives in Denver, doesn't she?"

"She does. She married a man named Thomas Leonard.
A lawyer. They're very good at minding their own business. You've never had any in-law problem there."

"I'm not trying to create one. I'm not proposing us as
house guests. But I thought if we went to an hotel in Denver, we could see a little something of them, and they could
tell us what sights are worth seeing in their beautiful state."

"Sure you're not thinking more about showing your children off than you are about seeing the sights in Colorado?"

"The two are not mutually exclusive: to see and to be
seen."

"You were never without an answer, were you?"

"It may have happened, but I can't recall an instance."

They went ahead as she suggested. Harriet and Tom
Leonard turned out to be very nice people, with an only
son who was in summer school in the state university. The

Andrewses spent a week in Denver, another week exploring the state. That was long enough to keep the children away this first time.

Saylesboro in August. The lovely autumn coming on. The little boys frolicking with Stub in the fallen leaves. The round of entertaining beginning. Cocktail parties, and dinner parties too, with dinner sometimes followed by a session of bridge. Charlotte was an indifferent player, but she generally held good hands. Bill was excellent, and he liked to win. Charlotte saw a side of him at the card table that she never saw at home. She could understand now how in business he held his own against competitors.

Thanksgiving, with the traditional big bird for the big dinner. Benjamin Franklin had wanted to make the turkey instead of the eagle our national bird; perhaps hospitality rather than aggressiveness should be a leading national trait.

On Christmas Eve Santa Claus came around again. Will was old enough now to hang up his own stocking. Charlotte read to the boys that wonderful poem "The Night before Christmas." They saw no discrepancy between the Saint Nick who arrived behind eight tiny reindeer that deposited him at the top of the chimney and their own Santa Claus who came to the front door. Or for that matter between these two and the Santa Claus who filled their stockings.

It seemed to Charlotte that the rest of that winter passed all too quickly. In July she and Bill took the children on several brief trips to Chicago, where they saw the sights of a big city and marveled at them. Already Charlotte was dreading the change that September would bring into her life. She would start Charles in school this year.

The other children in his class may have had something

to do with it, or perhaps Charles was simply growing up and observing for himself. At any rate, the following Christmas Eve when Santa Claus appeared at the Andrewses he said to the little boy, "Charley, I've heard that you say I'm not Santa Claus at all, I'm just Mr. Parker."

"Oh no!" Charles said, shocked and grieved at the misunderstanding. "I never said that, Santa Claus. Mr. Parker is much crosser than you are."

Santa Claus hastily covered his mouth with his mittened hand. Bill Andrews snickered audibly, but Charlotte succeeded in turning her laughter into a cough.

She was fairly quiet the rest of that winter; her third baby would be born in late spring. This time she and Bill agreed that they would like a little girl. A third boy would be welcome, of course. But a little girl, a doll baby, "sugar and spice," was really what the parents ordered.

It was what they got, too. A lovely seven-pound blue-eyed girl. "We put in our order," a complacent Bill said to a smiling Charlotte. But when little Will saw his new sister, he asked, "Where did you get her?" And his father replied, "The angels brought her."

That was as good an answer as any. Motherhood, so grossly physical in many of its details, still had about it an element of mystery, of the divine.

"Charles is named for you, and Will for me," Bill reminded her. "For whom are we going to name this one?"

"Well, since Charles is the masculine for Charlotte, and Will takes care of your end of it, I think I'd like to have our little daughter named the feminine of Paul."

"Pauline? For your father? That sounds to me like an excellent idea."

"Pauline Andrews it is, then. Papa will be properly puffed up. I think I'll write him tomorrow. Since this is his namesake as well as his granddaughter, it would hardly do for him to get the news merely from a card."

A first baby is a novelty, a second a satisfaction, a third a bonus. Charlotte was not only a proud and happy mother, she was really satisfied. She was standing on the island of Monte Cristo. The world was hers.

Book III

AFTERNOON

🌷 1 🌷

"ALL GRANDCHILDREN are wonderful," Paul Emerson announced to Charlotte. "Of course, I get rather tired of hearing my contemporaries brag about their little prodigies—"

"While you're waiting for your chance to hold forth about your own," Charlotte interrupted.

"Who has a better right, I'd like to know? Mine are all scrumptious, to put it mildly. But this little newcomer is my namesake as well as my granddaughter. She is also the prettiest one of the quartet—and that's going some."

Quartet? The word brought Charlotte up sharp. But of course Agnes's daughter was as close kin to Papa as his new namesake was. She was first cousin to Charlotte's offspring, too. The kinship was there, all right, but Agnes and Charlotte had been just too far apart in age—or something. Charlotte hoped it wouldn't be like that with her children. At least Charley and Will were great companions, even if they did manage to get into so many fights.

They were left with their grandparents in Saylesboro two weeks that summer, while Charlotte, back home in Euclid, had her new baby all to herself. Those lovely first months while a baby was still a baby, all hers and all potentialities. There for a little while Pauline belonged to Charlotte almost as much as she had before she was born, and in a vastly more interesting way. The young mother could see her and handle her, bathe her and change her, feed her at her own breast, in that deep communion which meant so much to a young mother. The sight of them together like that thrilled Bill Andrews as nothing else could. His baby at her breast!

When Charlotte and the baby and the nurse girl joined the party, small Will informed his grandmother, "Now you're going to see *my* little sister." The temptation was too much for Charles, who said loftily, "She's mine more than she is yours. I'm the oldest, so the most belongs to me."

Those were fighting words, of course. Charlotte jumped in to settle the fracas. When it was over and the disputants out of earshot, she said to her mother, "Have they been acting like this all the time they've been here?"

"Well, not all the time." Mamma smiled.

Charlotte shook her head. "They *are* nice when they're in their cradles."

"They're always nice. But they do grow up and grow away from us."

"Yes, that's what we have to expect." Charlotte impulsively reached over and kissed Mamma's cheek. At that moment they felt very close.

Prohibition had brought with it not only increased drinking, but two features which were absolutely its own special product. One was the bootlegger. In many circles people asked, "Who's your bootlegger?" just as naturally as they might ask, "Who's your family doctor?" or "Where do you buy your hats?" That didn't affect Papa or Bill—at least as yet; their cellars were too well stocked. But nobody wanted to sit at home all the time, or wait to be asked to a friend's house. So here came that great new institution, the speakeasy.

In order to gain admittance to a drinking place of this

description, or more often an eating and drinking place, the customer had to be known. That was the one point which all speakeasies had in common. In one class of such were Italian joints where red wine was made on the premises or bought from an Italian who dealt in it. In another type, hard liquor was on sale, sometimes of doubtful quality, sometimes good stuff smuggled in. Saylesboro, being right on Lake Michigan, was very easily reached from Canada.

So on two different occasions, after Bill joined them for a fortnight's rest and change, the Andrewses were taken to a speakeasy. All that business of being eyed through a peephole before you were let in was fun; so was the sense that you were putting something over on somebody you didn't like. For the rest, the surroundings were quiet and the provender good. If people drank more than they would have under other circumstances—well, that was the way things were going these days.

Then it was back to Euclid for the opening of school. Both boys were in school now, Will as a neophyte a little bit timid, Charles swaggering like a veteran. The baby was now sitting up in her crib. She recognized the rest of them. When Bill got home from the office, if it was anywhere around his usual hour, he had an interval when he played with her and talked to her. She recognized him with a little whoop and a sort of sitting dance. Bill had always been an attentive father, but it seemed to Charlotte that he was tenderer with her than he ever had been with the boys.

Just before Christmas Charles announced to his mother, "I know that Santa Claus really is Mr. Parker. But I'm not going to tell him so. I won't tell Willie either."

Oh, no, he didn't tell Mr. Parker! All he did was address

him as "Mr. Parka Claus." To which Santa Claus replied sweetly, "You're a little wrong there, Charley. A parka is fine in Alaska, maybe. But it wouldn't do for me at the North Pole."

"Some little boys are fresher than a new-laid egg," Bill Andrews said in quasi-apology.

"I don't bother so much about how fresh an egg is," Santa Claus returned. "Eggs keep very well at the Pole."

Charles was defeated on this attempt to get a rise out of the grown people. But he thought up a new one a few weeks after that. Careful to say it in front of Will, he informed his mother, "I know where babies come from."

"So do I," Charlotte said coolly. "But once they're here, I don't see that it matters much."

"It's before they get here. That's what's interesting."

"It may be to you, Charles." Charlotte remembered that Bill had told Charles on his little brother's arrival, "The angels brought him." On Pauline's arrival he had said the same thing, and little Will had exclaimed, "My, ain't she a flier?" Charles hadn't said a thing, but he had looked a little smug. Some children learned more on the school playground than they did in the classroom—or at least, it was more interesting to them.

Charles went serenely on, "Babies come out of—just where other things come out of."

Startled, Charlotte snapped, "And where is that?"

"Out of where other babies come from," Charles wound up serenely.

"That's a good answer, Charles. It just about closes the subject." Charlotte hoped that her eldest did not hear her involuntary sigh of relief. He was just trying to startle the adults. And succeeding very nicely, if you asked his Mommy.

When she related the incident to Bill that evening, he shook his head in mock despair. "I don't know what that boy will be up to next."

"Neither does he," said Charlotte. "But he'll think of something."

"Your much desired first-born," Bill said softly.

Charlotte nodded. "At least he brings home good report cards," she reminded Bill—and herself. "As to what he hears on the school playground, well, I suppose it's foolish to make too much fuss over it."

"You've handled the one situation very nicely, my dear. I'm sure you can deal with the next one."

"Oh Bill, you're such a comfort to me!"

"Didn't I promise to cherish you? This is a part of our life together. It has its funny side, too."

"It has—now. I didn't see anything funny about it at the time."

"Wouldn't you like an evening drink on that, Charlotte?"

"I'd like an evening drink anyhow. Thank you for reminding me. And if you feel like lighting cigarettes for the two of us, I'd like that, too."

While Bill was mixing their drinks, Charlotte stole in for a glance at her first-born—her namesake. Mighty sweet and innocent he looked, lying there asleep. What if she and Bill had never had any children? Charlotte shuddered at the very idea. She leaned over and kissed the little boy's smooth warm forehead.

On a sudden warm afternoon which gave a fallacious promise of spring, her darling pulled another fast one. Rushing in after school with his cap in his hand and little beads of perspiration showing on his forehead, he burst out, "Mommy, do you know what I heard a boy say on the playground today? The boy said—" Then followed two short sentences, each beginning sweetly "Will you kiss—?" and each terminating with a brief word which Charlotte hadn't heard in years, and had heard then very much *sub rosa.*

But she betrayed neither amazement nor shock. She said simply, "I don't think I'd say that, dear. Those are dirty words, and I wouldn't use them, any more than I'd breathe dirty air or bathe in dirty water."

"That's what I thought, Mommy." Charles was all bright-eyed agreement. "I thought they were dirty words, so I decided *I* would never say—" and promptly repeated the original offense.

Charlotte rumpled his hair and kissed him. He was a smart lad. All little boys were a curious mixture of angel and gutter pup, she supposed, but the gutter pup in Charles only added to his endearing quality.

That evening, upon hearing the episode, Bill guffawed. "I remember having my mouth washed out with soap for using one of those words. I had overheard it from a bigger boy, and I hadn't the vaguest idea what it meant. But after that, I made it my business to find out."

"Bill, I have an idea that a successful parent sees and hears only about half of what goes on."

"An excellent principle, Mrs. Andrews. The only question left to be decided is, which half?"

This time he got her a drink and lit their two cigarettes in his own mouth without being asked. Bill approved her. Bill stood behind her. If he left the discipline of the children almost entirely to her—well, it was that way in most American families, Charlotte supposed.

The weather that spring was trying; not quite so bad in Euclid as it was in Charlotte's native Saylesboro, perhaps; but still, bad enough. The boys both had colds, Will's much the worse. Little Pauline in her turn sneezed and coughed, and looked at her mother with wide, reproachful eyes which seemed to say, "Can't you do something about this?" Charlotte could, of course; she held the baby, fed her orange juice, gave her tiny bites of toast softened in hot water. Eventually she caught the baby's cold, but she did feel that she had soothed and comforted the child.

Then, just when the children were convalescing, Mrs. Khaut took to her bed. Charlotte, summoned by the second maid, found a very sick and suffering old woman. She called the doctor. He diagnosed pneumonia, and suggested either hospitalization or a trained nurse.

Mrs. Khaut snapped at him, "A hospital, with its nasty hospital smell! And I don't want any nurse fussing over me, thinking she knows what I want better than I know it myself."

The doctor soothed, "We're not trying to tell you what you want, Mrs. Khaut. We wish to help you get better."

"Then go away and let me manage to suit myself."

The result was that Mrs. Andrews in person took care of her, and also helped out a demoralized household staff. She was really fond of the old lady, who was a holdover from Bill's bachelor days, who had been consulted by the new bride and had helped her settle in this big, comfortable house which was still home to both of them. But Charlotte realized now that Mrs. Khaut was beginning to look and sound like a very old woman.

Mrs. Khaut realized that herself when she was able to get out of bed and totter around. "You've been awfully kind to me, Mrs. Andrews," she said. "I've always enjoyed looking after Mr. Andrews; he was an easy man to work for. But it's time I got out of the way and let some younger person take over."

Charlotte's heart leaped. This was what she had herself been thinking, but she was afraid to bring the matter up and hurt the old woman's feelings. She temporized, "I should hate to see you go. But if you really feel that way about it—"

"You might promote Minnie and get a new second girl. Or you might decide to get an altogether new cook." A faint smile flitted over her worn old face. "I'll leave my recipe book here if you do decide to promote Minnie. An altogether new person might turn up her nose at it."

"You can leave it here for my benefit," Charlotte said quickly. "Thank you very, very much."

So Mrs. Khaut, an old woman free at last to lead her own life, went flat-hunting. She had a very neat sum in savings, and she looked forward to a snug little nest where she could lie in bed an extra hour any morning she chose, and could have a cup of coffee at any hour of the day or night.

Having lived so long under somebody else's roof, she was appalled by the rents that were demanded for anything like good accommodations. When she returned, weary and discouraged, from a fourth quest, she poured out a tale of woe to Charlotte. "I may have to wind up in a furnished room with only a gas plate to depend on," she wound up. "I could afford a boarding house, of course, but I'd hate to try to get along on the messes they shove at you on boarding-house tables. And I had wanted to be all by myself, so that I could have a little peace in my few remaining years."

"I'll consult Mr. Andrews about this," Charlotte promised. "Being a businessman, he probably knows more about such things than you or I would."

"Oh, if you think that that's the thing to do—!" Mrs. Khaut sighed with relief.

Bill listened to Charlotte with an understanding smile,

and answered promptly, "Something can certainly be done about Mrs. Khaut's problem. Ask her to go out again and have a look, and then decide which flat of all she has seen she likes best. Maybe she'd better make a second choice, too. Have her make a note of the price and the landlord's name and address. I think I can do something about it."

"You're pretty sure you can, aren't you?"

"For a good and faithful servant, I'm willing to go to a little trouble."

When Charlotte relayed these instructions to Mrs. Khaut, the plain old face lighted up with hope, though after an instant the flat-hunter demurred, "But suppose the places I like best are also the ones that cost the most?"

"I wouldn't know, I'm sure," Charlotte said demurely. "I've never been in business myself. But I've been married to Mr. Andrews long enough to know that he generally manages to get things done."

"Mr. Andrews is wonderful. And he takes such an interest in people!" Charlotte had never seen Mrs. Khaut show such enthusiasm before, and wouldn't have believed her capable of it. But perhaps that was what the mere idea of her coming emancipation would do for her: the idea that she was no longer simply the Andrewses' cook, but a person with a home of her own and a well-earned independence.

Mrs. Khaut lost no time in handing Charlotte the required information. Bill, looking over the shaky scrawl on his return home, said, "I suppose it would look suspicious if I negotiated the first place on this list. Second choice might be a little more plausible."

"Bill, are you planning to subsidize the old lady?"

"No harm in that, is there, as long as she doesn't catch on?"

"It's a wonderful idea. An idea like that, and the means to carry it out—I only wish that combination occurred oftener in this fascinating but muddled world of ours."

Bill nodded his thanks, then went back to the scrawled memorandum. "The landlord agrees to knock a third off the proposed rent because I guarantee the respectability and trustworthiness of the tenant?"

"That's a little large, isn't it? Oh, wait a minute! A third off the best and most expensive of these places, a quarter off the other. That way the old lady has some choice, and while she's choosing, she won't have time to become suspicious."

"Fine! I'll see both landlords tomorrow, while you explain to Mrs. Khaut. Tell her there is often a difference between asking price and what the seller is willing to take."

"That much is often true, isn't it?"

"Yes, Mrs. Andrews, it is. You might say that is what the stock market is all about."

So Charlotte went ahead with her part in their little drama. Mrs. Khaut looked dazed at this turn in her fortunes. She faltered, "It's almost too good to be true."

"Not at all!" Charlotte said stoutly. "People often try to take advantage of a woman alone, but a good smart businessman is generally onto their little tricks."

Mrs. Khaut gave in then and decided on the apartment that had been her first choice. Charlotte made her a present of her bedroom furniture and went with her to help select sheets, pillowcases, towels, and washcloths. "I declare, it's almost like being a bride!" Mrs. Khaut cried out, gloating over the freshness of her purchases.

"A new home is a new home," Charlotte sympathized. "There's nothing quite like having a home of one's own. But I won't forget all you've done for me in my home over all these years, Mrs. Khaut, and for Mr. Andrews before that."

So here was Mrs. Khaut finally out of the picture. Minnie moved into the cook's bedroom, with brand-new furniture in the selection of which she had been allowed some voice. Minnie, with Mrs. Khaut's recipe book to help her out, but with very definite ideas of her own. Charlotte hired a new second girl, and went through all the business of breaking her in. It was Memorial Day before she again had a chance to draw a long breath. Memorial Day, with the flags all flying in honor of little Pauline's birthday.

Charlotte sat back and let her breath go. For a few nights she slept so deeply that she wasn't even conscious of Bill there beside her in the bed. She thought of Mamma, preparing her young daughter for marriage—how many years ago was it? Not really before the Flood, but somewhere around the time that Columbus discovered America. Mamma, preparing Charlotte for the facts of married life, had succeeded only in embarrassing the bride-to-be. A little wise counseling on the subject of servants might have been more to the point.

Or perhaps not. Mrs. Khaut had been a part of Charlotte's married establishment, with priority rights. And Bill had known the proper way to deal with Mrs. Khaut. That was all very fine, fitting, and proper. Charlotte had learned a lot from Bill, and with Bill. As for those facts which had embarrassed Mrs. Emerson, Charlotte was being schooled in them by her own children.

2

WHEN CHARLES ANDREWS was old enough to be awarded his first bicycle, he was the biggest thing in Euclid. The houseman taught him to ride, and he learned in no time at all. He had now entered a magic world, where he could go far and fast with as little effort as it takes a bird to fly. Weekdays he rushed home from school so that he could go for a spin before it got too dark. Saturdays, and often on Sunday afternoons, he and his cronies took little spins in the country; if they could inveigle packed lunches out of their elders, they would be gone the greater part of the day. Some grown person, also mounted, went along on these expeditions, but even grownups were different on a bicycle trip, not like a teacher or a policeman or a cranky neighbor.

The boys learned to brag about the gears of their bicycles; the point was to prove that your machine had the highest, though often to an impartial eye the bikes might have looked identical. The juggling with figures would have astonished the great mathematician for whom their city was named.

Will used to look after them longingly sometimes, but he would return to his own concerns and his contemporaries —and of course he could always lord it over his little sister. He had something to look forward to, anyhow; his day was coming.

It came soon enough; Will was presented with his own bicycle. Charles had a new one; his old bike was given away. It was a good deal the worse for wear, but it had been fitted with new tires. A second-hand bike could be a mighty fine present, Charlotte supposed, when a boy had been getting along with no bike at all.

Will was much slower to learn the gentle art of cycling than Charles had been. Charles was now up to tricks. He would stand up on the pedals and wave both arms in the air. "See, Mom, no hands!" He would coast down a small hill, hands off the handlebars and feet off the pedals. He would ride backwards, trusting to an occasional glance over his shoulder to keep him out of harm's way. Most of these feats were performed out of his mother's sight, naturally, but Charlotte witnessed just enough to keep her nerves on edge.

Charles never came to any harm. Will, a far more cautious rider, was the one who would skid and come up with a skinned knee or a bruised forehead. Thank goodness Pauline was still young enough to be under the charge of a nursemaid. A mother couldn't hope to keep the children always small and dependent.

There was such a thing as luck, of course, though people were too much inclined to blame their luck for what was really their own fault. Had the William Andrewses used up too much of theirs on their first-born, so that there was nothing left for the second in order?

No good thinking that way, of course. You just got yourself upset, and some of your nervousness was bound to spill over on the people around you. Charlotte wondered what had ever happened to poor little Miss Kaminski back there in Belair, Wisconsin. She had intended to keep in touch with her, and of course hadn't done so. It was perhaps negligence on Charlotte's part. Yet what was there to say? "I have a wonderful husband. I have three remarkable children. I am happier than I ever expected or deserved to be." A bitter mockery. If kept down to skeleton facts—"I have a husband and three children"—it was shorn of all interest, but it still sounded like bragging. Charlotte thought that her son Will was unlucky because he sometimes had a wistful look and had fallen off his bicycle a few times? Charlotte should be ashamed of herself!

She should be ashamed of herself anyhow, to have so much when so many people had so little. Or no, not ashamed perhaps, but just a little fearful. She and Bill had given hostages to Fortune. That was the drawback about having a family: what might happen to the children. But a person had to take chances. That was the universal law of life. If it hadn't been for that great push, we should all still be back there in the primeval ooze.

It was far more to the purpose when Charlotte turned her attention to the domestic department. Minnie turned out to be an excellent cook, and ambitious. She followed Mrs. Khaut's recipes only occasionally. Generally she thought she could improve on them, or follow one of the standard printed works, or even try an improvisation of her own. At their conferences over menus and marketing, Charlotte was always more detailed and decisive than she had ever dared to be with Mrs. Khaut. An employee of her own was easier for Mrs. Andrews to get along with than an old family retainer.

The summer that Will got his bicycle Charlotte took all three children and their nurse up to Saylesboro for a lovely three weeks; she had the boys' bicycles sent there by express. Then in August the bicycles stood in the garage for a fortnight. This time Bill Andrews took his Mrs., all three children and the nurse, to New York City for an enchanted fortnight.

To small Pauline it was like a trip to Fairyland. Much of the time she was left with the nurse, and went on with something like her home regimen; but she saw and heard enough, and perhaps in her childish way she would remember some of it. The boys took in everything: rides up Fifth Avenue on the double-decker bus, the boat ride around Manhattan Island, the climb to the top of the Statue of Liberty, a few matinees as the opening season got under way, eating around at various restaurants, and having a wonderful time with the menus and the crowds.

"Gee! I'd like to live here!" young Charles cried at the height of the excitement. "Or no, I wouldn't either. I'd miss my bike and the dogs. But it's a great place to visit."

"That seems to be the general verdict," his father said dryly. "I'm glad it is. I'm sort of attached to my home and my business in Euclid."

"You can always be in one place and think about another," young Will said quietly. "Now that I've seen New York, I can take some of it back to Saylesboro with me."

Charlotte beamed, and big Bill caught her eye and nodded emphatically. Their quiet Will had said something this time. One of the greatest pleasures of any expedition was getting home and thinking it over afterward.

So then they were back home in Euclid. Charles was bragging to his bicycle gang about his travels. Will was playing with the dogs, an aging Stub and the Boston bulls Jack and Jim. Charlotte arranged autumnal flowers for the dining table and the living room, and began the business of buying new fall outfits for the family. The shadow of school's reopening sometimes flitted across the boys' horizons, but when that day came, they found they didn't mind too much. There was always Saturday to look forward to, and some teachers weren't quite such meanies as others.

For Christmas the boys now gave as well as received, and Charles smiled condescendingly and Will wistfully when Santa Claus gave a wide-eyed Pauline a Chinese fan. Then he gave each boy a peppermint cane and a pat on the head. They knew the legend for what it was, but we were all friends here.

Charles was now the one who read aloud, " 'Twas the night before Christmas." And after Pauline had been put to bed, the boys were treated to a reading of the *Christmas Carol*, with their father and mother taking turns at the text. There are a few special books for which each repetition only adds to the novelty of the event; Scrooge's saga heads the list of those.

Suddenly that year Charles developed a great interest in arithmetic, or maybe he simply decided that since he was there and had to go through the motions, he might as well do the work. He tackled it in dead earnest, and turned in perfect paper after perfect paper. Those high marks on his report card looked so lonesome that he began to sail into spelling and geography, and to take a little more trouble with reading and composition. Those high marks gratified his father and mother, and pretty well put the kibosh on brother Will, who had to work his head off to stay in the upper 80's.

Snow, sledding, and skating in the long Ohio winter. Popcorn balls made by Minnie to celebrate Saturday evening. Small friends in for games of checkers or dominoes, followed by hot chocolate and cookies. The first winds of spring, with the hunt for pussywillows. The delights of spring clothes and Easter. Bicycling again, with the long vacation to look forward to. This was life. This was living. This was—what was it Mommy called it? Oh, yes, "standing on the island of Monte Cristo." That must be a great story. All books about the Wild West were fun, and *Treasure Island*, and all that about fighting in different wars. Now Charles was thrilled by any mention of New York in a book; he had been there and seen it. Of course he had been to Denver, too, but Denver was different.

This next summer they spent the usual three weeks in Saylesboro. The bicycling there was just as good as it had been last year. And the young Andrewses saw more of their mother's native city. Mommy took them out to Madison, too. She said she had gone to college there. "I danced almost as much as I studied. But I studied quite a lot, too." Then in August Daddy took the family and the inevitable nurse to Minneapolis and from there on to the Pacific coast. He made some business calls, too, in various cities on their way. This country of ours was very large, very beautiful, very exciting. They told something about it in the geography books, but to get any real idea, you had to see it for yourself.

So here they were back in Euclid again, with a new school year beginning. The routine and the confinement had ceased to irk Charles, now that he was doing so well in his studies. He liked the work both for its own sake and because it was a contest between his will and the teacher's. Let the old crank try to flunk him if she could; he would show her that he was smarter than she was.

But his mother came up with a fresh and awful blow. This fall, he would be required to attend dancing classes. Over his howls of outrage she said soothingly, "You won't be alone, you know. Your brother will be with you."

"Oh but gee, Mom! It's not fair! You said yourself how well I'm doing in school now. So when I go to school, and do my homework too, you think you can bundle me off to —to—"

"I never made you take music lessons, did I?" Charlotte reminded him. "If you'd like to start in now with the piano, maybe I can arrange that. But you'll have to practice an hour every day, and that *will* cut into your playtime."

"Piano lessons!" Charles screamed.

"Or if you would prefer to study the violin, that can be arranged. It's harder on the nerves of the family, but we love you so much we'll try to put up with your scrapings and slidings."

"Oh Mommy, you—! Oh, I see! You're making a joke. You know I haven't any talent, and pianos are for listening to anyhow, not for playing. Mommy, how come you never play the piano?"

"To me," Charlotte said serenely, "music is something to dance to." Thus, with parental shrewdness, she brought the conversation around to its original topic. Then, while Charles grinned a little sheepishly and held his tongue, she began to hum a waltz melody, "The Beautiful Blue Danube," to which she had waltzed so many miles while she was still Charlotte Emerson. Waltzed with so many different men, who were gone now, like the toy balloons, into the blue unknown.

Presently she began to dance to her own music, to glide and turn and glide, waving her arms in time with the melody. Charles stood transfixed. This was somebody he had never seen: somebody who was not his own beloved familiar Mommy, yet in some strange way went along with her. Then after a few minutes the graceful shape came to him and took both his hands. Somehow she drew him into the rhythm with her. Stumblingly, but catching on after a fashion, Charles danced with her.

When she stopped humming and released him, Charles let go his breath, which he had been holding without knowing it. Charlotte reached around and rumpled his hair; his head came to her shoulder now. "That wasn't so bad, was it?" she asked softly. "Remember, too, in a real dance it is always the man who leads."

The man! Charles was not only soothed and interested; he was elated. Girls were always *there*, of course. In school, where the annoying creatures often got good marks and seemed to stand in with the teachers. Around the neighborhood, where they flocked together as if they formed a separate tribe. On their own bicycle trips, with their machines designed to make room for their silly old skirts. Pauline was different, of course; she was still sweet and babyish, and anyhow she was Little Sister, not a member of an alien tribe. But in dancing, when he was required to associate with the specimens one by one, *he* would lead. Always, inevitably, by virtue of his innate maleness. The man! Charles yielded, but with one stipulation. "If you say so, Mommy, I guess I'll have to. But it lasts only the one year, doesn't it? Next fall I won't have to put up with any such foolishness?"

"You may like it so much that you'll ask me to let you go back for a second year."

Charles guffawed. He knew a grownup joke when he heard one. It was only later that he thought of an appeal to his father. "Daddy, Mommy says that I'm supposed to go to dancing school this year."

"Yes. You'll need special clothes for that, I suppose. Your mother will attend to that for you."

"But Daddy, if I didn't go to dancing school, I'd save

all that time. You'd maybe save some money, too."

"And have you grow up into the kind of young man who goes stepping all over his partner's feet? That's no saving in the end, son. It's a massacre."

It suggested a new game, anyhow. Charles went looking for the luckless Will and shouted, "We're going to dancing school, to learn how not to step on each other's feet. Like this! Wow!" Then he proceeded to stamp all over Will's feet. Will of course stamped back, and one of their old-fashioned brawls ensued. Those brotherly fights didn't occur so often any more, but the old habit lingered.

So Friday afternoon no longer meant the beginning of the weekend freedom. Instead, the Andrews boys were now corraled, scoured even more thoroughly than they had been in the morning, compelled to put on the dressy clothes which were laid out for them. They were delivered at a big ballroom in Ivanhoe Temple downtown. There they and some twenty other boys and slightly more than that number of little girls were greeted and lined up by Mrs. Leighton, a gray-haired lady in a full skirt which barely came to the tops of her shoes. Under the eyes of the mothers seated around the walls, she began to teach them the various dance steps, which they performed to the music of a piano played by a man in a little balcony at the end of the big ballroom. Imagine a man playing the piano for little girls to dance! Charles could not imagine it, but he saw it happen.

The steps came easy to Charles, a little harder to Will. Everything always came a little harder to Will. But every time he mastered a new step he looked for approval to Big Brother, and Charles was careful to catch his eye and nod.

The next thing they knew, the boys were dancing with the girls. What was more, Charles found himself liking it. There was something about the touch of the soft little hand in his, and the sweet flowery smell so like Mamma's, and the way they did things together—why, this was fun! Almost as much fun, in its very different way, as riding his bicycle "no hands" or chasing around with the dogs in the autumn leaves or the new-fallen snow.

During Christmas vacation Daddy and Mommy gave a big party for Charles and Will and some of the children from Mrs. Leighton's class. The Andrewses' piano, so seldom used, was specially tuned for the event, and the man from dancing school played it. This was quite the best party yet. It was the best vacation yet. Dancing school was a great idea. Parents did sometimes know what they were talking about.

For Easter that year they had a school play. Charles was cast for the part of the Easter Rabbit, and delivered his lines with a flourish. There was no question about it—he adored having the center of the stage. But of course somebody had to take the leading part, or how would the rest of them have anybody to act around?

Back in Saylesboro in July for their annual three-week visit, Charlotte gave a balloon party for her own three and as many of Mamma's friends' grandchildren as could be collected. There was some dancing on the lawn, too, and Charles disported himself grandly with the local girls. "They're coming on," Papa said with a smile that was half sad. "Making a place of their own, while they're waiting to take our places."

Charlottte could see a change in Paul Emerson. His hair was snow white now. He moved a little slower, and sometimes with an effort. Once Charlotte thought she saw him feeling his own pulse. But he caught her eye and smiled reassuringly. Perhaps it was all her imagination. Perhaps she loved him so much she couldn't even bear to think that some day. . . . No sense in worrying about "some day," though. Charlotte herself might be the first to go. Meanwhile he was perfectly happy with his small namesake. There seemed to be a special rapport between them. Pauline would far rather sit on his knee and talk small nothings with him than play with the other children.

The news from the Stantons was not good. Agnes was even now arranging a quiet divorce from her awful husband. Young Inez and her husband were tiffing off and on; right now her grandfather had given her a trip to Paris with a woman friend, in the hope that a little cooling off would help matters.

"Oh, dear, when another generation gets to the marrying stage—" Charlotte sighed. "I'm not even going to think about mine in that connection."

"It is a little early," Inez said with a sweet, sad smile. There for an instant Mamma too looked her age. But what was so terrible in that, pray? The only way to avoid growing old was to die young. After an instant's thoughtful silence, Mamma asked, "What are your plans for the rest of the summer, daughter?"

Charlotte was glad to tell her. Those things were fun to talk over. That was another of the pleasures of a trip, talking it over in advance with somebody who would listen and understand and be happy with you.

❦ 3 ❦

THERE WERE so many different ways of noting the passage of time. Those pencil marks on a door jamb recording the children's increasing heights. Birthdays. Anniversaries. A woman's first gray hair. (Charlotte hadn't reached that stage yet.) The increasing use of automobiles, with the horse-and-buggy days gradually vanishing into history. Rising prices. Elections coming and going, always with so many "able, fearless" men seeking office, who then turned out to be pretty much like their predecessors and their opponents. The newspapers getting bulkier all the time, and having less and less interesting news in them.

These topics were thrashed out pretty thoroughly at the meetings of Charlotte's bridge club. She had never been much of a "joiner," and her card-playing was largely an evening affair in which husbands and wives both took part. But Miriam Prince from the house in the next block talked her into it, and Charlotte found that she enjoyed the sessions and even looked forward to them. Her card-playing was mediocre, but she liked eating those company luncheons, and in her turn trying to do the others one better. There were eight members of the club; they met every fortnight with fair regularity. When Charlotte was invited to join a second and larger club, which met every week, she backed out as gracefully as she could. Fun was fun, but there was no sense in dedicating one's life to finesses and slams.

The summer before Pauline was to start school, the Andrews family visited New York again. This time they all took a boat trip up the Hudson to West Point. The little girl would gaze wide-eyed at the sights which were pointed out to her, would ask a few questions, look again, then suddenly turn and smile up at her father. Charles was quite the veteran sightseer; he reminisced about previous trips, enthusiastically rather than accurately. Will occasionally jotted down something in a small notebook. "I want to remember," he explained. "Besides, if I have to write a composition in school next winter—"

"Next winter, haw!" Charles snorted. "This isn't next winter; it's this summer. This isn't Euclid; it's New York. Anything you can't remember, you ought to forget. Who is going to care what you see or think, anyhow?"

"Young man!" his father admonished. To Will he said, "Write down anything you like, of course, son. Just don't worry. Worrying won't get you any place."

Once out of earshot of the boys, Charlotte said softly, "Our first-born is as bright as they make 'em, I think. But sometimes I tremble for his future."

"You well may!" Bill snapped. "He's the one who will get into trouble. He's the one who will have the illegitimate children."

Charlotte retorted instantly, "If Charles has an illegitimate child, I'll take him and take care of him."

The couple stared at each other in amazement, almost in hostility. Then they both burst out laughing. Here they had endowed their eldest with ill-begotten offspring, and made it a boy, and arranged for its care and upbringing— all out of the blue!

Then Charlotte shook her head ruefully. "I don't see now how people ever have the nerve to have children."

"It's a little late to think of that," Bill reminded her.

"Oh, I'm not regretting it! You know I think our children are quite the most wonderful anybody ever produced. But still—"

"There you go, taking thought for the future, just like your little Willie. What say we go nightclubbing tonight, young lady? Here where we are strangers, nobody will know that we're husband and wife. They may think we're just out stepping when maybe we ought not to be."

It took a little arranging, but nightclubbing they went. Their anonymity turned out to be a delusion, since the first people they ran into were a member of Charlotte's bridge club and her husband. They had to leave early, too, because they faced another day of sightseeing with their tribe in tow. But this *was* New York, and they *were* behaving as proper out-of-towners should. Nobody could take that from them.

That Christmas Eve Santa Claus came in just a little sadly. He could not bring himself to skip the Andrews children, though now even Little Sister knew him for what he was. But we was not prepared for the reception they gave him. Lining up in the order of their age, they chanted,

> Thank you, Santa Claus!
> Thank you-ou-ou, be-cause
> You make little children happy!
> Thank you, dear old Pappy!

This time Santa Claus didn't have to conceal his mirth; instead he blinked fast for an instant. But Charles broke the tension, as Charles had a habit of doing. He shouted, "Isn't that a pretty song, Santa Claus? I made it up for you. Mommy taught it to the other children, but I was the one who made it up."

"It's a lovely song," Mr. Parker said. "It isn't every rundown Santa Claus who has a song written to him. Now won't you sing it for me again, so that I can be sure to remember it?"

Without urging they sang it for him, not only a second time but a third and a fourth. Even after the younger ones had tired of it, Charles went on caroling. It was only when Mr. Parker remembered his peppermint canes and produced them that the minstrel was silenced.

There was no hanging up stockings this year, but there was a great to-do over setting up the tree and distributing packages. Then, just before the children's delayed bedtime, Charlotte lined them up and led them in singing, "Silent night! Holy night!" Charles caught on fastest and sang loudest, of course. But even he looked impressed. There seemed to be in children's minds no conflict between the Santa Claus story and the Jesus story. It was all a part of the wonder.

The children had been safely disposed of, and Bill and Charlotte were busy about the tree, when Charles reappeared. Bill had already opened his mouth to begin the familiar "See here, young man," when Charles put up a hand for silence. "When I'm a big man, and maybe an old man," he announced, "I'm going to be Santa Claus and go around and make the little children happy. That's what Christmas is for, and Santa Claus and the Christ Child, to make little children happy."

His mother seized him and hugged him. Then she took him as far as the head of the stairs and again kissed him good night. Returning to Bill, she said softly and very sweetly, "That one minute was worth all the trouble he has cost us. Yes—" she threw up her head defiantly, "—and all he ever may cost us, too."

During holiday week she consulted Bill about another point of procedure. On New Year's Eve the two of them were accustomed to celebrating with a quiet drink at home. This year she suggested that they enlarge the celebration a little. They would have their usual champagne at midnight, with Mein Host Andrews popping the cork and pouring the fizz into chilled glasses. But couldn't they have another bottle earlier, just before the children's bedtime— and make that bedtime later than usual, say ten or even half-past? They could pour each of the children a small drink, proportioned to his age. This would give the trio a manificent feeling of being grown-up, and would at the same time teach them that the use of some things is proper and delightful; it is only the abuse that is to be shunned.

"I'm afraid it's a little too early for that," Bill demurred. "In another year or two, perhaps—" Then at the sight of her disappointed face he pulled up sharp. "No, you're right, dear. It's a splendid idea. You go ahead and have your way. And can't you just hear old Charles bragging to his gang about the champagne party he had on New Year's Eve?"

Charles adored the little festivity; he merely stipulated, "I don't have to brush my teeth again after this, do I?" Will took a sip, hiccupped, and said to Charles, "Here, you can have my share." Pauline tasted, licked her lips, tasted again. Then she looked around the table and smiled at everybody.

It was all over in half an hour. The children were escorted upstairs. Pauline was put to bed first, after being kissed all around. Will was kissed only by his parents, of course. He murmured half apologetically, "Thanks for everything. I really liked it, only—" Charles, crossing his wrists, held out his right hand to his father, his left to his mother, and said, "Shake. You're sports, both of you."

Downstairs again, Bill cleared away the children's glasses and refilled his own and Charlotte's. Then he said quietly, "We've already welcomed the New Year in, and the old one is still briefly with us. Let's drink to this little interlude, reserved for just the two of us."

They did so, then sat very quiet. It was a relief, and at the same time a letdown, when the actual hour struck.

It was during the next term that Charles asked his teacher to excuse him from singing class. "My voice is changing." He started something; the voices of his male classmates promptly began changing. Perhaps they did, at that. But Charles sometimes walked a girl home from school now, carrying her books for her. On the second or third such trip they might stop in somewhere for a soda; it was rather out of their way, but they were in no great hurry.

Another autumn it was another girl. Then, between school and play and long diversified summers, the eldest Andrews reached the eighth grade, got through it, and triumphantly graduated from grammar school.

Halfway through his formal education! The next step was preordained: high school. But after that came the choice of a college. The first of the three great choices. With Yale indicated, because Dad had gone there; but it wasn't compulsory. Then the choice of a vocation. There again, a family business was waiting for him; but there was still a lot of in-what-capacity and even whether-at-all—a lot to be determined. Finally there was the choice of a life mate. But at his present age this was the least of Charles's troubles.

High school was a strange world in many ways. Didn't

Charlotte remember how it had overwhelmed her? But there was a lot of free choice here. Charles met many new people, too. He began to date girls for Saturday afternoon movies. In secret he practiced his old dancing school routines. Sometimes in assembly room he passed notes. A wide world was opening before him. He was growing up, and the process couldn't go too fast to suit him.

Charlotte had now learned to drive, and there were two cars in the Andrews garage. "When can I have a car of my own?" her son demanded.

"Not for some time yet. You can have a new bicycle in the spring, perhaps, though you don't use the old one as much as you might."

"Bicycles are baby. Everybody knows my dad makes cars. They wonder why I don't have one. They keep asking me."

"Tell them you're too young to get your driver's license."

"When can I learn to smoke?"

"When you're eighteen. I'll light a cigarette for you myself at your birthday party." As if he hadn't already experimented behind her back! Did he expect her to come out and accuse him of that?

"How about drinking?"

"Champagne every New Year's Eve, of course. Next time you'll get a full glass, and you always drink most of Willie's for him. Claret cup on your birthday when you're eighteen. Maybe a little wine some time next winter with your Sunday dinner. You might let me look your Latin paper over before you hand it in. Algebra you do better than I, but you're pretty careless sometimes."

Charles had tackled geometry and Caesar, and Will was rounding out his grammar-school life, when a curious episode occurred. The Andrewses had seen Mrs. Khaut now and then during the years since she left their service; she paid them a visit occasionally, and a few times Charlotte had encountered her downtown or observed her sitting on a park bench. Now they received word of her death, and attended her small, bleak funeral. Soon after that, Bill had a letter from a lawyer. It turned out that the old lady had left all her belongings to "my friend and benefactor, Mr.William Andrews."

"Bill!" Charlotte gasped. "Do you suppose she found out that you had made a deal for her about her rent?"

Bill shrugged. "She may have found out. She may have guessed. There's no telling. But the poor old soul hadn't anybody who really belonged to her. We were the closest to a family that she had."

"I wish I'd been nicer to her than I was," Charlotte said with compunction.

"Well, you got along with her all right, and you did appreciate that recipe book of hers."

Much better to get along with her present concerns, of course; and Charlotte had enough different matters to see about. Beginning in the spring of his sophomore year, Charles began to go to dances. He led now; the man always led. Daddy provided the means of transportation; Mommy sat up for him and either listened to his account of the festivity or watched him go up to bed, disgruntled or starry-eyed as the case might be. Those good old high-school "crushes"! They didn't last, of course. They weren't meant to last. But they had a strange charm which nothing in later life exactly matched.

When Will in his turn entered high school, Charles was ready to show him the ropes. Almost too ready, indeed. Will needed time to adjust to the new environment. He liked to sit in the assembly room and look about him; liked to watch the comings and goings of those superior beings, the upperclassmen. He liked to see all these girls, now "Miss" this and "Miss" that, as much a spectacle as actresses in a play, yet still his fellow students here in this vast complex organization. He took home hordes of new impressions with him. Alone in his own room, when he was supposed to be busy about his lessons, he often sat vaguely dreaming. Or he would draw girls' profiles on his theme paper, and remember those long-ago dancing lessons, and imagine himself whirling through a waltz with the Miss Gibson who sat just ahead of him in Latin class, or the real unknown who sat two rows to his right in the assembly room, and whose hair curled so enchantingly across her wide, smooth forehead and around her delicate little ears.

But after only a few weeks Charles was at him. "If you like a girl, tell her so. How's she going to know it if you don't? Girls aren't mind-readers." Or again, "It's time you got out and had some fun for yourself, kid. You can't just go mooning off on bicycle trips or stay home with your nose stuck in a book. You'll turn into a schoolteacher if you do."

Will listened, and agreed, and went back to his studies and his dreams. But the time came when Charles's new girl had a sister about Will's age. The elders arranged a double date, being careful to impress it on their juniors what a favor they were doing them. Strange to say, Will and Eleanor took a real liking to each other. They were still going to movies and eating ice cream together that next year, when Charles and Natalie were off on other paths; and the first girl Will ever invited to a dance was his Eleanor.

"I suppose I ought to be glad that the boys get on together as well as they do," Charlotte fumed to Bill. "But I declare, sometimes I get sick of the way Charles bosses Willie around."

"Your Willie stands up very well under all that bossing," Bill reminded her. "I would say that of the two he is probably the happier, though he doesn't make nearly so much noise."

Charlotte grinned ruefully. "I know. When they're unhappy, it makes me unhappy. When they're happy—which thank Fortune is most of the time—I worry for fear their happiness may have some dire results. Maybe I should think up some substitute for worry. What should you say to solitaire? Or maybe playing checkers, the right hand against the left?"

At least, her daughter was different. Being a girl, she was not a direct rival of her brothers. She was an excellent student. She learned a lot on the family trips. She did well at dancing school. But there was something curiously self-contained about her. Much of the time when she could have been with other people she preferred to stay in her room, or in fine weather in a remote corner of the back garden, and read. She went to other children's parties and entertained them in her turn. But a great deal of her life seemed to center on animals.

Another generation of dogs had succeeded Stub the Second and his contemporaries. Pauline had a huge tomcat, too. She had brought him home from the pet shop herself and named him Tiger-Tiger. She had a tankful of goldfish which she tended sedulously. Finally she procured a parrot, and taught it to talk. She would take it from its cage and let it strut around the room, and she held long conversations with it. Charles made fun of Pollykins at first, but when the parrot began to imitate his teasing, he thought it better to lay off.

Pauline would often study with Pollykins perched next to her book. She occasionally took one of her dogs to school with her, and the dog always behaved beautifully. She wrote frequent letters to her grandfather in Saylesboro: letters mostly about her pets. Paul Emerson answered those letters promptly and preserved them carefully; to him they represented a real achievement. Pauline took a selection of pets with her when she went to visit in Saylesboro. When she was away on a trip to New York or Denver or the Pacific Northwest, she always left detailed instructions as to the care of her pets during her absence, and sometimes sent postals to Pollykins or Tiger-Tiger.

"I hope she's not going to turn into an old maid," Charlotte said to Bill. "A parrot and a cat are supposed to be the standard equipment for a life of single blessedness."

"She might do worse!" Bill retorted savagely. His sons would get married some day, he supposed, and carry on the name and the business. But the boy was never born who was good enough to grow up and marry Bill's darling Pauline.

That day was pretty far off, however, if indeed it should ever arrive. Right now only one of the nestlings was about to try its wings, and that one wasn't Darling Daughter.

Bill Andrews had endeavored to talk seriously to his eldest on other subjects, and had usually been cheeked for his pains. But when it came to the question of his going away to college, Dad couldn't allow himself to be sidetracked. "You're a lucky dog, Charles, to have both a chance at a fine education and the brains to make use of it. This is no time for mistakes. If you care to go to Yale, I'm sure my old Alma Mater will take you in. A broad general education is a fine preparation for a business career. You will meet people who are worth meeting, too. But the choice is entirely up to you."

In his reasonably good baritone, Charles intoned,

> Here's to good old Yale,
> She's so hearty and so hale!
> Drink her down, down, down,
> Drink her down.

Then in a mincing tone he said, "Blue is such a pretty color. Looks awfully nice on young girls."

Trying to keep his face straight, Bill ignored the flippancy. "I infer that you contemplate honoring some other institution with your presence?"

"You may indeed, dear old Eli. You may indeed."

"And what *is* your choice?"

"I plan to enter the University of Wisconsin, if they will have me."

"Wisconsin? That's your mother's university. Are you planning on liberal arts, or—"

"They have a very fine College of Engineering. One of the best in the country." Charles was simple and direct for a moment. Then he again relapsed into his act. "And the university is coeducational. Plenty of girls there, plenty! Girls to the right of me, girls to the left of me. I shall dance where my mother danced. Between dances, I shall study where my mother studied."

"If you do as well as your mother did on both counts, I shall be satisfied," Bill said. They shook hands on it.

When Bill relayed their son's decision to his wife, she was surprised, happy, excited. "That rascal! To make such a decision, and keep it under his hat!" Then in sudden compunction she added, "Bill, I hope you're not *too* disappointed!"

"On the contrary, I am both pleased and relieved. Charles has made a sensible decision, and one that has a touch of sentiment in it. I'd love him just the same if he went to Harvard, but it's wonderful to realize all over again that he is *your* boy."

Wonderful, too, to realize that Charles would be near at hand, though his horizon would no longer be theirs. Wonderful to realize that brother Will would be free of so much example and pressure. Most wonderful of all, for Bill at least, to sink into the comfort of the thought that young Pauline, menagerie and all, would be right here with them for some time to come.

🌷 4 🌷

THESE BRIGHT AUTUMNAL days the big Andrews house seemed strangely empty and forlorn. Every morning at breakfast, and weekdays in the middle of the afternoon, Charlotte would catch herself looking at the table, so dismal with only four places set, or waiting for a noisy entrance and very likely a quick departure. She knew better. She *knew* better. She knew her first-born was away, knew where he was and something of what he was up to. But there was the old maternal pull at her heart strings.

Bill had done what little he could to bridge the gap. He had presented Charles with a packet of envelopes which had Mr. William Andrews' name and address neatly typed on them and stamps affixed. He had also said, "Call us long distance as often as you feel like it, and always reverse the charges." But the fact remained: the focus of Charles's life had altered. A wider world had claimed him.

It wasn't as if Charles had been an only child. Charlotte could now help Will expand a little. The comradeship between the brothers had been close, but there was no question that Charles had dominated Will. Pauline assuaged her own loneliness by ministering to her mother's. "Do you think you could take Tiger-Tiger for a walk this morning while I'm in school, Mommy? He gets tired of prowling around all by himself." Or "Put Pollykins through her repertory this morning, will you, Mommy? She needs a more thorough examination than I can ever give her, and you know you used to be a schoolteacher." Or "I've written down some notes about my goldfish. Won't you read them over, and then watch the fish a while and see whether you agree?"

Charles spent Thanksgiving with his grandparents in Saylesboro. For Christmas he came home and brought two pals with him. One boy lived in Colorado, the other in Montana; that was too far for them to go for the holidays. He was so busy showing them the town that his parents didn't see a great deal of him. But how much better off they were than the parents in Colorado or Montana!

Things settled down after that; the new routine established itself. In no time at all it was summer again. This year Charles went off by himself to visit his western pals. The others visited Saylesboro in July, then New York in August.

In another year it was Will who was going away to study for a degree and plan for his future. He went east to study architecture. It wasn't quite such a wrench to have him go. "Luckily you and I are still on speaking terms, Bill," Charlotte reminded her husband. "It doesn't take the presence of children to keep us from throwing things at each other."

On this July's visit back in Saylesboro, Paul Emerson managed a long private talk with his daughter. "I'm getting on in years," he said, "and the old pump isn't what it used to be. Oh, it's nothing to get upset about! I shall probably be around to vex my competitors and annoy my friends for a good many years yet. But I'm arranging the business so that I shall have less and less to do with its active management. I'll soon be Chairman of the Board, which is a nice green pasture to turn the old horse loose in. I've lately made a new will. When I die, a trust fund will be set up for your sister Agnes, who is—well, she's not been the luckiest or the brightest woman in the United States. Half of the rest, and this house, goes to your mother. The rest will be yours."

"But Papa—" Charlotte faltered.

"I've lived to see my grandsons grow up," he went serenely on. "And although I have two granddaughters, I have only the one namesake. Now go ahead and talk to me about your children, please. It's a subject I never tire of."

He sank back in his chair and closed his eyes. For a minute he looked like a very old man. Charlotte's throat contracted and her head throbbed. Not Papa, dear God, not Papa! Other men do grow old and die, but this man mustn't. Then after a pause which seemed endless, though by the clock it could have been measured in minutes, she said quietly, "I just don't know where to begin on that subject. But when I do begin, there will be no stopping me."

Papa opened his eyes, and smiled. Instantly everything was all right. Why bother about the future, which was anybody's guess anyhow? Here the two of them were in the garden, overlooking their lovely lake. Theirs was the golden present, this moment snatched out of eternity. Their moment. They must enjoy it to the full.

They did, and in after years that moment often came back to Charlotte. But it was something she never mentioned. Never once to Papa. Never even to Bill.

Charles did brilliantly in his engineering studies. When he was allowed a car of his own, he flashed about Madison and its environs, and sometimes drove to Saylesboro to greet his grandparents and air his views on cars and current celebrities and world problems. If he got an early enough start, he sometimes brought along a girl. Never twice the same girl. He didn't want to get the sweeties' hopes up too high.

Repeal was with them now. Charlotte and Bill still had some of their pre-Prohibition liquor left, and even a few bottles of champagne. How nice to feel that Americans were again being treated as adults, not as naughty children who didn't know what was good for them! If Charlotte sometimes had her doubts as to whether the War to End All Wars had really done so—well, she wasn't saying too much about that.

Will wrote home better letters than Charles ever had written, and never called long-distance. He loved his work. The fellows he went to school with were awfully nice. The nature of architecture was changing very rapidly. Did Dad and Mommy ever think of selling their old place and having something absolutely modern and up to date built just for them?

"At one time we discussed that possibility," Bill reminded Charlotte. "We haven't said anything about it for quite a while now."

"I like it here," Charlotte answered. "Maybe if we had built some years ago, I could have thought of things I'd like a little different. Maybe the time will come when I'll collect some ideas and at least talk them over. But with our children at the stages in life where they are now, I think we'd best hang on here a while longer. After all, this has always been home to them."

This was home to them. The old place in Saylesboro was still their home away from home. Both houses had advantages. Both had associations. She would wait and see. Was this middle age? Was it philosophy? Was it simply common sense? Anyhow it was a satisfactory policy for Charlotte Andrews in this particular year of grace. She would wait and see.

But she sat down and wrote to Will at some length.

I'm interested in new ideas about houses, of course. A new idea is not necessarily an improvement, but at least it's a change. If it doesn't work out, a person can always change back, and maybe, due to experience gained, he can modify the old idea. If our forebears hadn't welcomed change, that would be just too bad for us. We would still be living in mud huts and caves, or maybe swinging from the top branches of trees.

So I hope I don't sound like an old fogy, though in your eyes I must look fairly old. Old enough to be your mother, anyhow—which is not at all strange, seeing that I *am* your mother.

But suppose that your Dad and I were customers of yours. Or does an architect say "clients"? I'm sure the word is not "patients." Size up our situation. We need a house which will accommodate a family of five, an adequate domestic staff, and your sister's menagerie. We require room for overnight guests, too.

A house which is compact, streamlined, filled with the latest gadgets, would not seem like home to us. We would miss all the dear old associations, the tender memories—yes, and the fixed habits. It would look as unsuitable, too, as I should in clothes designed for a girl Pauline's age.

But picture a couple ten, or better say twenty, years older than Dad and I are now. The children all have homes of their own now. The domestic staff is reduced. But there must still be room for visiting children and grandchildren. Mommy would still prefer to go upstairs when she went to bed; it seems more respectable, somehow. Cherished possessions, some of them really good stuff and some simply dear to the owner, would not look too good against a sleek, self-consciously "functional" background. Of course you could attempt to compromise. But where's the fun in that?

She paused, drew a line across the page, resumed:

Reading this over, I realize how like a schoolteacher I sound. Yet I actually taught for only one year, and that was a very long time ago. Is there something of the dominie in all of us? Or is it that I missed my vocation, and should still be correcting theme papers and inveighing against the dangling participle? Where would you be now if I had done that? Certainly not off somewhere in a technical school, writing challenging letters to your fond but distracted parent.

Will answered promptly and in some detail. In later letters he kept referring to that epistle of hers; by this time he must know it by heart, and Charlotte herself could reconstruct it from his references. At length she went so far as to write:

I suppose everybody likes to get a letter from home. But perhaps one written about the things you are especially interested in is more to the point than a lengthy account of what Mrs. So-and-so gave us to eat at the bridge party this week, and how Mrs. Such-an-one plays a very slipshod game, but always seems to have all the luck.

To that Will answered:

Would you like a separate game room in that streamlined, functional house you are not planning to build? Or should there simply be a convenient storage space for folding tables and chairs? You will want plenty of electrical outlets, but do you really need one for a can opener? Presumably both you and your maid servant will be strong enough to wield an ordinary hand tool.

He gossiped on about the theoretical house for another paragraph, then wound up:

I don't envy your buddy Mrs. Such-an-one her luck at cards; everybody knows that means no luck in love, and after one gander at Mr. Such-an-one anybody could well believe that. But what did Mrs. So-and-so give you for luncheon? Do tell me, and make my mouth water. The chow here is good enough, but a little on the monotonous side.

Charlotte saved his letters. Glancing through them sometimes when she sat down to write to him, she would pick up a thread which she could somehow spin into her new effort. Taken together, they formed quite a neat picture of an active and versatile mind. They would be wonderful to reread when Charlotte was an old lady and Will himself no longer young and eager and ready to make plans for his vague but shining future.

Charles was dancing and studying his way through the university now. Like his mother, he went to Prom every year. He did take the same girl two years in succession. But that was not as serious as it might seem; their steps happened to fit together particularly well. By his senior year he had progressed to a different cutie. Three Prom girls in four years wasn't quite up to his mother's record with men. But it did very nicely. He was like her in more ways than his name.

Then, inevitably, he graduated. He and his mother were fellow alumni. The "bright college years" were past. The long stretch of maturity and man's work and making his place in the world lay just ahead. The only question was, just where and how would he begin? It had been understood all along that he was to come into the family business. Andrews Motors could use another bright young engineer; and he might as well get an early start in the business which was to be his—or at least partly his—eventually.

But now Charles had an offer to enter the employ of a large firm in Milwaukee as a draftsman. "I'd get a skimpy salary, and I'd have to live in a boarding house and like it," Charles acknowledged. "But that experience among strangers would be worth more to me than if I came to your plant right away as the Young Master."

"Don't worry about that!" his father snapped. "When you start in with us, now or later, you won't start as a draftsman; you'll go into the shop. And you can live at home, of course; but I'll ask you to pay board there."

"Board!" Charles snickered. "Board—at your board! Oh, how bored I should be at boarding with Baba and Maba and Baby Brother and Baby Sister.!"

Bill permitted himself to smile. "Token board, maybe you might call it. But you will be comfortable, and so far as I'm concerned you can have your evenings to yourself."

"My laundry—" Charles insisted.

"You'll have to make arrangements about that with your mother. The clothes you have now will do you nicely for another year."

"You've thought everything out, haven't you, Baba?"

"That is my custom."

"I'll want my own telephone, of course, but I shall pay for that."

"All right, son. Now for July you might go up and see your grandparents. Make them twice glad. Then in August I'll stake you to one last grand fling: two weeks in New York, no relatives in sight, and all expenses paid."

Charles gave a whoop of delight. "Gosh, Dad, as a father you're swell! I'm awfully glad I picked you. As an employer —well, that can wait a while. If we ever do agree to split, it can be arranged very quietly. We won't have to go to the divorce court or anywhere like that."

For Charlotte it was wonderful to have her eldest back under the family roof again. Thrilling, and satisfying, and more than a little strange. During these years when he had been away most of the time, Charles had altered greatly. Grown from boy to man, branched out on his own. His whole frame of reference seemed to have changed. She would have to get reacquainted with him, and she must do it very slowly. She gave him his evenings to himself without question. In an allotted nook in the refrigerator she kept beer especially for him. When she and Bill gave a cocktail party, he was invited as any other guest would be, and he was free to attend for just as long as suited him. If she had a tendency to overdo the "go your own way" line, that was better than trying to keep him tied to her apron strings.

She tried to keep her perplexity out of her letters to Will —or rather to make light of it, as she might have mentioned inclement weather or a minor disaster to one of Pauline's pets. "It's a little strange to see him going off to work every day, just like that! Charles and work!" Or "When we have friends in for cocktails and Charles mingles with the guests, it's fun to watch the mothers of marriageable daughters try to put a halter around his neck. He dodges very gracefully." Or "Your father reports that Charles gets along well with the men in the plant. He takes a real interest in his work; he gives them no chance to think that he's there just because he's the boss's son." Once even: "Some day when you're figuring on a house for that older couple with dependents, be sure you plan a lodging for the bachelor son. Semidetached, I suppose you would call it. I'm sure lots of young men would have no objection to living at home if their mothers didn't try to make it too confoundedly home-like."

Charles came seeking his mother sometimes as the days shortened and the cold increased. "Pity the sorrows of a wage slave," he said once. "Willie-boy will get the Christmas holidays off; not so Charles the chump." Or "I had forgotten how mild the weather is here in Ohio. Give me the rigors of dear old Wisconsin; I'm man enough to take them." On Christmas Eve he made a real confession. "I followed Mr. Parker on his Santa Claus rounds today just to see him go into all the houses where little children are. I knew just how happy he made them. It gives a person a glow inside just to think of those happy children." But for the most part he remembered to mind his p's and q's, to excuse himself from the breakfast table so as to get to work a little ahead of time, to withdraw to his own quarters in the evening or go out and amuse himself elsewhere. Sometimes on Saturday evening he condescended to invite Pauline to go to a movie with him. When he did, Pauline was the proudest girl in Euclid.

The "apprentice year" drew to its conclusion. Charles had proved his worth; he was now hired on a regular basis, but required to go on serving in various capacities at the plant, so as to get thoroughly grounded in the business. The men liked and respected him for his own qualities. He was pretty well off his mother's mind, if very often and most pleasantly on her hands.

During that summer when Charles was rounding out his first year with the firm, Will spent an entire month with his grandparents in Saylesboro. He was not only a guest; he came for professional reasons. He explained to his grandfather that he had always loved this house as a person; now he admired it professionally. It was a very fine example of its type: a type which he was inclined to call "Baronial Middlewestern." It was a mansion: a house built for home and hospitality, but likewise for ostentation. Also, it presupposed an abundance of domestic help. The type was destined to extinction, as all highly specialized types were. But he would like to make a complete record of it just as it stood, and take the record back east with him. It would really show something.

Paul Emerson was interested, amused, and piqued. He hadn't realized that this sightly home of his was practically in a class with the dodo. He told young Will to go ahead. He even helped him a few times with his photographs and measurements. But a good deal of the time that summer Paul Emerson was satisfied to put in short hours at the plant, and to sit for long periods in the beautiful back garden overlooking Lake Michigan. Sometimes Inez sat with him. Sometimes a friend from the dwindling circle of his contemporaries came in for a quiet drink. But for the most part he sat there by himself, thinking, remembering, dreaming.

Will was there again briefly a year later. He had run up

from Chicago. Having finished his schooling as an architect, he was going to work for a big firm in Chicago. A firm which specialized in buildings thoroughly up to date, rational, functional. The kind of buildings that, in Paul Emerson's opinion, made it hard to tell which was a church and which was a warehouse.

Later that month Paul Emerson confided to Charlotte, "I'm afraid I'm turning into the kind of old person who thinks that nothing nowadays is as good as things were when he was young. Nothing is the same, to be sure. But why should it be?"

"Many things are the same," Charlotte insisted. "Others are changing, not always for the better. But that doesn't matter too much, does it, so long as you're here and I'm here?"

"We've been very happy here, haven't we, little daughter?" Papa said, almost in a whisper.

"Oh, indeed, indeed we have!" Charlotte whispered back. "You remember the balloon poem that was sung for my birthday when I was about as big as a minute? I'm thinking of something like that right now." Softly she sang,

> Take the word to the wide blue sky,
>   Tell it to wind and tide.
> People are still being happy here!
>   Spread the news far and wide.

He picked it up and sang with her. Sang it through twice. It was just what the two of them needed, and wanted. It voiced not only their thankfulness but their defiance. Oh, yes indeed, defiance! There were times when defiance was very much in order.

5

THAT SPECIAL SUMMING up, and their little song together, came back to Charlotte so often during the first
strange months after Papa died. For a brief but blessed
interval her sense of fulfillment overcame everything else.
Whatever had happened or might happen, Charlotte had
the finest father in the whole wide world, and she was his
tenderly cherished and all-sufficing daughter.

No matter how long it has been expected or how carefully prepared for, death is always a blow. The idea that she
would never see Papa or talk to him again was strange and
bleak and bewildering. It was especially hard to imagine
life in the big house without him, though as long as she
thought of him and loved him, he was right here with her
at her own home in Euclid.

After Papa died, daughter Agnes proposed to come and
"make her home" with Mrs. Emerson in Euclid. Perhaps
she was none too clear in her own mind about the trust
fund which had been set up for her, though she found it
very convenient to have a nice fat check coming her way
every month. But she did realize that the sumptuous big
house in Euclid and a nice tidy fortune had been left to
Mamma. Why shouldn't she come and live there, and lord
it over old acquaintances, and have her running expenses
paid, so that she could save her own money? It would be
fine for young Inez, too, who was not getting along any too

well with that person she had married. Men were brutes anyhow. But in the house on the lakeshore, Mrs. Emerson and Mrs. Stanton and young Mrs. Winthrop could all be very cozy together. "That is, of course, when young Inez chooses to come for a visit," Agnes amended. "She and dear Harry are very happy together, but I think it sometimes does a woman good to get away and just be with other women for a while."

"You may think what you please," Inez Emerson said sharply. "Just don't bother to do *my* thinking for me."

Agnes looked bewildered. "Now Mamma, you know I only want to do what's best for your happiness."

"I know that. But I cannot allow you to sacrifice yourself just to keep me from feeling lonely."

She did not always elude as neatly as that, but on Agnes's subsequent returns to the subject, Mrs. Emerson maintained a firm stand. She was somewhat at a loss about her own future; she had been married for so many years that it was hard to get used to being single again. She missed Paul around the house. She was rather miffed to find how, after her term of mourning was over, couples whom she had supposed good friends now let her severely alone. An odd woman at dinner parties; a superfluous woman. But her woman friends still made as much of her as ever; she found herself with plenty of opportunities to serve on committees and plenty of chances to give away money. But she would have given—well, perhaps not her eyeteeth, as the old saying had it—but certainly her next several dividend checks for a new interest in life.

Then all at once she had a brilliant idea. She remembered her grandson Will's interest in the old house; suppose it could be diverted into a new channel? She needn't commit herself, but at least she could investigate.

Since his grandfather's death he had come on fewer weekend visits; but he did come, and she always filled him up with home-cooked food and found that he enlivened the place and gave her something to look forward to. Now on his next visit she tackled him. "Will, I have an idea which I want to put up to you when you feel like listening for a while."

He grinned. "Nice introduction, Grammie. There's no time like the present. Go right ahead."

"What would you think of remodeling this house? Making it over into an apartment building? I know it's simpler to put up an apartment building which is designed from the start for that use. But if you took this place, which is very soundly built—"

"Built to last for centuries. 'Has the strength of Gibraltar,' " he threw in.

Mrs. Emerson nodded. "If you divided it up into small apartments, you could still retain the period charm while making the new accommodations very modern and easy to take care of; suitable for small families with little household help. The lovely outdoor surroundings would be the same. This is what is known as 'a good address,' I believe. The place could yield a reasonable income to its owner."

She was amazed at her own eloquence; she hadn't realized that the idea was so well developed in her own mind. Then almost instantly she feared that she had gone too far. "I'm not saying that that's what I plan to do," she added hastily. "I just want to know what you think of the idea."

Will grinned, shook his head, took his time about answering. Then he drawled, "As an idea, it's fascinating. But it would take a lot of time, make a lot of mess, cost a lot of money. In the end it might turn out a disappointment."

"Then you don't think much of it?" For an instant Mrs. Emerson looked like a disappointed child.

"I think it's wonderful, marvelous, extraordinary. But it would need all the skill in the world, careful planning, a certain run of good luck. I'm trying to think of all the objections to it, but it's all so new it makes my head whirl. Mind if I sleep on it? I might know my own mind a little better tomorrow."

Mrs. Emerson also slept on it, to the extent that she said to him the next day, "This idea of remodeling the house into apartments—if we go ahead with it at all, I want it to be something just between you and me. Your firm is not to come into it in any way. Do you get that?"

Will's face lighted up. "I had supposed as much, Grandma, but I didn't quite like to ask. The thing is in such an early stage as yet, there's no telling what may come of it. But if I can have a free hand to go ahead with it—"

"Mind you, I'm not saying that I *will* go ahead and re-build. But I'll pay you anyhow for the work you do on the plans. Do I pay by the piece, or should I put you on a salary?"

The undertaking took possession of both of them. They agreed not to say anything about it to anybody for the present. It was nobody's business but their own, to begin with. They feared a shower of cold water on their brightly glowing idea. And anyhow, the less you said about what you were going to do, the better chance there was that you would really go ahead and do it.

Mrs. Emerson made memorandums and drew rough sketches. Will measured, made sketches of his own, investigated the plumbing and heating systems in great detail. He came up here from Chicago almost every weekend now; he worked harder here than he did at his regular job. He and his grandmother agreed to get the whole thing on paper, an architect's finished plan, before they said anything to anybody else about it.

The few weekends that Will was in Chicago, he usually took a girl out to dinner and to the theater. It was generally the same girl: a very nice young woman who lived with her parents and attended some classes at the Chicago Art Institute. On those Saturdays and Sundays, his aunt Agnes Stanton was generally invited up to Saylesboro, where she reluctantly observed that her mother seemed cheerful enough and hadn't much to say for herself. The few times that young Mrs. Winthrop went with her, Mrs. Emerson was affectionate toward her granddaughter, but not at all effusive. Once, when Mrs. Stanton was detained at home by a severe cold, Harry Winthrop escorted his wife. His verdict, expressed on his way home, was that the old lady served good booze and wasn't stingy with it, but she looked like the cat that had just swallowed the canary.

Charlotte Andrews knew that her son Will was spending a great deal of time with his grandmother. The arrangement met with her hearty approval. Her mother and her second son were great company for each other, and it got them both off her hands and mind.

Charlotte really hadn't too much to complain about in her personal life. Charles was forging steadily ahead in "the company," and kept out of his parents' way carefully enough to avoid all friction. Pauline was cramming into her high school work all the science and mathematics she could possibly take. She displayed very little interest in clothes. She liked to go to Saturday matinees with her mother, but if Charlotte bought the tickets and suggested that she invite a schoolmate to go with her, that too was all right. She dated boys, but not half as often as she had a chance to. When her mother ventured to question her about her coolness at an age when she might very well have appeared boy crazy, she said tartly, "It's nothing for you to worry about, you know. I don't dislike all men: just all the men I know."

"I worry about her because she doesn't give me anything to worry about," Charlotte summed up to Bill. "How silly can a person get? And without half trying, too."

When she stepped outside the confines of her own family, however, or read anything in the daily newspaper except the society column and the recipes, she found plenty to worry about. The War to End All Wars certainly hadn't done so: there were rumblings and threatenings on every side. And how the prophets of doom enjoyed themselves! Reacting from their years of euphoria, they howled, "The next war will be the end of civilization!" And the accepted procedure was to agree with them, and shake one's head dolefully.

"The next person who says that to me is going to get a pretty sharp answer," Charlotte threatened. However, she confined herself to the four words "How do you know?"

The prophet was indeed taken aback, but only for the moment. She recovered herself enough to say, "Why, it stands to reason!" Then other speakers put in their two cents' worth. Charlotte wasn't convinced, but she was silenced. She had one private consolation, however: the end of civilization, if and when it came, would at least put an end to such prophesyings.

Charles had another new car now; he would be going to glory in style. He was at home less than ever; often on weekends he would simply say, "Don't expect me until you see me." His father probably saw more of him at the plant than his mother did at home.

Then one blithe spring Saturday he telephoned in the

middle of the afternoon, "Mom, are you and Dad going to be at home later in the day? Along toward dinnertime, perhaps?"

"I plan to be, and I believe your father does, too. May we expect you then?"

"Yes, you may!" Charles snapped, and hung up.

He arrived at the appointed time, and he was not alone. He ushered in a tall, blond, very self-possessed girl whom he introduced as Katherine Nelson. "Call her Kay. Her parents have moved here recently. I've been trying to show her that Euclid isn't such a hole as it must seem to a graduate of dear old Wellesley."

Greetings were exchanged, drinks offered and accepted. Then Kay, after an introductory sip and a complimentary remark about the drink, ordered him, "Go ahead and tell your news. Don't leave them in suspense."

"It's your news too. Don't tell 'em. Show 'em," Charles ordered.

She set down her glass and extended her slim left hand. Then on the appropriate finger she twirled a ring until the diamond showed.

Charlotte caught her breath audibly. Just for an instant her head swam. Then she got to her feet, seized the girl by both hands, and pressed them warmly. "Welcome into the family, my dear," she said just a little louder than she intended to. "Welcome to your new home." Then she dropped Kay's other hand, and fell to admiring her engagement ring.

Perhaps that was the best way to do it: confront them with the established fact, and get it over with in a hurry. But Charlotte's cocktail had a curiously salty taste, and when Bill lighted a cigarette for her in his old loverlike way, she took it with a shaking hand.

Into the group walked Pauline, fresh from a matinee and

eager to get back to her pets. Pauline eased the situation; as soon as things were properly explained to her, she took Kay off to meet her menagerie. And when she brought her back, she shaped with her lips to her mother two words, "She'll do."

Pauline's enthusiasm throughout the subsequent proceedings was of a similarly temperate character. Meeting the parents of the bride. The announcement in the newspapers. The plans for a big June wedding, at which Pauline would be a bridesmaid. "All a lot of foolishness," she grumbled to her mother. "Why don't they just get married? Marriage is a very simple biological function, when you come right down to it."

"Marriage is more than that," Charlotte protested. But she said it weakly. She herself felt strangely out of place in all these goings-on. Mother of the Groom. Take your place in the ranks of the has-beens, Mrs. Andrews. Climb up the family tree, and try to get used to being a looker-on at life.

Mrs. Emerson came to Euclid to bear her own share in the proceedings. Since she wore lavender, Charlotte was forced to dress in a medium shade of blue. A big splashy wedding, with Will as his brother's best man. The same set speeches to guests at the reception, many of them from out of town and strange to her. "I don't feel that I'm losing a son. I feel that I'm gaining a daughter." All that sort of thing. Mamma was very serene and impersonal; the extra generation's remove made all the difference. Also, Mrs. Emerson kept an eye on Mrs. Stanton, whose awful husband was now mercifully a thing of the past, and on young Mrs. Winthrop, whose Harry had been detained in Chicago "on business."

The newlyweds went to New York for their honeymoon. They would "make their home" with Charlotte and Bill until they found an apartment of their own. "They'd better do that in a hurry," Bill growled to Charlotte. "The house never existed that was big enough to contain two families."

He gave Charles an extra fortnight's leave from the company so that he could devote his entire attention to apartment hunting. "That's the same as saying 'Here's your hat,' " Charlotte reminded him.

"All the better if it is. I don't believe in delicate hints. They are too likely to be misunderstood."

Five of them at the breakfast table for a while there, with the new Mrs. Andrews often sleepy and cross, though she tried hard to let on that everything was absolutely lovely. Then she and Charles took to breakfasting a little later; they just got worn out by their quest, Kay explained. But the quest was narrowing down, and when they finally found a place that "would do," Bill Andrews gave them their money-down-on-signing-the-lease "as an extra wedding present."

"Buying yourself a little peace?" Charlotte teased her husband.

"Sure. Might as well take full advantage of what little peace is left to us now, for 'the next war will be the end of civilization.' "

"I wouldn't be too sure of that," Charlotte cautioned. "Prohibition didn't prohibit, and we lived through that."

"Right you are, Mrs. Andrews. It just makes you wonder, 'What next?' "

Charles and his Kay duly set up housekeeping, and threw themselves heartily into the social whirl. The Andrews name was now oftener in the society column than it had ever been before; considerably more than half the men-

tions were of Charles and his wife. Charles's work suffered
for a time, but Bill was careful to remind him that he
wasn't being carried on the payrolls simply as his father's
son. Charlotte was so afraid of becoming the interfering
mother-in-law of tradition that she tended to let the young
people rather severely alone. She accepted another commit-
tee chairmanship, though she still wasn't much of a
"joiner." She sometimes visited the schools in her neighborhood, just to see what modern education was like. She
often worked the puzzles in the newspapers; a puzzle involved some mental activity but absolutely no emotional
involvement—not even as much as was brought on by a
magazine story or a run-of-the-mill novel.

Almost two years after his brother was married, Will too
entered the honorable estate. He married a Chicago girl
named Marjorie Boyd. It was a quiet relatives-only wedding, and the young people, after a brief honeymoon,
moved into a little Chicago apartment which they had already leased and partly furnished. Marjorie was a small,
brown-haired girl, charming rather than pretty, but when
she looked at her Will, with all her love shining in her eyes,
she became singularly beautiful.

So now Bill and Charlotte had only Pauline at home with
them. Their "little" daughter, two inches taller than her
mother, good looking, serious, and extremely reserved. She
never made any trouble for her parents. Sometimes she
appealed to them very prettily for an opinion on some
question of general interest, or gave her own views quite
modestly about what the two of them were discussing. She
did not fall victim to high-school "crushes"—at least, not
so that anybody could notice it. She was what in a past
generation would have been called strong-minded. Yet her
parents were totally unprepared for her announcement of

her future plans. One evening when the three of them were just ready to rise from the dinner table, she said calmly, "I've made up my mind what I'm going to do with my life. Want me to tell you?"

"What's his name?" Charlotte asked rather sharply.

Bill grinned teasingly. "Now Pauline," he drawled, "you're too young to think seriously of marriage. But if he's a nice young man, bring him in and let us meet him. I think you were the girl who said you disliked all the men you knew. So if you've finally met the great exception, that will be good news."

"There isn't any 'he,'" Pauline said quietly, without smiling. "Not in that sense, anyhow. I'm due for college very soon now, and I know what I want to do after that."

"You have your college all selected, I assume," Bill said.

"Yes. The University of Wisconsin."

"Good!" Bill cried. "That's where your mother danced four happy years away, and so did your big brother."

"They have a very good premedical course there," Pauline went on quietly. "A person needs as solid a foundation as possible. From there I can go on and get my medical degree. I plan to be a doctor."

There was a minute's stunned silence. Then Charlotte tried to sound facetious. "A woman sawbones, egad! You're sure you don't mean a veterinarian? Your menagerie has always meant so much to you."

"I mean a regular M.D., the same as any other practicing physician. I'll take temperatures and write prescriptions. Or I may decide to specialize. So many doctors do nowadays."

Bill swallowed hard. "I—I'm proud of your independence," he stated. "I'm prepared to send you to school as long as you care to go, of course. But I wish you would

reconsider your decision. The things that any doctor—
or for that matter any medical student—has to see and
do—"

"Are all a part of human life," Pauline said quietly.
"Knitting little pink booties is not the major part of maternity. Even such a minor matter as tonsilitis requires to be
dealt with. The human heart may be regarded as the seat
of emotion, but it's subject to all sorts of diseases. In the
course of every twenty-four hours even a healthy human
being is subject to functions which do not form a fit subject
for conversation at the dinner table."

"Then we'll leave it at that," Charlotte said, rising.
"Have you studying to do tonight, dear, or do you want to
listen with your father and me to a few records on the
victrola? Even our disease-ridden bodies have moments of
pure enjoyment. People write music and other people per-
form it. That's as real in its different way as a fulminating
appendix or a broken arm."

Pauline sat with them for nearly an hour of music; twice
she put in a request for a record. It was a very pleasant
session, and it left Bill considerably soothed. But after Pauline withdrew he again fumed, "That I should live to see the
day when a daughter of mine—"

"Nonsense, Bill!" Charlotte chided. "I suppose you'd
hate to see the day when a daughter of yours changed a
baby's diaper."

He grinned reluctantly. "I suppose a man does tend to
sentimentalize his only daughter. I can't expect Pauline,
just because she's mine and I happen to have amassed a few
shekels—I can't expect her just to follow easy, ladylike
pursuits, to—how does the old rhyme go?—to 'sit on a
cushion and sew a fine seam, and feed upon strawberries,
sugar and cream.' "

"A monotonous diet," Charlotte agreed. "It sounds fattening, too."

He laughed, but he had one last uneasy word. "She's young yet. She may change her mind."

She might, of course. It was not absolutely impossible, like parallel lines meeting. But it was certainly nothing that Charlotte would have cared to count on.

❦ 6 ❦

MEN WERE LIKE that, of course. Fathers were like that; it was the way fathers were made, and Bill Andrews was a wonderful father. He loved his sons; he gave them every advantage in life, and was delighted that he was able to do so. But even closer to his heart, in a way, was his daughter, his one ewe lamb, the perfect crown of his marriage. The boy was never born who was good enough to grow up and marry Bill's little Pauline; no, not even if he were a Yale man who had landed a football between Harvard's goal posts, and then inherited a fortune from a Senator father and had excellent prospects of some day being elected President of the United States. Still, when the time came he would have had to knuckle under and give his daughter as splashy a wedding as her dear little heart desired, and himself take part in the ceremony by giving the bride away.

That would have been bad enough, though it was years in the future: one of those things which strike a chill to a man's heart, but can be shrugged off with the good old saying, "I'll cross that bridge when I come to it." But now Bill was faced with a much direr prospect, and one which did not even yield the promise of grandchildren. He was supposed to sit back and watch Pauline walk into the most exacting profession in the world. It was also one, Bill feared, in which there was a great prejudice against women. Perhaps that was all the more reason why courageous women should insist on making their way into the field. But leave that to the natural hard-shells and the crusaders, if you please; don't call in the young, the sweet, and lovely.

True, after Pauline had got her secret off her chest, she was more companionable than before around the house. When the time came for her to enter the University of Wisconsin, she willingly pledged Gamma Delta, and Charlotte had for a time the pleasure which she had occasionally experienced before—that of reliving her own life in her daughter's.

That winter Charlotte and Bill were left alone in the house which they had bought to shelter their growing family. Charles had two children, boy and girl. Will had one, a boy. They were carrying on the family name. As for the family business, it had grown but was again in process of conversion. For that "next war" which would be the end of civilization was already upon the world. There was no Woodrow Wilson to keep us out of it. The Andrewses and their friends made the best of a bad situation, even to the extent of a newly popular toast: "Well, here's one drink that Hitler won't get!"

It was during these years of strain and suspense that Charlotte's mother died. Inez Emerson had ignored certain symptoms. When Charlotte inquired, she evaded a direct response. Sharp-eyed Pauline too was disturbed, though as yet she was barely headed toward the goal on which she had set her sights. But when Mrs. Emerson finally consented to enter a hospital "for observation," it was already too late. The surgeons operated, made their dire findings, sewed her up again, and sent her home to die.

Mrs. Emerson had day and night nurses in attendance, and they administered morphine whenever they thought it was needed. Without making too much of a point of it, Charlotte managed to spend most of her time there in the old place in Saylesboro. It was there she learned about her architect son's designs for remodeling the mansion.

"I'm not saying anything to Agnes about this," Agnes's mother stipulated. "She has her trust fund, and she keeps her distance. But I'd like to know just how you feel about the idea."

Charlotte thought it was wonderful: a second blooming for a lovely place which had seen its day come and pass. To have Will do the great work was a satisfaction all around. Some things in this world did come right. So many things did. A person had to wait—and to trust.

When Mrs. Emerson grew worse, she allowed Charlotte to summon Agnes. Mrs. Stanton made a considerable fuss about not having been sent for sooner, but her effect on the patient was not the happiest in the world. Agnes seemed to feel that all attention should be centered on herself. And it was of herself, and her diet, and "your darling namesake Inez," and the brute young Inez was married to that she talked—on and on and on. Sometimes Mrs. Emerson's eye would meet Charlotte's and she would shake her head slightly. Sometimes she would go so far as to say, "I won't keep you here any longer just now, Agnes. Sick people are so tiresome. Feel free to go to your own room whenever you like."

Both daughters were staying in the house when the end came. The night nurse called them both, but it took Agnes a few minutes to collect her slow wits and get into her dressing gown and slippers. Charlotte had lifted her mother in her arms and whispered close to her ear, "I'm right here, Mamma. It's Charlotte, right here." Just for an instant Mrs. Emerson's eyelids flickered. A ghost of a smile touched her lips, and she whispered faintly, "Charlotte, daugh—" Then in the middle of a word she was gone.

She had made a new will long before she went to the hospital, before she confided to her younger daughter the enterprise which she shared with her architect grandson. She left the house and grounds and the plans which she had had him make for its remodeling to Will Andrews, with half her money. He was free to do what he liked with what was his, of course, but the implication was clear. The rest of her money Mrs. Emerson bequeathed to her two daughters, share and share alike.

The estate was still being settled when America was drawn into the war. This was no great crusade to "make the world safe for democracy"; it was a grim battle to save our own skins. We were fighting on two fronts, too. But in the European Theater of Operations, as it was officially styled, this war was an improvement on its predecessor in one respect. This time the English weren't telling us what to do.

Charles Andrews had a deferment because of his job. But Will, with all his brilliant prospects interrupted by this national emergency, went rushing off to training camp; it was in aviation that he was qualified. "I want everything as up to date as possible," he explained to his parents with his slow smile. "Anyhow, let the government pay for my education. When it's all over, I may buy my own private plane and commute between Chicago and Saylesboro, with occasional side trips to Euclid."

Again the terrific strain and anxiety of war. Agony on all sides, so that a person was half ashamed even of a brief respite. Long stretches of boredom, when it seemed as if this war had been going on forever and would last for a future eternity. Writing and receiving letters. Charlotte wrote not only to her aviator son but to buddies of his and sons and nephews of friends. It didn't matter so much what she wrote, though she did take pains with her letters; the important thing was to show the young men that somebody cared.

Will's young wife took their little boy and moved into the big house in Saylesboro. That way she could keep an eye on things. "I simply rattle here," she told Charlotte. "But I do so want Will to come back here and fulfill all his lovely plans, and here I can feel that I'm helping him a little."

"I'm so sorry for young people," Charlotte confided to Bill. "Because it's the first time a thing has happened to them, they think it's the first time such a thing has happened in the entire history of the world."

"For them it is," Bill pointed out. "But while you're feeling sorry for them it keeps you from feeling sorry for yourself. That is very important."

So there was poor sweet Marjorie, living in the surroundings which meant the glorious full future to her Will, but where everything was strange to her. Marjorie, born Boyd but now another Andrews, showing her little son a photograph and teaching him to call it Daddy. Since Marjorie's father, as well as the baby's father and the Andrews grandfather, were all named William, the baby was almost inevitably one more William; but when he was very small his own father had taken to alluding to him as "Billy Dilly," and the nickname stuck. Charlotte, visiting her Wisconsin grandson, made up rhyming sequences—"Billy Dilly, never silly, ride a filly, pick a quilly, go to milly, country hilly, willy nilly." He laughed and imitated her. Marjorie wrote it all down, so that she could recite it to him in his grandmother's absence. Gunner Will Andrews let his mother know that the word had been passed on to him. If War was the villain of the piece, Home was the heroine.

"In one way," Charlotte told her husband, "war is more cheerful than peace. In time of war, you can always look ahead to peace. In peacetime, what you have to look ahead to is the next war."

"Which is not quite the end of civilization?" Bill suggested.

"Which we're getting through somehow, on a wing and a prayer and with our fingers crossed."

Questions of rationing and shortages and difficulties with domestic help were simply to be met and dealt with. They were nothing to be thankful for, but they did take a person's mind off the main issue. A mosquito bite was not a boon, but for an instant it did make you forget everything except the infuriating itching.

War casualties were not the only ones that occurred, of course. Harry Winthrop, young Inez's husband and sister Agnes's barely tolerated son-in-law, was killed in a traffic accident. He was by no means sober at the time, and the person who walked away from the scene of the accident was not his own wife. But Inez put on deep mourning, and talked to anybody she could buttonhole about her deep loneliness, and went back home to Agnes, where the two of them could quarrel intimately and at their leisure.

There were other marital troubles closer at hand. Two or three times when Charlotte walked into a meeting of war workers, she thought that the conversation ceased rather suddenly. Coming out of a movie late one afternoon, she caught a glimpse of her son Charles with a woman who was definitely not his Kay. Weeks later she caught sight of him in his car, with still another woman.

Then one day just as Bill, in dressing gown and slippers, was asking Charlotte whether she would like a cocktail or a glass of sherry, he was called to the telephone. On his return he looked amused but a little worried. "That was my darling daughter-in-law," he reported. "She says she wants to see me here this evening, alone."

"I'm sure you're welcome to her society," Charlotte snapped. "Am I asked out of the house as well as out of my own living room?" Then her mood veered abruptly. "Bill, have you been hearing things about Charles and—"

"And another woman?" Bill finished for her. "It would be my guess that Kay has."

When Kay had been and gone, Bill reported to Charlotte, "She says Charles has been running around a lot lately. In fact, she has definite proof of his 'misconduct.' She doesn't want to hurt the business, but she plans to take the children and go home to her parents."

"Why doesn't she tell Charles that instead of telling you?"

"She says she has done so, and he just laughs at her. I promised her I'd speak to Charles."

"If Charles is tired of her—"

"He is, undoubtedly. But his income is as good as ever."

"There are the children to be considered," Charlotte said.

"Yes. She's using them to put the screws on me."

Charlotte was sympathetic with the children, but they were somehow not quite as close to her as Bill. And she was bitterly ashamed of Charles and Kay for bickering, when Charles's own brother was in imminent physical danger. War wasn't the only calamity abroad nowadays, but it certainly underlined human folly.

There was a ripple of gossip when Kay took the children and went home to her family. It died down quickly enough in the interest of other, larger questions—and of fresher gossip. Charles simply stayed away from the offended lady. He might miss his children, but he was tired of the "home" they had shared with him.

The war in Europe terminated. It came to the only possible end. But relieved and jubilant as the American people were, they were simply more determined than ever. For them, this was not the end.

In that last stretch of the war, Gunner Andrews was wounded, seriously but not critically. His real ordeal was long hospitalization and a series of operations. He would walk stiffly for the rest of his life, and his right hand, his good drawing hand, was rehabilitated only after many more months.

Will was bored and resentful when he came home. He wouldn't have minded dying for his country; at least that would have been soon over with. But these long weeks in traction, and then all these deadly exercises and manipulations, were dull, irksome, very difficult to endure.

Charlotte doubled her efforts to write amusing letters. She saw to it that Marjorie managed to visit Will as often as possible; she herself stayed in Saylesboro and kept Billy company until his father was well enough so that seeing him would not be too much of a shock to the child. When people behaved themselves, no matter how hard their luck was, there was always something you could do.

Then Will Andrews was finally in Saylesboro, a pensioned veteran, trying to realize that this was all true, that it wasn't simply a beautiful dream from which he would awaken to hospital routine and hospital tedium. He had his son to get acquainted with, a wonderful little reality who sometimes seemed shy and at other times acted as if he remembered his daddy. Here was the mansion which was to be his magnum opus and his home. Here were his plans, which could be changed and enlarged. He had the money, the plans, the time. Here was his mother, who had helped them through these long, trying months. Here in a way was his grandmother, for although he would never see Inez Emerson or talk to her again, it was she who had made this whole thing possible for him, and in remodeling the big Emerson homestead he would be creating a last memorial to her.

Here, too, was his sister, Pauline, for a brief visit. She regarded him partly as a brother, partly as a hero, but principally as a case. Some of the questions she asked about his symptoms and treatment were downright embarrassing. Will hoped if he had a second child it would be another boy. Or perhaps a sweet thing like Marjorie. Certainly not a lady medic.

Charlotte knew when to make herself scarce. Now she could go back to her own home in Euclid, perfectly happy about Will, very well satisfied about Pauline. As for Charles, well, his father had predicted a long time ago that he would be the one who would get into trouble. His guess had been wrong as to particulars, but prophecy is an uncertain business at best.

Charles and his wife arranged a "friendly" divorce. As if

a divorce ever could be friendly! If a husband and wife were really friends, they would agree to stay married. Kay got a handsome settlement and custody of the children. Charles had "visiting rights." That proved to be not half so hard on the children as Charlotte had feared it might. The children liked him and associated him with treats. He was more like a favorite uncle than like the author of their being. He did good work for Bill at the plant, which was once more reconverting, but in private life his parents saw almost nothing of him. Still, it might have been worse. It might have been much worse. The senior Andrewses were in no mood for carping.

"Bill," Charlotte said one night after the war, "this time I really *am* standing on the island of Monte Cristo."

Bill grinned. "To listen to you, anybody would think that Monte Cristo was an archipelago. Or is it that you love the spot so much you keep having your yacht bring you back here?"

"It's a nice feeling, this Monte Cristo feeling."

"Yes, and you were a stranger to it too long. You are, of course, leading up to something?"

"I just thought, why don't you and I go somewhere to celebrate? Go off by ourselves and have a good time, and forget that we ever had anything else?"

"Sort of a second honeymoon?"

"Honeymoon and Thanksgiving and V-J Day all rolled into one."

"Sounds great. It will take some doing, but—sorry, honey, I didn't mean that 'but.' I repeat, it sounds great. What special spot do you have in mind?"

"New York is a great place to visit. We've been there before, but we've never really exhausted its wonders. It keeps changing all the time."

"I thought for an instant that you were going to fall back on that oldie, 'New York is a great place to visit, but I'd hate to live there.'"

"Those dear old clichés! I used to love to reverse them when I was a kid. 'It isn't the humidity, it's the heat.'"

"All right, New York it is. Two weeks and the adjacent weekends. As soon as I can make arrangements at the plant."

"Bill, we're really doing it? This isn't just another fine scheme?"

"We're really doing it. I've kept my nose to the grindstone so long it's badly abraded. I don't want the skin to be worn off completely."

Actually, they made it three weeks and the "adjacent weekends." The shops had never before looked so glittering. Every play that they saw seemed a masterpiece. The taxi drivers were marvels at weaving their way through traffic, and many of them were mines of droll humor. Strolling in Central Park was like walking in the Garden of Eden. They went to bed late. They got up when they felt like it. They were happy. They almost seemed to be young again, and this time with full consciousness of what a boon youth was. They felt singularly irresponsible. It was the loveliest trip that they had ever had. Charlotte was sorry to find herself on her way home.

Still, it was nice to be back in the house that had been home to her for so many years; to install her new possessions, try on her new clothes, and decide what was to be done with the old ones. Charles brought his visiting children around to see the Andrews grandparents. Marjorie came lugging Billy in for a week—"It's so nice to get into a place completely out of earshot of workmen." The bridge club resumed its sessions.

"This is sort of a plateau," Charlotte informed her listening husband. "After the long climb—no, after a series of long climbs—here is where we pause to get our breath back."

"I didn't notice that you had run out of breath," Bill remarked. "But I know exactly what you mean, honey. I'd be satisfied to spend the next twenty years right here. Or maybe twenty-five, or even thirty."

It was only two nights after this declaration that Charlotte awakened suddenly in the middle of the night. She felt a curious sense of alarm, but there, in the darkness and silence she did not know at first what was the matter. Then she realized that Bill was groaning in his sleep. He must be having a nightmare.

Somewhat relieved, she spoke to him, spoke louder, then shook him. She could not awaken him—and now he not only groaned, he made curious gurgling noises.

Thoroughly alarmed, Charlotte realized that she would have to summon help. She crossed the bedroom to the extension telephone, tried to get her doctor's number, realized that she couldn't remember it. In a panic she searched for her list of "numbers often called," found it, found the doctor's number. Now the blood was drumming so loud in her own ears that she had trouble hearing anything else.

She got through to the doctor finally, roused him, told her story as briefly and carefully as she could. "I'll be right over," he assured her.

Relieved that help was on the way, Charlotte started back toward the bed. Even before she got there, she realized that the room was suddenly very quiet. Much too quiet. Help was on its way, but help would be too late. Her Bill was gone. Suddenly, as he would have wished it, and right here with her, the end had come. He would never open his eyes to the old familiar surroundings, would never enjoy that final twenty years on the beautiful vast plateau. He had gone on to scale new heights.

Book IV

THE WITCHING HOUR

1

DEATH IS ALWAYS a shock to the survivors, even if it comes after serious illness or in extreme old age. Sudden death has a numbing effect. Charlotte simply could not realize that Bill was gone. She went through all the usual motions at this time of crisis, even to writing personal notes of thanks for all the floral tributes and the many messages of condolence. She attended to the legal matters which required a widow's attention. She kept an eye on the reorganization at the plant. (Charles really showed his mettle now; for his conduct in the family business, Charlotte had no fault to find with him.)

She couldn't get used to missing Bill. Time after time she dreamed about him: he was there vividly before her eyes, as a young man or in early middle life, but there was something strangely wrong between them, and she could not quite get to him or feel the touch of his cheek against hers or understand what he was trying to tell her. Other nights she would wake from a dreamless sleep and move toward his side of the bed, only to find that he wasn't there any more. He wasn't there, and he never would be, no matter how far the long years stretched ahead.

She considered sleeping in another bedroom, but that seemed like deserting him. She put off the hour of bedtime, and sat in her living room reading a book on which she couldn't concentrate. She smoked endless cigarettes instead of the one or two she had smoked with him. Nothing really helped. Nothing. Oh, countless widows had been through this ordeal before, her own mother among them! But this was the first time that Charlotte had ever been through it.

She got a lot of good advice, of course. She might look up another widow of her own age and similar tastes, and invite the lady to come here and live with her; the house was plenty big enough, and luckily finances were no problem. She might travel for a year or so and see still more of the wonderful world that stretched so far beyond her present knowledge. She might have Will do a little additional remodeling on the old place in Saylesboro, and provide her with a special apartment which would be near her beloved Lake Michigan, within reach of him and his Marjorie if she ever needed help, yet at the same time quite independent of them. A dwelling which would recall her premarital days, and would be free from too many associations with Bill.

Once when Pauline was at home for all too short a visit, her mother confided in her to the extent of saying, "There are so many things I might do, you know."

"Don't do anything until you are sure it is just what you want to do," Pauline said. "But you might go away for a while, just to get a better perspective. Why not take a trip to New York? You've always enjoyed your visits there."

Her last visit there had been with Bill, just before the shattering end came. But the place did not teem with associations and memories, the way the house here in Euclid did. Hadn't the two of them agreed that "New York is a nice place to visit, but—"? And hadn't Charlotte been reminded of one of her old reversals, to make it, "New York is a nice place to live, but I'd hate like thunder to visit there." Could she possibly—? Maybe she could. Maybe she could actually try living there. It wasn't like taking a one-way trip to Robinson Crusoe's desert island. Trains ran every day back to Ohio and to good old Wisconsin. If you were in a hurry, you could even fly. Lots of people did nowadays.

The sheer audacity of the idea was a delight in itself. Charlotte wouldn't mention it to anybody until she had considered it more carefully and decided whether it was worth acting on. Maybe she wouldn't mention it to anybody even then. Better either give it up as something to dream about rather than to do, or confront people with an accomplished fact.

There was nobody who could forbid Charlotte Andrews to do what she chose to do. Loneliness was a big price to pay for independence. But she had already paid the price. Why shouldn't she take what it had bought her?

That evening, because Pauline was there, Charlotte didn't smoke a single cigarette. Pauline didn't smoke, and it would be rude to go puffing clouds into her face. The next evening, alone, Charlotte reached for her first cigarette, then laid it down unlighted. Nicotine was a poor substitute for human company. Anyhow, it was a bad idea to become a slave to habit. That was what lots of people were when they fancied they were contented. They were simply in a rut, and hadn't enterprise enough to get out of it.

Here by herself in the evening, Charlotte now began to wear some of the gay new clothes she had picked out with Bill's approval. She cut her cigarettes down to one or two an evening, and presently to none at all. Somehow she was beginning to get a little taste of freedom, and freedom was a heady brew.

Finally she went to New York for what might be a long visit. She told both Charles and Will so. Charles said,

"Don't make it too long. Euclid will miss you."

Will said, "Call us if there's anything we can attend to for you. The change will do you good. You've been looking a little peaked lately. Isn't that what you used to say when I was a little boy? 'Peak-ed,' in two syllables."

So here was Charlotte Emerson Andrews, a native-born American, a widow, and considerably more than twenty-one years old, setting forth on what might be just another sightseeing trip, or might be the beginning of a great adventure. Anyhow it was a beginning, a setting forth. She wasn't just plain old Charlotte stick-in-the-mud.

She registered at a small East Side hotel where she and Bill had sometimes lunched or dined, but never stayed. She brought with her the gay clothes she associated with him. The very first afternoon she was there, she located a neighborhood bookstore and bought two new novels. This was good preparation either for a short visit or for an extended sojourn.

She bought matinee tickets which would commit her to a three-week sojourn in the big city. She wrote to all three of her children to give her present address and to say she was enjoying herself. Then she gave all the New York newspapers a good going over, trying to decide which one she would read regularly in case she did decide to become a resident.

Exploring, sometimes by cab or bus, sometimes on foot, she made up her mind to one thing: if she did come to New York to live, she would dwell within sight or easy reach of one of the rivers. That gave her a wider choice than might at first appear, for if she went high enough up in an apartment building and chose the right direction, she could see either the Hudson or the East River from a considerable distance. Of course, she might live permanently in an hotel.

That would do away with all housekeeping problems, and would leave her free to come and go as she pleased. On the other hand, she couldn't have so many of her own things about her—and to a woman her age, those dear familiar possessions were almost a part of herself. She couldn't take an active part in the housekeeping, either—and although Charlotte had generally depended a lot on competent help, she enjoyed managing a household and having it just a little different from other women's households—and, in her own opinion, just a little better.

So Charlotte used her matinee tickets, went to art exhibits, read late, and had her breakfast sent to her room. Then, when the fourth week of her stay opened before her, she decided she had had enough vacation. She turned to the serious business of apartment-hunting.

The end of vacation; the beginning of school. Alack-a-day! Yes, but this was a beautiful big school that Charlotte was due to attend, and it was her own choice. Lovely, lovely feeling, the freedom to choose. Wonderful wide choice, with nobody to please except her fastidious, but she hoped not captious, self.

It had been different on her other house-hunting expeditions. An apartment for a growing family; a house for a real family. Had Charlotte reached the age where everything in the present reminded her of something in the past? Very well, then, she had reached that age. She was all the richer for having that past on which to draw for comparisons—always provided, of course, that she didn't turn into the kind of older person who complained that nothing was as good as it used to be. A good many things were pretty much the same; of those that changed, some had actually changed for the better.

So here was Mrs. William Andrews, a mature woman

looking for a fair-sized, convenient apartment, with a river view if possible. A well-to-do widow, destined victim of wily real-estate men. They were not exactly out to fleece her, but they certainly were not pointing out the disadvantages of the accommodations which they had to offer. Mrs. Andrews called on three different firms and answered three ads in the newspapers. At the end of ten days she was a little tired, a little bewildered, a little disgusted with herself. She had seen so many places which said, "You will do all right here," but not one which commanded, "Come in here and stay with me." Did she expect this to be like meeting Bill Andrews? A case of the one and only?

She did some revisiting, a little re-revisiting. Eventually she narrowed her choice down to three. She wrote those three locations on three slips of paper, turned them face side down, and shuffled them. Then, with her eyes closed, she drew one slip. Leave the decision up to Chance, the great blind goddess. Then if anything went wrong she could blame her luck, not herself.

When she looked at the slip she had drawn, she was tempted to go back on the arrangement. If she repented of her own folly, nobody would be any the wiser. Then she shrugged, and decided to follow through along the line indicated. There was nothing irrevocable about renting a place. You could always move again when your lease ran out.

This apartment of Charlotte's was on the top floor of a middle-aged apartment building pretty well downtown. All the buildings to the east of her were lower, so that she had a wonderful view from her living room windows of the East River and beyond it another borough stretching off into the distance. There were two big bedrooms with their own baths, and two smaller bedrooms with a connecting bath. "You can let your maid use one of those," the agent explained. "Of course, in New York people have mostly sleep-out servants, but maybe you'd like two, so that they could take turns."

Mrs. Andrews could do quite nicely for herself, if she were put to it, and there were plenty of places to go for food if she didn't feel equal to the exertion of broiling a lamb chop or poaching two eggs. She wasn't asking for advice, simply for information. The agent did give her information: the name and address of an "intelligence office" where he and his wife had had satisfactory service in the matter of hiring servants. One maid would be a small staff indeed, and, of course, in New York there would be no need of a houseman or a gardener. Moving here would mean giving up her own car; Charlotte wasn't going to get into any negotiations for garage rent, and to drive in New York traffic struck her as the shortest and quickest way to a nervous breakdown.

So now Charlotte could go back to Euclid and face her family and her friends with an accomplished fact. She was deserting them to settle in New York City. Yes, her arrangements were all made. No, she hadn't set any date for leaving. To be sure she would miss Euclid. Yes, of course she might find it lonesome in the big city—but how could she tell until she tried?

All this was fun; now came the ordeal. Had anybody ever written a doleful, mostly cacophonous ditty entitled "Moving Day Blues"? Oh, the music and the poems and the stories that Charlotte herself could have written, provided only that she had been endowed with the ability!

She sorted and packed. She gave away and she threw away. To Will went a vanload of possessions which had been in the family for some time, and which he might wish to hand on. The Good Will Industries profited enormously. Charles and Pauline had special articles reserved for them. The house in Euclid was put on the market. Since everybody knew she wanted to get rid of it, it wouldn't fetch half what it was worth, but at least it would be off her hands.

(That house she had never got around to building! Now she never would get around to it—and that was nobody's loss.)

The last thing Charlotte got rid of was the connubial bed. She hadn't slept in it during these days of selection and upset; she never would sleep in it again. It brought back too many memories of comradeship, of bliss, of ecstasy, and of that one dire night when Bill had left her for good.

Bill's clothes had been given away, a few to Charles, whom they fitted beautifully, a dressing gown to Will, two mufflers to Pauline. Packed with her own things for transport to New York, Charlotte took a well-worn crimson wool dressing gown and a pair of shabby bedroom slippers. She put a slipper in each of the great square pockets, and hung the gown in a corner of her new bedroom closet before she unpacked most of her own clothes.

Settling, of course, was fun, though fatiguing, because then you were working toward an end. The fresh paint and the newly waxed floors were an opportunity and a promise. The tricky new electric stove did everything except plan your meals for you. A new bed for Charlotte's room was her first purchase. Some new rugs would be required, of course, and new Venetian blinds and curtains. Fixing up a place was fun. Her own place, where she could look out over water and dream of that other water so far to the west, and remember the balloons which had sailed away into that great dim beyond where balloons do go when they vanish. (*Is that where you've gone, my Bill who were once so close to me?*

You must have gone somewhere; you couldn't simply cease to be.)

Charlotte phoned the intelligence office and got amazingly quick service. (A convenience. And an omen?) An hour later her bell rang, and in walked a very comely Negress, young enough to be Charlotte's daughter. In her violin-string voice she said, "I'm the guhl from the office, Mrs. Andrews. They said you wuh lookin' foah someone to wohk aroun' the house."

"You're from the South, aren't you?" Charlotte asked.

"From Chahlotte, Nawth Ca'olina. The finest state in the Saouth."

"Charlotte?" Mrs. Andrews echoed. "Why, that's my given name!"

"Well," said the brown girl with a flashing smile, "that just shows."

They had taken an instant liking to each other. Charlotte motioned toward a seat. "I think you will find that chair comfortable. Your name is—?"

"Mamie Lee Jackson, ma'am."

"Those are two fine Southern names you have there, Lee and Jackson. Do your employers generally call you 'Mamie Lee'? It's prettier than just 'Mamie,' I think. Has more of an air."

"You *do* think about things like that? Oh, Miss Chahlotte, I know I'm going to enjoy working for you."

Just like that it was settled. Charlotte never hired Mamie Lee; Mamie Lee hired her. The arrangement worked right from the start. Not only was Mamie Lee a fine cook and an excellent housekeeper; she took a great load of responsibility off her employer's shoulders. Best of all, it was done with such good feeling. Southern style, she never called her boss-lady "Mrs. Andrews" except in front of a tradesman. It was always "Miss Chahlotte," or "Miss Chahlotte, honey," or sometimes, saucily, "Miss Lottie, love."

While they were settling the apartment, Mamie Lee worked hard, throwing out remarks about what would look best where, giving her own opinion almost as often as she consulted her employer's. Sometimes she was encouraging: "Go ahead and try it thataway. We can always change it back." Sometimes she shook her head in silent deprecation. Rarely she ventured as far as, "Miss Chahlotte is the boss-lady. Mamie Lee does as she's told."

But when they sat down together for a breather or a cup of coffee, she often waxed confidential. She was a high-school graduate, knew shorthand and typing, was qualified to work in an office. "But lans' sakes, Miss Chahlotte, a body might as well *be* a typewritah as run one all day long: just one machine running anothah machine. Besides, I always had a hankuhing—" She broke off and shook her head.

"Go on, please," Charlotte urged. "I'm very much interested."

"A hankuhing foah New Yohk. I always read the New Yohk news in the newspapahs. At the movies, I always got excited when I saw the skyline of Manhattan."

"Good old skyline of Manhattan!" Charlotte agreed. "It means New York, just the way the Eiffel Tower means Paris or Trafalgar Square means London."

"Yes, ma'am, only diffunt. Moah exciting, somehow. You think moah of some places than you do of othahs, just the way you think moah of some people."

Some people! Charlotte felt a deadly stab at her heart. Just for an instant she was right back there in the dear old home in Euclid, in that awful deadly silence which had meant the worst to her. But the moment passed, as such moments will. She was once more here in her new home in New York, and it was high time she took to sleeping in her new bed in the master bedroom, instead of living in the second bedroom and postponing things.

Perhaps Charlotte had betrayed her disturbance; perhaps it was simply that Mamie Lee thought she had talked enough about herself for the present. Anyhow, she rose then and went about her work. There was always plenty for her to do. They were getting settled, yes; but real order was still only a gleam on the horizon.

At a later session Charlotte encouraged her. "You came to New York, Mamie Lee, and you started to work as a general helper. You surely haven't worked for many different people?"

"No, ma'am, not many. Only two, really. The fust job was with an old bachelah. He was nice enough, and lib'al with the pay an' the food, but he stahted to get ideas."

Charlotte laughed. "I can imagine that. You went from him to a family?"

"To a doctah who was ma'ied and had just the one child. It was nice theah, and I loved the little guhl. But then the Alexandahs left New Yohk; he went to Boston to join some fancy outfit—a clinic oah somethin'. They wanted me to go along, and foah a while I did think about it. But I like it heah in New Yohk." Then with her saucy grin, "I like you, Miss Lottie, love."

Mamie Lee was told that she could stay in one of the back bedrooms whenever she felt so inclined, but she did that only when the weather was very bad or she had worked unusually late. Her weekends were her own right from the beginning. She marketed and cooked on Friday; the other days went to the settling.

Then things fell into order rather suddenly. Charlotte, installed in the master bedroom, had her own dresser and tall chest of drawers, and her bedside table with her clock and radio on it. The room still looked a little large and empty, so Charlotte moved a small bookcase in here and spent a rapturous evening selecting volumes for it, mostly anthologies and books with which she had very dear associations. One shelf she carefully left vacant for the new books that she would buy. That night she went to bed deeply satisfied. For once, her sleep was dreamless.

One more small, intimate task remained. Charlotte unpacked and arranged the framed photographs of her dear ones which she had brought with her. She grouped them around one taken of Bill about a year after they were married.

She brought Mamie Lee in here the next morning to look at it. The girl picked it up and studied it long and earnestly. Then she set it carefully back where it had stood. Just above a whisper she breathed, "He was a ve'y lovely gentleman."

"Yes," Charlotte said. "He still is."

❧ 2 ❧

CHARLOTTE HAD MADE her banking connection as soon as she signed her lease, of course. Her first check to her landlord was drawn on a Euclid bank, but now her checking account was here, and she had a sizable deposit box where her securities and most of her jewelry were kept. She had opened accounts at the big city's two leading department stores, at provision shops in the neighborhood, at her local drugstore. Once a month she settled major bills, and she took good care to keep a substantial amount of money on hand. Her account-keeping was rough, but satisfactory to herself. As long as you knew you had money, the precise sum didn't matter too much.

Money in the bank. A spic-and-span apartment nicely settled. Domestic machinery running smoothly. Now there was one more connection Charlotte must make before she could think herself quite established. She must look up a doctor.

She had noticed a doctor's brass plate on a big building just two blocks north of her apartment. She had seen a man presumed to be that doctor coming out of the building. A large, handsome man, sixty or better, with his medical bag in his hand. Charlotte liked the looks of him. There would be no harm in inquiring further. She went into the corner drugstore, got her usual pharmacist aside, and began to ask questions.

"Dr. Sanborn? Dr. Louis F. Sanborn?" the druggist repeated. "Yes, he's very well thought of in the neighborhood. He's on the staff of a big hospital just across town. He was a successful surgeon for years, but now that he's getting older, he is going in more and more for geriatrics."

"Geri—?" Charlotte stammered.

The druggist grinned. "That wouldn't apply to you, of course. It's the branch of medicine which deals with the ailments of old people."

"Thank you for those kind words," Charlotte said. "Now I'd like a bottle of lavender cologne, please. And where are the latest in paperback books?"

Charlotte gave herself no chance to cool off. She walked into the doctor's waiting room that very next afternoon and announced to the office nurse, "I'm Mrs. William Andrews, a newcomer in this neighborhood. I'd like to arrange for Dr. Sanborn to give me a slight going-over some afternoon when he isn't too busy."

"There are two patients ahead of you now, besides the one who is with him," the nurse reported. "I can't tell just how long he will be, of course. Would you rather wait now, or make an appointment for another day?"

"Thank you, I'd rather wait," Charlotte said, and picked up a magazine.

The examination was not much of an ordeal. Dr. Sanborn took her heart and blood pressure readings, looked down her throat and up her nose, and asked a few questions. Then he said, "Sound as a bell, I must say. Come back again in six months. Or call me, of course, if you should happen to come down with anything." He began to scribble data on a card.

The afternoon was now pretty well advanced. When he opened the door for her into the waiting room and glanced outside, there was only one person there besides the nurse: a middle-aged woman in a very stunning hat, with a paper shopping bag on the table beside her.

"Hello, Greta," Dr. Sanborn said. "I hoped you'd be here by this time. This is a newcomer in the neighborhood, Mrs. Andrews. You two go ahead and get acquainted while I doff my white coat and wash up."

The woman smiled. "I'm Mrs. Sanborn. I think the doctor forgot to mention that. This is a nice neighborhood. I hope you are going to like us."

"I already do," Charlotte said.

This time they both smiled. Then Mrs. Sanborn shifted the big shopping bag on the table beside her. "Do you keep house? I've just been doing a little marketing. I take great pains with that. You see, I'm the doctor's second wife. Dr.

Sanborn was a widower for seven years before he married me. For seven years he took all his meals out. Isn't that dreadful? Now I see to it that he gets proper home-cooked meals. That means so much to a man."

Dr. Sanborn took a long time cleaning up; perhaps he relaxed for a few minutes in his office chair to give the two ladies time to become acquainted. By the time he emerged they were chatting away like old friends.

Charlotte was settling in. People were very nice to her. It was pleasant, too, to know that there was nothing the matter with her medically. This would give her something to write Pauline.

That next week everything ran as smoothly as a perfectly functioning car. As an Andrews sedan, of course! Friday evening, after Mamie Lee Jackson had finished the dinner dishes, she took her Miss Chahlotte honey for an inspection tour of an immaculate apartment; she wound up by pointing out just where she had put the steak and the cold chicken and the two-thirds of an apple pie which had been left over from dinner. Then she set out for Harlem and two lovely long days to herself, with her job not only off her hands but off her mind.

Charlotte spent a full hour that evening by a darkened window, watching the river and the sky and the myriad lights which showed where other people were living and loving, breeding—yes, and dying, working and loafing, all of them unconscious of that observer on the top floor of an apartment building, none of them suspecting that they were really putting on a show for the benefit of Charlotte Emerson Andrews.

Saturday morning Charlotte bathed and breakfasted, tidied everything, roamed around the apartment with a terrific sense of house pride. She got out some letters from the

children and reread them. They had all been answered. She
didn't like to call long-distance to her relatives at this busy
time of the week. She wasn't one bit lonesome; of course
she wasn't. It was just that she hadn't quite got used to her
new-found leisure and independence.

Eventually she settled herself with a book, and became
oblivious to everything except the interest of the story. She
lunched on a cup of coffee and two pieces of apple pie: a
delicious snack, if not one that would be recommended by
health cranks or reducing faddists. By dusk she had finished
her book. It was a day well spent, and a whole lovely evening stretched ahead of her.

Charlotte changed to street clothes and went for a leisurely walk around the neighborhood. She could dine out,
if she pleased, and maybe go to a movie afterward. Or she
could pick up a theater seat at the last minute; singles were
always easy to come by. Or she could wander back home
and finish the pie and dawdle the evening away with televi-
sion or radio. Fine freedom of choice! And in all the passing
crowd nobody knew who she was, and among the distant
people who knew and cared about her, nobody knew where
she was.

She turned down a street where she was not accustomed
to walking, and paused before an attractive shop window.
Glancing over the display, she turned slightly toward the
right and then lifted her eyes. There mirrored in the glass
was a man's dim shape. A man's—his! Charlotte started,
and gave a faint shriek.

It was all over in an instant. This was no shade of Bill
Andrews returned from the Great Beyond to haunt her. It
was simply the reflection of a man standing beside her. A
flesh-and-blood man, watching her and very much amused
by her perturbation.

"I think so too," the man said. "I think I've met you somewhere before."

"You think?" Charlotte said saucily. "With what?" It was a childish piece of repartee, but it was the first thing that came into her head.

The strange man laughed. He had a nice laugh, a nice voice. He didn't really look much like Bill Andrews, except that he too was a man any woman would notice. He went on coolly, "If we haven't met before, it's time we did now. I'm known in this shop. Won't you walk in with me, so that we can be properly introduced?"

That question was like the old standard, "Have you left off beating your wife yet?" Whether Charlotte said "Yes" or said "No," the answer would be wrong. "Some other time, perhaps," she said curtly, and turned on her heel.

He fell into step beside her. "The name is Hiestand," he informed her. He spelled it for her. "Joseph Hiestand. I will not try to deceive you by telling you it's Smith. I once knew a man named John Smith. John W. Smith; the 'W' adds a final touch of unreality. Hotel clerks always looked very knowing when he registered with that snappy brunette who was actually his legal wife."

"This is a thoroughfare, Mr.—is it Standish?" Charlotte said at the corner. "I won't trouble you to walk any farther with me. I'm quite safe here, and very close to home."

"It's no trouble," her escort said. "The name is Hiestand. A nice time of the week for a leisurely stroll, isn't it? I always have a nice relaxed feeling along about now, though I'm really a lonely man."

"You mean your wife misunderstands you?" Charlotte flashed.

"Oh, Mrs. Hiestand and I called the whole thing off! I'm a free man again." Suddenly his voice lost its flippant tone. "It was different when Mary was alive."

One wife dead and one divorced, she thought. Well, King Henry VIII had done three times as well as that. "My building is just two doors down. Thank you for escorting me," she said firmly.

"The pleasure has been all mine," he said. At her building he heard the doorman greet her by name. He gave a little nod, lifted his hat and said, "*Au revoir,* Mrs. Smith. Mrs. John *W.* Smith."

Charlotte went on up to the top floor. The decision had been taken out of her hands; she was spending the evening at home.

Ten minutes later her phone rang. "Mrs. Andrews, this is Joe Hiestand. I don't usually go around making a nuisance of myself. But the moment I laid eyes on you I somehow felt—"

"You needn't go on," Charlotte said, and hung up on him.

Twice more her phone rang. She did not answer. Men were like that, she supposed. Made that way, for a purpose. But there was no point in letting a fresh egg think he could spatter over her, just because she went out for a quiet stroll in her own neighborhood early in the evening.

At nine o'clock she was called to her door. A large box of roses was delivered to her. Sure enough, the scrawled message was "Happy Sunday from Joe." Roses! Love's flower! The nerve of him! But roses were lovely flowers, no matter who sent them or when or why. Charlotte selected three, which she arranged in a little vase and set before Bill's picture in her bedroom. The others kept the living room sweet all the rest of the evening. Charlotte was conscious of their perfume every time she glanced up from her book.

It had been a pleasant episode, but one that she could scarcely reveal to anybody. Mamie Lee Jackson, spotting the flowers when she came to work Monday, smiled her sauciest smile but said nothing. And that was that.

Only it wasn't. Tuesday's mail brought Charlotte a letter, most beautifully typed on expensive stationery, from the firm of Alfred Morrison & Company, Stockbrokers. It stated that the writer had the "matter of which we spoke last Saturday, under consideration," and that he looked forward to another interview with her. At the end was typed "Joseph R. Hiestand, Vice-President," and above the name was scrawled a scarcely legible "Joe."

"If that big fool thinks that I—" Charlotte stormed. But she was not nearly so angry as she tried to pretend. She was her own boss, and she had seen a lot of men and their monkeyshines. But there might be a few more moves in the game. It looked as if she hadn't seen the last of Mr. Joseph R. Hiestand. She was curious to see what he would do next.

He sent roses again on Thursday. Then on Friday he phoned. "I know you will be busy during the weekend," he said. (Liar! He knew she hadn't been busy last Saturday.) "But how about having dinner with me, say next Tuesday? Some quiet little place where we can talk. You may bring along a duenna if you choose."

"A duenna? Oh, I'm far past the stage where I need chaperoning! In fact I'm quite an adequate chaperone myself. I'm a widow with three grandchildren."

"Don't brag!" he snapped. "I once knew a woman who had six."

She laughed, and gave up. When you laughed, you were lost. Memory drifted back to the afternoon when a little girl had to stay after school and write fifty times, "I laugh at nothing." Charlotte and Bill had laughed together so many times. You did miss a man, when you and he had laughed together.

"You'd better not get me started talking about my grandchildren," she said into the telephone. "Tuesday will be fine, thank you. Your small quiet place will probably be quite new to me; I've lived in New York only for a short time."

"It's a date, then. And while you call me Joe, I can't go on calling you Mrs. Andrews."

"My given name is Charlotte. It isn't often abbreviated."

"It abbreviates very prettily, Lottie lady."

"Have it that way if you like. Just don't be surprised if I don't answer."

He took her uptown to a small restaurant where the lights were dim and soft music was piped in from outside. There they were seated at a corner table, which gave them just the right amount of privacy. Joe Hiestand consulted her taste in food and drinks, but Charlotte refused to be drawn. She went only so far as to say that if they were having wine with their dinner one cocktail would be enough for her, and she had no allergies.

He treated her to a magnificent steak and all the proper accompaniments. The usual small talk took them as far as dessert. But over the coffee he relaxed and confided, "You touched a sore spot with me, Lottie lady, when you threatened to brag about your grandchildren. I haven't any. My son was an only child and a late child. Mary was always afraid of making him a Mamma's Boy, so we sent him away to school very early and kept him away very consistently. Sometimes I wonder whether we did the right thing."

"Anybody would wonder," Charlotte said softly. "Who can tell?"

He smiled ruefully. "I suppose it's silly to dwell on your own mistakes."

"The only way to make no mistakes would be to do nothing whatever. And that would be the greatest mistake of all."

This time his smile was brilliant. "You do have a telling way of putting things. I noticed that very early in the game."

As if it were still not "very early in the game"! Unless, of course, he intended to make this a very short game. Charlotte sipped coffee and said nothing.

"It might have been worse," Joe Hiestand went on. "I expected Jim to go to college, of course. College is the minimum social requirement nowadays, whether or not a person learns anything. After that I thought he might be satisfied to come into the business. But no! Mr. James D. Hiestand must go back to college, and keep on going back. He must get not one degree, but three. He must turn into a blooming professor."

"I know," Charlotte sympathized. "Neither of my sons went to Yale, where my husband graduated. Our eldest did go into the family business; he's still there. But our daughter must needs turn into a doctor. A pill-pusher. A taker of temperatures and signer of prescriptions. Her poor father never got over the shock."

"But he must have been very proud of her, too. That sort of thing takes brains."

"Your son must have brains, too. All that hard studying, year after year!"

Joe Hiestand grinned. "Sometimes when I pretend that I'm complaining about him I'm really bragging. I try not to do too much of either. I hope I haven't bored you. How about a cordial now? Or would you like more coffee?"

"Nothing more, thank you. I've had just enough, and I've enjoyed every morsel of it."

Joe signaled for the check. "What do you want to do now? Catch a movie, or ride around in a taxi for a while, or maybe go somewhere where we can dance?"

Charlotte started to decline all three propositions. But the evening was yet young. She had enjoyed it so far. Why not prolong the pleasure? "Ride around is a good idea," she said. "Why not take a taxi across the Brooklyn Bridge? So often in the evening I look at Brooklyn from this side of the river. Now I'd like to try it the other way around."

"That's a very good idea," Joe Hiestand said.

"That steak was an inspiration. Come around and test me some time after I turn vegetarian."

"Some vegetarians allow eggs and milk. I always like a good omelet," said Joe. Was he answering a foolish remark in earnest, or was he merely making her acquainted with his tastes?

They made the proposed excursion across the East River, and viewed the city from Brooklyn Heights. For the most part they were silent. The wonder and the beauty of the lights! Here for an enchanted hour Charlotte could almost believe that it had been created for herself. Sometimes she forgot her companion briefly, but for the most part she was conscious of his presence there beside her, and aware that he shared her delight.

Back once more in Manhattan, he said, "Shall we go somewhere now for a nightcap? Or are there other sights you'd like to view before I take you home?"

"I've seen enough to carry me for some time."

"How about a mushroom omelet then, and maybe a bottle of beer? A vegetarian doesn't have to be a teetotaler, does he?"

"My acquaintance with vegetarians is limited, and teetotalism brings back strange memories of Prohibition."

Both their tongues began to wag then; they reminisced about that incredible era when defiance became the rule. Joe knew another small place where Charlotte had never been before. Although she didn't care much for beer and let him finish her bottle, the omelet was delicious, and they sat and talked for a good half-hour after they had finished eating.

When he landed Charlotte back at her apartment, he worked her latchkey for her and waited until she had switched on a light. For an instant a strange embarrassment came over Charlotte. It was gone almost as soon as it came, but it did cause her to falter when she said, "It's—it's late, or I'd invite you in."

"Yes, it's late," he agreed.

She drew off her gloves and turned to shake hands; somehow a gloved handshake was just too stand-offish after the marvelous time they had had together.

He took her hand in a firm, warm grip, and held it while he said, "There are lots of other places to go in New York. May I take you somewhere again, soon?"

"You know my phone number," Charlotte said.

They both laughed. Yes, he knew her phone number. And when he called this time, Charlotte wouldn't hang up on him.

3

WILL ANDREWS CALLED from Saylesboro to invite his mother to spend Thanksgiving with them in Saylesboro. He put his sweet-voiced Marjorie on the wire, too, and that girl was a wheedler. "Thanksgiving is the season of home-coming, and you know this is your old home," she pleaded.

But Charlotte was adamant. "It's too far to go just for a slice of turkey."

"You can have two slices," Marjorie offered. "Or we'd even see that you got the wishbone."

"You can give me my wish right this minute. Ask me for Christmas."

"Oh, Mother, you will, you really will? It's a date, then." She put Will back on the wire to confirm it So Charlotte was nicely booked up ahead of time. That in itself was something to be thankful for.

She had other plans for Thanksgiving. If they fell through—well, there were plenty of ways to spend time in New York. That was one of the things that had always impressed Charlotte about the big city; so many people could always manage to stop and watch a steam shovel work. They didn't seem to feel under pressure to get on with the job, the way people did in places like Saylesboro and Euclid.

So she got on the wire to son and namesake Charles in Euclid. She called him at the plant, and when a smooth-voiced secretary inquired who wished to speak to Mr. Andrews, Charlotte answered in an authoritative tone, "This is Mrs. Andrews, his mother. I'm calling from New York City. Please put him on." Oh yes, she could sound definite when she had to! If it hadn't been for her, Mr. Charles Andrews wouldn't have been there in Euclid to hold down his big job.

Charles's voice over the wire was warm and affectionate, but he seemed a little taken aback by the inclusiveness of the invitation. "I'd love to come. You know that, Mom. But I'm not so sure about the children. There might be—difficulties."

"Come alone if you have to," Charlotte answered. "But I don't really believe that you'll have to. You are pretty good at talking your way around difficulties."

He laughed, and just for an instant he was again her little Charley reassuring Santa Claus that he wasn't Mr. Parker. Dear Mr. Parker! He had gone to his reward now, but he had left such lovely memories behind him!

"I think I can manage to talk my way into bringing them," Charles assured his mother. "My 'ex' knows which side her bread is buttered on, and if necessary I can add a dab on the under side."

"Bribery and corruption!" Charlotte teased.

"Maybe, when the other fellow does it. But when you yourself cross the gypsy's palm with silver, two pieces will get you a better fortune than if you used only one."

He called back an hour later. It was all arranged; nothing remained but to set the times and make Charlotte's own arrangements. "I think the Nelson grandmother's nose is slightly out of joint," Charles confided. She 'wants only what is best for the dear children's happiness,' you know. She takes such an interest in other people's misfortunes."

"Yes," Charlotte said, "I know."

Charles's children had been named after their parents, with their mother's maiden name for a middle name. For purposes of identification they were called Nelson (or very often "Nelse") and Kitty. They were nice children, intelligent and well spoken. They had never been to New York before. Whenever Charles's "ex" or Mrs. Nelson took such a trip she had always made a shift which would leave the children in Euclid. And of course in these days summer camps for children were very much the vogue.

Charlotte assigned Kitty the second bedroom and bath—and called her Katherine when she did so. Katherine beamed at her, took a look around the room, pronounced it "super," and walked to the window, where she stood entranced at the prospect. Charlotte left her there, to enjoy it at her leisure. She gave the two back bedrooms, with their connecting bath, to Charles and his son. That way they could wash each other's backs, and thus strike up a real friendship.

Mamie Lee Jackson was as delighted with the visitors as if she had invented them. "That li'l Miss Kitty, she's jes' the sweetes'," she pronounced. "She looks jes' like you, too, Miss Lottie. An' that Mastah Nelse (who else?), he's goin' to b'eak a pow'ful lot o' ladies' heahts befoah too long."

She cooked a magnificent turkey dinner, to which the Andrews clan did full justice. In return for her working on a holiday, she had Friday off. The Andrewses wouldn't have had much need for her services anyhow; they were perpetually on the go.

They started in with the theater Thursday evening, an elaborate musical revue which made the Midwesterners sit up and take notice. This was followed by a Broadway stroll and supper at a big noisy restaurant. "This is seeing life. *Night* life!" young Katherine sighed blissfully.

She helped Charlotte get a late breakfast Friday. While the two of them cleared away, the men folks tidied up and made the beds. Not as well as Mamie Lee Jackson or Charlotte would have done, perhaps, but no one was coming in to inspect. Then the four of them went on a sightseeing tour: Trinity Church standing at the head of Wall Street, the Statue of Liberty, Radio City. Dinner in that neighborhood, and in the evening the show at Radio City Music Hall. In the taxi going home, little Katherine went to sleep against her grandmother. While she was being helped to bed she murmured drowsily, "Two days gone already! I never knew time go so fast."

"Time goes fast in good company," Charlotte whispered back. This was the best of company, this charmer who was so closely related to her, yet whom she was only now learning to know and to love.

Charles found a chance to tell her much the same thing about himself and his son, when the guests were leaving Sunday evening after the theater twice on Saturday and another round of sightseeing on Sunday. "Visiting rights are fine so far as they go, but they do hold a man at a distance. Here under your roof I've really felt like a father."

"That's what grandmothers are for," Charlotte assured him.

"Humph! Not all grandmothers are like you. Some of them 'want only what is best for the children's happiness.' But you proceed to give it to them."

At the actual moment of departure, the young ones bade Charlotte characteristic farewells. They both thanked her very prettily, but it was Katherine who said, "I love you

very, very much. I'm going to write to you and tell you so."
Nelse contented himself with a brisk "Wait till I get home
and tell the other kids about this!"

Then they were gone. The apartment seemed very large
and empty; seemed in a way as if Charlotte didn't live here.
And she was tired, dog tired. "New York is a nice place to
visit," Charlotte muttered to herself. "The visited-upon
sometimes almost wish that it wasn't quite so nice."

She was still a little forlorn Monday when Mamie Lee
Jackson came back to work. "Lan' sake, Miss Lottie sweet,
you is jes' plumb tuckahed out," Mamie Lee sympathized.
"Let me make you pancakes foah youah breakfas', an' then
you lie down again a while an' snooze. Next thing you
know you'll feel like yoahself, pinin' to get up an' get
stahted thinkin' about Ch'istmas."

"That's right, Christmas is coming too," Charlotte said,
and groaned. But already she felt better. Right here and
now, she could do with a little quiet. But prolonged quiet
was not desirable. All too soon it would run into
monotony.

Charlotte did full justice to the pancakes. She did not set
foot out of the apartment all that day, and she went to bed
early, for once quite satisfied to rest even if she could not
sleep.

A well-known voice reached her ears the next day
shortly before noon. "You been away, Lottie lady, or just
gadding your pretty head off? I've been trying to reach you
for days, and your phone wasn't answered."

"Do you expect me to sit here and twiddle my thumbs,
just on the chance that you might call up?"

"That is a reply of sorts. I'd scarcely consider it an answer."

"All right then. I've been out on the town: entertaining guests and showing them the sights."

"Friends or relatives, if I may make so bold as to ask?"

"Relatives, but I don't hold that against them."

"Out-of-towners are just too sophisticated nowadays. There isn't a chance of selling them the Brooklyn Bridge."

"You were the one—who sold me—*on* the Brooklyn Bridge," Charlotte said in a soft, full tone just above a whisper. She heard him gasp, and laughed wickedly. Joe Hiestand liked her, and had taken pains to make her like him. But he had hinted to her of his second marriage, which had had a very sour ending. Obviously he was scared to death that he might be trapped again.

He got his breath back fast enough, and informed her, "There are still bridges that I haven't shown you. Or would you rather just go somewhere where we can have a quiet dinner and you can tell me about your trippers?"

"Prepare to be bored," she said. But he was not too alarmed. They set an early date. Yes, it was great to live here where Charlotte knew so few people, where everything was on such a casual, take-it-or-leave-it basis. But it wouldn't have been so much fun to live here too long as a stranger. A person could get very lonesome in the midst of crowds.

That very afternoon Charlotte encountered Mrs. Sanborn, out to do her little marketing. "Do come with me and give me the benefit of your ideas," that lady begged. "If I can feed Louis something and tell him you suggested it, I know that will perk up his appetite."

She was sincere enough in her plea, but there was a touch of pride about it. She was doing something important for her man, and she had a man of her own to minister to. It was all very pleasant and friendly; it added to Charlotte's sense of belonging here. But while she was about it, she bought a few items for herself. There was no point in letting even the most dutiful and doting wife have everything her own way.

That little shopping for food had been fun. Why not go on now and shop for something to drink? Charlotte had been buying what little she needed at a liquor store just around the corner. She phoned and had it sent up; she had stuck to brands familiar to Bill, and hence known to her, back in Euclid. But it occurred to her now that she might well branch out a little. Good enough was not the whole story; there might be something better.

It was late in the afternoon when Charlotte entered the Superior Wine & Liquor Store. The proprietors, brothers, were both behind the counter and both reasonably busy; one was entrusting an order to a delivery man who had sometimes brought up Charlotte's bottle, the other was waiting on a woman who obviously believed in taking her time. Charlotte caught his eye and raised her eyebrows slightly. It must be tough to be in business and have to be polite to customers.

She thought that again an instant later, for there following her into the store and waiting the turn after hers was a man she surely had seen before. Not just glimpsed in the street either, but seen inside somewhere. Seen with his hat off.

He recognized her almost instantly, took his hat off, and said, "I've seen you in the bank, haven't I? I work there. I don't remember that I've had the pleasure of waiting on you, but I certainly do remember you."

That wasn't just another version of Joe Hiestand's come-on, but it was very definitely a come-on. "In the bank, yes,"

Charlotte said. "You sit behind a desk labeled 'Manager,' and give the customers a suspicious stare when you haven't some special wretch squirming in the chair on the wrong side of your desk."

The man laughed. "That is a very nice description from a customer who obviously never has to come to us for a loan. You are Mrs. Andrews. Mrs. Charlotte Emerson Andrews. I wasn't christened 'Manager,' either. I'm Sidney Miller."

"No middle initial?" Charlotte asked.

"Middle initial W. Stands for Watson, if you want to know. Oh, it's your turn at the counter now. You were ahead of me."

"You two are near neighbors," said the brother who was now free. "What would you like today, Mrs. Andrews? I believe you often buy gin and dry vermouth."

"I'm in here looking for information," Charlotte said. "I'm a very moderate drinker, but I'm getting just a little tired of the inevitable dry martini."

She got a little advice from Mr. Waring behind the counter, a lot more from Mr. Miller on her side of it. When they left the store Mr. Miller was carrying Charlotte's order as well as his own. He said he would be saving the delivery man one trip, and it wasn't a bit out of his own way; he lived just around the corner from Charlotte.

When they reached Charlotte's apartment she had to invite him in, of course. He said he wouldn't stay a minute, and he didn't; he stayed fifteen. He said this was a lovely apartment. So homelike. He himself kept bachelor quarters with another man. He was not married; never had been. "The fellow I live with, Sam Groom, he's married all right, but he doesn't work very hard at it. He's a very big bug in the library world; teaches library work at Columbia and has an active job besides. His wife is head of a library up in Massachusetts; breaks in new talent while she's living with her aged mother and keeping an eye on her. Samuel goes up there for holidays. She sometimes joins him here for a few days. When she does, I make myself scarce. It's an all-around odd arrangement, maybe, but it suits me."

Charlotte did not offer to open her package while he was there, and when he left he almost forgot to take along his own. This must be a relief after putting up a front all day in the bank. But what characters there were around New York! Or was it just around this part of New York? Or was it just that they were somehow attracted to Charlotte?

It was unbankerlike conduct. Charlotte was curious to see whether she would notice any change in his conduct the next time she went into the bank. When she did so, Mr. Miller, Manager, was sitting at his desk busying himself with some papers. He happened to look up when she was leaving; Charlotte smiled and spoke. He barely nodded in response, and his lips remained closed. Very well, then. He had a nice soft job dealing with other people's money. But he needn't think he could come around again after hours making eyes at a well-to-do widow just in from the wilds of the Middlewest.

That evening her phone rang. A man's voice said, "Mrs. Emerson? Good evening. This is Sidney Miller. You know, your neighbor from just around the corner."

"Yes," Charlotte said coolly.

"I've been telling my housemate, Sam Groom, about you, and he is anxious to meet you. We are giving a little cocktail party Saturday, before people get too busy with their Christmas shopping. We would like it if you could join us then."

"I don't care much for cocktail parties," Charlotte said, more truthfully than politely, perhaps.

"I don't blame you a particle. They are rather ghastly. But I thought you might like to join us for a little while, just so that you can meet Sam and perhaps a few other of your neighbors."

Maybe he was genuinely being hospitable. Anyhow it would be a new experience for her. She needn't stay long or drink much. Charlotte's tone warmed. She thanked him, inquired about the hour, got his apartment number. "Thank you. I'll try to make it," she wound up sweetly.

There was so much to do at this time of the year. Charlotte had made out her list of gifts to be purchased, and had already bought her Christmas cards. It was such fun to go into the gaily decorated shops, to see the children being taken on their rounds, especially the very small children, the true believers. Memories came crowding back, lovely, tender memories. If nothing could ever bring back the past, in another sense nothing could ever take it from her. It was Charlotte's to recall at will.

On Saturday afternoon Charlotte arrived at the cocktail party fairly early. That gave her a better chance to size up Sam Groom, and also to have a look around the apartment. The apartment was sightly, convenient, just a little impersonal. Mr. Groom was in his middle forties, nice looking, sleek, very quick and incisive in his speech. He didn't talk half as much as Sidney Miller, whose banking manners were evidently strictly for banking hours.

Charlotte had a cocktail and a cheese wafer, and presently a second cocktail and some salted almonds. She strolled around and met ten or twelve people, most of whom arrived in couples and then uncoupled themselves at once. Charlotte exchanged the smallest of small talk and listened to two fairly uninteresting scandals. Taking her empty glass back to the improvised bar, she caught a glimpse of herself in a mirror. Her face was slightly flushed, her eyes very bright. She looked very pretty—yes, and amazingly young. Yes, life in New York agreed with her. Yes, a couple of drinks at this hour of the afternoon and this time of the week were an amazing pick-me-up.

Then all at once there came over her a sickening revulsion. She could stay here as long as she pleased; nobody was waiting for her at home. She could go on drinking until her head swam and her feet refused to track; nobody cared. She was a stranger in this no-man's-land. She no longer belonged either in Euclid, where her wonderful married years had been spent, or back in Saylesboro, where she had been born, and had laughed at nothing, and had grown up to dance her way through four successive Proms. She no longer believed in Santa Claus; she knew he was just poor old Mr. Parker being kind.

It was all over in a flash. Charlotte picked up a third cocktail and a stuffed olive. She moved over to her second host and asked, "Are you going away for the holidays, Mr. Groom?"

He nodded. "For part of them. I'm joining my wife in Massachusetts."

"How lovely! You'll have such a lot to tell each other!"

"She's coming here with me for New Year's. It makes a nice change for both of us. And you?"

"I'm going back to Wisconsin, which is next door to the North Pole. I've enjoyed meeting you, Mr. Groom. It was kind of your banking buddy to bring me up here."

"Not going so soon, are you?"

But she was, before she had quite finished that third drink. She felt just right now. She was amused by a man who had a wife in Massachusetts and exchanged visits with her. At least, that kept other women at a distance. This kind of party, where the guests came and went as they liked, was just right for such an establishment, just right for tonight. Charlotte had enjoyed seeing all these good-looking people, some of them rather hard. She wouldn't know most of them if she saw them again. She wouldn't be heartbroken if she never saw any of them again. Right here and now, they simply added to her feeling of holiday.

She found her coat, retouched her make-up slightly, started for the apartment door. She wouldn't bother to say good night to Sidney Miller. She had already told the other host that she was going.

But her unbankerlike banker had had his eye on her. With his own overcoat over his arm, he intercepted her. "Just a minute, young lady. I'm seeing you to your door."

"It isn't necessary."

"It is customary."

He saw her into her own apartment, where she had left a light burning. "It was a lovely party," she said. And turned toward him. And waited for him to go.

He raised his right hand toward her face. Charlotte was startled, and flinched. But all he did was put back a stray lock of her hair. Then he was gone, but not before Charlotte had had a whiff of very fine imported soap tinged with cigarette smoke. She felt an instant's touch of excitement. Which was all nonsense, of course. It was Joe Hiestand who was dating her in New York, and Joe, though he was fine in his way, was not exactly the answer to a maiden's prayer. Or a widow's.

4

EVEN WHEN YOU could have work done for you, things required a certain amount of arranging. Charlotte had agreed to spend Christmas in Saylesboro with Will and his family; that meant she could take their presents with her. She was in doubt about Charles's arrangements and didn't like to ask, so she sent gifts for him and his children to his address in Euclid. It was a special pleasure to select gifts for Nelse and Kitty, now that she felt she really knew them.

Charlotte gave Mamie Lee Jackson an extra week's pay as her Christmas present. She would have a nice ten days to herself, too, and she received permission to come and stay at the Andrews apartment if she wanted a change, and to bring along any of her friends she would like to entertain. Joe Hiestand took Charlotte out for an early dinner and gave her a foot-high toy Christmas tree which was also a music box; when wound it would play "Silent Night." Charlotte hadn't prepared any gift for him; he probably had more handkerchiefs and neckties than he knew what to do with, and she didn't know his size in socks. But she laid the first two fingers of her right hand against her own lips and then against his, and whispered, "This is for the mistletoe I forgot to buy." He kissed her fingers heartily, took them in his hand for a minute, then kissed them again. Her hand lay warm in his, and he breathed a little faster. Then he let her go, and again picked up the music box to wind it. That was just as it should be. Charlotte wasn't thinking about any old image in a lighted shop window or rides over the Brooklyn Bridge; she was thinking about Santa Claus, and balloons released over Lake Michigan, and an old house made new again for many different families.

Here she was once more embarked on a long train trip. Sleeping in a berth, eating in the dining car, feeling a kinship with her fellow passengers. Charlotte had lovely memories of journeys with Papa and Mamma as far back as she could remember. Those long-ago experiences had been voyages into the unknown, with everything the little girl saw or heard or felt new and strange and marvelous. If nothing later could quite come up to that first freshness for sheer marvel, still added knowledge had made later journeys richer if less novel, and tonight the rails were singing to Charlotte, "Christmas—children—Santa Claus —lullaby—Christmas—children—Santa Claus—lullaby." She would half waken, and listen to the melody, then fall asleep again in time to that lovely rhythm. Then the next thing she knew they were in Chicago. Charlotte changed trains—and here it was the twenty-fourth of December, and here she was back in the town where she was born.

The day was all too short. Will had to show her his latest improvements. She admired them, and Billy, after the first few minutes' strangeness, warmed up to her and told her all the news of his schoolboy world. Marjorie said, "I hope you will stay longer than you had planned to. We've waited all this time for you to come!" They trimmed the tree. Billy read to them "The Night before Christmas." "Just the way I used to have it read to me." They had oyster stew for supper. It was lovely. It was heart-warming. It was just as it should be. But once or twice Charlotte had a strange feeling that it wasn't really happening, that she was back in her New York apartment and was simply imagining all this.

She stayed in Saylesboro six days. Long enough for Will to say to her, "Wouldn't you really like to come back to Saylesboro to live, Mom, now that you've got New York out of your system?" Then in response to her refusal, "You could at least let me rig you up some kind of summer home here, and keep your New York apartment for use during 'the season.' " But Charlotte liked things just the way they were. She enjoyed being a visitor instead of a commonplace —or a has-been.

Charles had let himself be heard from. So when she left Saylesboro, Charlotte went to Euclid. Charles took her through the plant and demonstrated the fine points of the new model that was now going on the market. He took her to see the children, who made their little speeches of thanks for their Christmas presents and then proceeded to tell her how they had enjoyed visiting her. "My grandma in New York City" was big-league stuff in their world.

"You'll stay here for New Year's Eve, won't you?" Charles asked.

"Aren't you going to a New Year's Eve brawl?" his mother asked.

"I can always get out of it."

Charlotte hesitated. She was still hesitating when his phone rang. The caller was a woman, his mother could tell by the tone of his voice. His replies were brief and noncommital, but he wound up, "I'm busy right now. Won't you let me call you back later?"

"It's your New Year's Eve date?" Charlotte asked as soon as he had hung up.

"Yes, and she has started to act proprietary. Mom, do stay over and—"

Charlotte shook her head. "You can't stand her up at this late date."

"Mom, please, please, pretty please?"

"Certainly not. If you were a lad still in high school, or even a sophomore in college, I'd be delighted to help you out of a small scrape. But you should have learned the ropes by this time."

That was the way it stood. Charles finally went to his party. Charlotte had a glass of champagne all by herself in Euclid and listened on the radio to the Times Square jamboree in New York City. It was nice to be quiet and listen to the din. Nice, just this once. But this wasn't setting any precedent. Less than ever did Charlotte intend to be an onlooker at life, or just a listener.

She stayed in Euclid two days more. Long enough to put an icebag on Charles's aching head. Long enough to call up the members of her old bridge club and ask for their news, but not to make any dates. Euclid without Bill Andrews just wasn't home to her. She thought it was a nice place to visit, but Charlotte would hate to live there.

She arrived in New York at five o'clock on a miserable January afternoon. Her taxi was caught in a traffic jam, and it took her almost an hour to get downtown to her own building. She was dog-weary, travel-smirched, faintly lonesome for the dear ones she had left behind. But she was going back where she could rest and readjust and think things over. It had been good to go, but it was doubly good to get back.

A beaming Mamie Lee Jackson was waiting for her. Charlotte had a long hot bath in her own bathroom.

Stacked up newspapers were waiting for her, all her December bills, some late Christmas cards, a short but pleasant letter from Pauline. "Dinner in half an hour, Mamie Lee," she called out. Then while she glanced over the newspapers she set her little music box going and listened to "Silent Night."

Later she sat at a darkened window and watched the lights of the city. Just before she went to bed she took Bill's old dressing gown from the farthest corner of her closet, buried her face in it for a minute, and felt closer to him than she had felt during those days in Saylesboro, where they had been married, or in Euclid, where they had lived so long together. Then she hung the dressing gown back in its corner and pulled some of her own clothes sharply in front of it.

She lay in bed late the next day, pleasantly conscious that she hadn't a single social obligation to meet. Time to herself —what a luxury! A home of her own. Freedom to come and go as she chose. All the rest of January ahead of her. All the other months after that. Twelve months in the year. Fifty-two precious weeks packed full of opportunity. Who invented the week, anyhow? Whoever did was a smart man; he handed us a unit small enough to deal with capably, yet not so small that its passing would leave a person without a sense of something accomplished.

Charlotte breakfasted in her dressing gown, made some housekeeping plans with Mamie Lee, finished her unpacking. Then, sure enough, early in the afternoon her phone rang and a well-remembered voice asked, "Is this Lottie lady, the traveler in the remote wilds of the Middlewest?"

"Who wants to know?" Charlotte demanded. "Surely not big old Joe Hiestand, that inveterate New Yorker?"

"A very sad Joe, who has felt how lonesome a big city can be when a certain person has left it."

"Don't make me cry, Joe-Joe. My Kleenex is in the other room."

"When are you coming out to dinner with me, Lottie lady?"

"I'm waiting until I'm asked. Oh, let's not keep this up any longer! Such back-and-forth is all right when people are still in high school. We're old enough to talk a little sense. I'm pretty well tired out right now, Joe, but a few days should see me rested. What do you say to next Tuesday night? I'm free then."

"It's five long days to wait. But I've already waited longer than that. Tuesday it is, then."

Charlotte went into the bank that afternoon. When her business had been transacted, she approached the desk with the "Manager" sign and said quietly, "I'm back, Mr. Miller. I won't disturb you when you're busy, but I do want to say I enjoyed your party."

"Sit down please, Mrs.—it is Mrs. Andrews, isn't it?" Sidney Miller rummaged among the papers on his desk. Then he seized a blank pad and wrote, "Again this coming Saturday? Same time, same place, but many fewer people. Please do say yes."

Charlotte wrote back, "I'll toss a coin on it." He nodded as if satisfied, then rose and escorted her to the door. His smile on parting was again unbankerlike.

Not twenty-four hours back in the big city, and already she had two dates! She would have to catch up on her sleep between times. She'd better look over her clothes, too, to see what needed to go to the cleaner's. And a visit to the hairdresser's was very much in order. She might as well go there right now.

She did so. It was half past five when she again approached her own building. Coming from the other direction was a shortish woman of about forty-five, with very bright brown eyes and a rather prominent nose; under her arm she carried a bulging briefcase.

"Good evening, Mrs. Andrews," the doorman said. "Good evening, Miss Coulter. Are you two ladies acquainted? You live only two floors apart."

"We're acquainted now, thanks to you," Charlotte said.

Miss Coulter smiled. "Are you and your husband in 12A, Mrs. Andrews?"

"No. I'm a widow. I live alone."

"I have an apartment mate, Jean Cochran. Won't you come in and meet her? She has the second rottenest job in New York. I have the rottenest."

"As bad as all that? Then you weep on each other's shoulders?"

"No. It's always her shoulder that gets wept on. She is *the* Jean Cochran."

Charlotte remembered then. That was the name of a columnist who conducted a regular feature in a leading New York daily. Under the heading "Love and Life," she answered a letter, sometimes two letters a day from readers who sought her advice on their intimate problems. Charlotte had often read that column casually, as she read so much of the news. It never occurred to her that Jean Cochran was not just a name in a newspaper, was indeed a woman like herself, living right here in this same convenient building with a view. Charlotte felt a certain curiosity.

When they left the elevator Miss Coulter led the way into an apartment similar to Charlotte's own. The living room was lighted, and from it came a faint whiff of cigarette smoke. "She's here," Miss Coulter said. "Jean dear, we have company."

Jean Cochran rose to greet her guest. She was about the same age as Miss Coulter, several inches taller, with a very smooth, pale skin and flashing gray eyes. After Helene Coulter's little speech of introduction she said, "Do sit down and let's get acquainted, neighbor. Would you like a beer?"

"There's sherry, if you would prefer that," her companion supplemented.

"Sherry would be fine. And my name is Charlotte."

They had a sherry all around, and an exchange of given names. Then Helene asked, "What luck today, dear Miss Cochran?"

"Good. Only one letter, and that from a teen-ager. I feel that I can usually help them. Their problems are mostly due to lack of experience, and the great youthful dilemma of not knowing which one you prefer. And you, dear Miss Author's Agent?"

Helene pointed to her briefcase. "Another script to go over. A novel. From an experienced author and under contract. Just not too bad."

Charlotte took a sip of sherry, and smacked her lips. It was very dry and had been properly chilled. "It must be great to do such interesting work," she said. "I've never had a job, except as a schoolteacher very briefly about a century ago. But I have an M.D. daughter. Gets her brains from her father's side of the family."

"You're a newcomer in this neighborhood?" Helene asked.

"A newcomer in New York. Everybody here seems to come from somewhere else. Or is it just that my experience has been limited?"

"Helene and I met in Chicago," Jean Cochran said. "But we both had gone there from other places: Indianapolis in her case and Denver in mine."

"It's a big country," Charlotte said; "and people do move around." She went on to account briefly for her own background and to quote Mamie Lee Jackson's "It just goes to show."

Both the other women smiled. Helene went to her bedroom to dispose of her wraps. Jean held out the letter she had received that day. "The spelling and punctuation are not beyond cavil," she commented. "But most of those letters require editing before they can be printed. I figure that when people have thought their troubles over to the point where they can sit down and write about them, the battle is half won."

"It must make them feel important to see their letters in print. But what does the party of the other part think about such public exposure?"

Jean laughed. "Often I suppose they don't recognize themselves in the pen portrait. Sometimes I get a hot rebuttal. To such letters I reply by mail. That is, when they remember to sign their names and addresses. And every once in a while, of course, there's a case of mistaken identity. He or she—usually he—recognizes himself when he wasn't at all the person intended."

"But don't you ever feel stumped?" Charlotte asked.

"Often and often. But I hate that 'Confide in your church pastor' stuff. If they had any such person to confide in, they wouldn't be writing to me in the first place."

Helene, returning with the decanter for a refill, summed up, "Jean lives off other people's troubles. But at least she does some good in the world. I'm the one who is caught between the upper and the nether millstones."

Charlotte sipped and smiled. "As bad as all that?"

"Oh, indeed! The publishers all want something which is completely fresh and strikingly original, but exactly like the latest best seller put out by a rival firm. The authors all think their baby is the original text handed down from Mount Sinai, and combines all the merits of *Vanity Fair, Gone with the Wind,* and Hemingway."

"I'm surprised you stick to it, then," Charlotte said. "A woman can always get a job working behind the counter in Woolworth's."

Jean Cochran snickered. Helene flushed, but she too smiled. Then she said, "Ah, but I haven't told you the whole story! The thing sometimes comes off. When it does, I'm like the head nurse on the maternity floor when she escorts the fond parents and the new arrival to the door of the hospital and beams on their departure. I act as if I had done it all."

"You did do something," Charlotte reminded her. "And it's a nice way to feel."

"She did do something," Jean Cochran echoed softly. "She does do a lot. She's the easiest person in the world to get along with, too, once you get used to her talking streaks."

Helene bowed in acknowledgment. Charlotte thought they were thoroughly nice people, both of them. She felt she was going to enjoy getting better acquainted. But she had stayed long enough for a first visit. She rose to take her leave.

"I'll walk you up to your own apartment," Helene volunteered. She was courteous, but perhaps she was also curious.

She was more than that. She had something on her mind. When they reached Charlotte's apartment she took a brief survey, complimented it, and, still standing, launched into what she had to say. "I was once a fit subject for Jean's column, but neither she nor anybody else could have helped me. When I was still fairly young I was married after a whirlwind courtship."

Charlotte murmured sympathetically.

"Such a lover! Such a pursuer! But once he had made sure of me, John Westerman changed completely. He was grossly inconsiderate in every way; he expected me to be at the mercy not only of his tastes and desires but of his whims and caprices."

"Some people are like that. I don't know what makes them behave as they do. But go on. You left him?"

"I got a nice respectable divorce on grounds of incompatibility. Afterward he was sorry and made overtures; but 'once bitten, twice shy.' Luckily I had some money of my own. I lived in Chicago for a time while I was getting my bearings; it was there that I met Jean. And yes, I did work behind a counter for a time. But it wasn't in Woolworth's, it was in a department store. Then I came here, because I wanted to do something really interesting."

"You are doing it, aren't you?"

"Indeed I am. Being an agent has its ups and downs, but even when authors and editors are at their worst, I always have the consolation that I'm not married to them."

"I know. Thank you for telling me all this. It always helps to know anybody's background."

"I've given you fair warning, haven't I? But before I leave, I must tell you about Jean." Helene hesitated, and a look of deep concern crossed her face. "She was a very popular girl in school and college, as you can easily believe. Then she was 'legman' for a big newspaper. On the eve of

World War II she met an aviation cadet. He was simply *the* man. Things do happen that way, you know. Not very often, I suppose, but they do happen."

"They do. Indeed they do."

"Jean and Bob Newcombe became engaged very soon, but they planned to defer their marriage until peacetime, when they could look forward to a home of their own and a reasonable amount of control over their future. Then Bob Newcombe was killed, not in combat, but by collision with another plane whose pilot apparently panicked."

"Oh, how cruel!" Charlotte cried.

"Cruel, yes. But while it lasted, their love was perfect. Sometimes I don't know whether to pity Jean or to envy her."

There was a moment's deep silence: the silence of sorrow, and of understanding. Then Helene moved toward the door. "I hadn't intended to stay so long. But somehow I just had to tell you." With her hand on the doorknob she paused to say, with a touch of brightness, "I think Jean will make popcorn for the two of us tonight. She often does, when we have a quiet evening all to ourselves."

It was a pleasant picture, the two women enjoying each other's society and a simple treat. A country treat, you might almost say. Charlotte's spirits lifted at the idea. Later on she reflected, did it ever occur to Helene during those tranquil sessions that she could have been making popcorn for her children years ago? Popcorn one of these days for her grandchildren?

5

CHARLOTTE READ Jean Cochran's column with renewed interest now. Knowing who wrote it made the whole thing come alive. Charlotte told Jean so a few days later when she happened to meet her in the elevator. "Don't your correspondents ever thank you for the help you've given them?" she added.

"Not often, but when they do, it's a very wonderful experience. I don't expect too much, you know. That's the best way, so then I'm not disappointed. Oh, Charlotte, just a minute!" She drew Mrs. Andrews aside. "Helene said she told you about my popcorn-making interludes. I can feel one of them coming on now. Would you like it if I brought you up some? It's a childish treat, but somehow people fancy it."

Jean was better than her word. She brought up not only a liberal helping of popcorn but also two novels in a state of shiny newness. "These are Helene's copies of two books for which she was agent," she explained. "She hopes you'll enjoy them more than she did. You may keep them as long as you like."

A very friendly gesture. A very friendly neighborhood. Perhaps any neighborhood was friendly enough, if you yourself were friendly. What was that old nursery-rhyme aphorism? "If you bring a smiling visage to the glass, you meet a smile." Nice going, Mrs. Andrews. Pat yourself on the back. Just don't sprain your elbow while you're doing so.

But here came another consideration. Charlotte had now lived in her New York apartment long enough to accept a certain amount of hospitality. She owed it to several people now to entertain them in return. The question was how and when, and to a certain extent whom.

To begin with, it would not be at a cocktail party. It would be at a proper sit-down meal. Cocktails, of course, but not as an end in themselves, only as a prelude to the great business of eating. When? Sunday was as good a day as any. Better, perhaps; by established custom it was pretty much official eating day. At what hour? Most people had to get up and go to work Monday, so say at six o'clock. Sunday at six. And a Sunday far enough in advance so that people wouldn't really be booked up. If any of those invited pleaded a previous engagement, Charlotte would know what that meant.

She consulted Mamie Lee Jackson on the subject. Her maid beamed. "Any day you say, Miss Chahlotte. I've been wondahin' when you was goin' to staht askin' folks in. You got a nice place heah. It's time you showed it off."

"Sunday is all right with you, then? It will make a lot of work for you over the weekend, which you generally have to yourself."

"You can give me some othah days off if you like. Oah just don't mind. It's genally powahful easy wohking heah foah you, Miss Lottie honey."

The menu then, and the guests. Eight would be a good number; seven besides the hostess. That would give a chance for general conversation and at the same time for private talk with one's companions at right and left. Six would do. If the party fell down to four—oh, even four congenial souls could make out very nicely!

Two unattached women beside the hostess. It was easy to guess who they would be—and they wouldn't be put to the expense of taxi fare, either. Three unattached or semi-attached men. Unless Charlotte missed her guess, they would be delighted to partake of a home-cooked meal. But that question of home cooking brought up the subject of the married couple whom Charlotte desired to invite. She wasn't indebted to them, and she had her doubts about how her invitation would be received. But she decided to go ahead and ask them anyhow. The only question was how to set about it.

She would ask them first, now that she had definitely fixed on the date. She decided not to risk a phone call on this one; that would be just too easy to deal with. That very next afternoon she dressed even more carefully than usual, and sauntered over to Dr. Sanborn's office.

There was only one patient ahead of her, so she hadn't long to wait. Dr. Sanborn raised his eyebrows when he greeted her. "Don't tell me you're having difficulties with your blood pressure. You look blooming as a rose."

"As the last rose of summer, maybe," Charlotte said pertly. "Go ahead and get your customary readings and have done with it. There's something I want to talk to you about afterward."

"Having something on your mind will send your blood pressure up," he observed. But he went ahead and did as he was told. Then Charlotte delivered her invitation, winding up, "I don't know how much you and Mrs. Sanborn go out. But it isn't as if I were asking you to a restaurant meal. My Mamie Lee Jackson is an excellent cook."

He asked particulars, phoned his wife to confirm the date, beamed at Charlotte, and said, "It's nice of you to ask us. We do go out sometimes, of course. But not often. We're pretty well out of the swim of things now." Then as Charlotte rose to go, he added, "I can't very well charge you for an office visit this time, can I, seeing you really came to deliver an invitation?"

So it was all over as quickly as that. Charlotte invited Joe Hiestand the next time he phoned her. "Just the two of us?" he demanded. "An intimate little dinner there in your own home? That will be lovely. But you shouldn't go to all that trouble just for me."

"I wouldn't," Charlotte retorted. "There will be other guests. You have been so kind to me that I felt bound to make some return for your hospitality. But—"

"But I'm not the only pebble on the beach? No, I wouldn't be." He heaved a mock sigh. "Tell me again when the party is to be. . . . At six? And I'll meet my hated rivals then? All the better. But that's too long to wait. How soon can you have dinner with me at one of those out-of-the-way places which are really desperately respectable, but do their little level best not to show it?"

He had to hand out a line; he knew it was expected of him. All the same, he was pleased to be asked.

She phoned Sidney Miller at home. He accepted, and said he thought Sam Groom would be free; he wasn't home just then. Sam called her back later that same evening. He too would be delighted.

So now there were only Helene Coulter and Jean Cochran left to be asked. They were both delighted to accept. "There won't be any misunderstood husbands or neglected wives there, I trust," Jean said, and Helene added, "Or anybody who has written a novel based on her own life— 'Just read it over, Miss Coulter, and tell me what you really think of it.' "

So they were assembling on Sunday at six. A choice of cocktails, martinis or old-fashioneds. Perhaps one of the men would be good enough to serve as bartender. Did Mamie Lee think she could fry chicken for that many people and serve it hot? That was like asking Paderewski if he imagined he could play the piano. Or asking Beethoven if he knew anything about writing music. Mamie Lee didn't even bother to answer the question. She just asked, "What else you want, Miss Lottie, honey?"

Everything was arranged, then, and Charlotte could sit here and look forward to her party. She had a satisfactory interval for doing so: not long enough for the idea to go stale on her, but long enough to have all the pleasure of sweet anticipation. To judge from her pleasure, anybody might think that she had never given a party before. That was hardly the case, but she had never given this particular party before.

She saw some of her prospective guests during the interval: Sidney Miller acting managerial in the bank, Jean Cochran perplexed by other people's problems, Joe Hiestand grinning at her over a restaurant table and making cracks about his hated rivals. They couldn't actually have changed much in such a short space of time, but to Mrs. Andrews they all looked a little different. They were her chosen few. Perhaps too they felt a little different. Or was she just imagining things?

The day came. Charlotte breakfasted lightly, got the Sunday newspapers out of the way in a hurry. For a time she tried to help Mamie Lee with the preparations, but she succeeded principally in getting between that lady and what she was trying to do. Finally Charlotte settled herself at a window and watched the passing traffic. Sunday traffic, so different from weekday traffic. Lots of people enjoying their welcome leisure. Young fathers getting reacquainted with their families. Young mothers trying to look as if theirs was not the most beautiful child in the whole turnout. Scores of people on their way to parties. There were hundreds of parties being given in New York today, though of course there was only one that counted.

Charlotte sat there until it was time to dress. At that, she was ready too soon. Better that way than the other, perhaps; she had known occasions when as a flurried hostess she had been grateful for guests who were just a conventional ten minutes late and gave the hostess a chance to get in under the wire.

Tonight's guests all arrived within a few minutes of one another. The rooms which had been so quiet all day were suddenly abuzz with chatter and laughter. The cocktails were produced and consumed. After the second round Sam Groom, who acted as bartender, raised his eyebrows at Charlotte. Contrary to her original plan, Charlotte nodded. But that third round was really final; Charlotte even left a little in her glass, as a hint that enough was enough.

Charlotte had provided place cards with two lines of doggerel carefully lettered on each. Some of the verses were not too bad: Mrs. Sanborn's "As the only wife present/Your lot should be pleasant," and the manager's "Sit here, Sidney Miller/ You old lady-killer." Some of them were very bad indeed. Like Joe's "Old Joe Hiestand/ You beat 'thees' band." But nobody was too critical after those cocktails. Under cover of the mirth Dr. Sanborn whispered to Charlotte, "Your prescription is better than mine. In the words of the great King Solomon, 'A merry heart doeth good like a medicine.'" Charlotte, who had once laughed at nothing, now felt that she had been justified.

Mamie Lee's fried chicken received full justice and a

round of compliments. Mrs. Sanborn went so far as to say, "Your fried chicken isn't just a dish, Mamie Lee, it's a gift." With the salad course people began to eat less and talk more. The dessert was raspberry ice and homemade angel-food cake, and the hostess said, "Anybody who wants coffee with dessert gets it, and if a large cup, so much the better." It was not too long before she progressed to "A second cup is even better than the first, isn't it? Do have another."

It had been nearly seven o'clock when they sat down at the table; it was almost nine when they rose. They ranged through the rooms then, exclaimed at the charm of Charlotte's arrangements, examined books and photographs. Some of them had come here as strangers to some others. They were not merely acquainted now, they were friends. This was the result of a successful party. This was what parties were for.

The Sanborns left at ten. Mrs. Sanborn kissed Charlotte good-bye and whispered, "It's done Louis all the good in the world. I thank you more than I can say." Dr. Sanborn himself not only thanked his hostess, he addressed the rest of the crowd. "Old Wet Blanket is taking himself off. That should encourage the rest of you to stay. Baking soda will still turn the trick, if you feel you really need something. But the best idea is just to let nature take its course."

"Did you hear that?" Charlotte demanded when the door closed on the Sanborns. "Doctor's orders to stick around and have a mild carousal. There's club soda, so anybody who wants a whiskey-and is welcome. Or I can stretch to a brandy, if you prefer."

They all said whiskey-and would be fine. They had it. They relaxed and gabbled. They were still at it when Mamie Lee Jackson came to the door of the room to smile good night at Charlotte.

Sam Groom was devoting himself to Jean Cochran now. They had got around to talking about her column. Sam said he had recognized her name at once, but he couldn't quite believe it was the same—that sage giver of advice ought to look more like an old gorgon. Presently he dragged in a reference to his wife. They both lowered their voices and became really confidential. Was he seeking some off-the-record advice, Charlotte wondered. Or was he telling her how adequately intelligent people could solve intimate problems?

Sidney Miller was well into his second post-dinner drink. His hair was a little rumpled, and he had a tendency to repeat himself. He explained carefully to his hostess that so many people misunderstood about an old bachelor. Some of them thought he played the field. Some thought worse things than that. But really it could be that a bachelor was a confirmed idealist, a man who refused to settle for second-best. Charlotte listened and agreed. Once she went so far as to murmur, "It's a mistake to suppose that people are all alike. There must be more than one reason why a man should remain unmarried. For all that I know to the contrary, there may be almost as many reasons for celibacy as there are celibates." That set him off again. And if he slurred a little on the word "celibate," well, this was no lingering remnant of the bluenose organization.

That left Joe Hiestand to partner Helene Coulter. Charlotte wasn't eavesdropping, of course, but she couldn't help catching fragments of the conversation. Helene wasn't complaining now about the hardships of her lot; she was telling him about all the interesting books she had been associated with and all the important people she knew. Joe listened and nodded and made short appreciative comments. Really, that was all very nice. It was very nice indeed. Charlotte was glad that they were hitting it off so well.

The party was a great success. Her first New York party. It meant that she was really at home in New York. She belonged here. This was a lovely place to be. This was a lovely way to feel.

Charlotte again turned her attention to Sidney Miller. He was saying, "I've been disappointed so many times, in so many different ways. Perhaps sometimes it was I who did the disappointing."

"Don't think about that," Charlotte soothed. "Think about here and now. That's what counts."

"Here, with you. Now, late on a lovely evening. I must sound ungrateful, growling about my past. I may have been disappointed, but you can't tell what I've been spared."

"That's a much better way to feel about it," Charlotte agreed. Was it always easy to be cheerful about other people's troubles? Anyhow she had soothed her guest. He took one more slow sip at his drink, and repeated, "Here with you—and your good friends."

In the silence Charlotte could hear the other two couples going on. Sam Groom was laughing at something that Jean Cochran had said. Joe Hiestand commented to Helene Coulter, "Well, that was droll." Over the quiet in the apartment Charlotte could hear the murmur of the city far below, subdued and intermittent at this hour, but always there. Always strangely, and blessedly, *there*.

Then Jean cried, "Twenty minutes before!" Helene chimed in, "Twenty minutes after!" They both laughed. Helene turned to her hostess to say, "Did you have that superstition when you were a child? That if a sudden silence fell, it was always either twenty minutes before the hour or twenty minutes after?"

Charlotte hadn't had, and started to change the subject. But attention had been called to the time; that was the signal for departure. They finished their drinks, and Sidney Miller had just a splash more. They stirred about the room, and talked to other people. But they did not sit down again. The evening was drawing toward its close.

Sidney and Sam said they would see the ladies home. "Very sweet of you," Helene jeered, "since it's only an elevator stop out of your way." Sidney protested that he hadn't known that.

Sam said, "The offer would have held good even if they had lived in the Bronx—or in Brooklyn."

"Brooklyn and the Bronx are part of New York, really," Jean Cochran pointed out. "But to so many people 'New York' means simply Manhattan Island."

"Provincialism," Charlotte said with a smile. "But then, I'm a provincial myself."

"Maybe so," Sam Groom agreed. "And a provincial from the provinces is nothing like as bad—or as good—as a proper Bostonian. Oh, I know, 'The home of the bean and the cod, where the Lowells speak only to the Cabots, and the Cabots speak only to God.' But for genuine provincialism, recommend me to the Philadelphia Social Register."

"Oh, Sam, must you?" Helene groaned. "Just when everybody was having such a good time!"

They donned their wraps. The two couples took off together. The door was still open, and they were walking down the public hall, but Joe Hiestand lingered for a word with Charlotte. "I wouldn't want to be the fifth wheel," he explained softly. As if he couldn't have gone out ahead of them! But Charlotte was pleased that he hadn't.

He swung the door almost shut behind him. Then he

faced her to say, "It was such a beautiful party, Lottie lady. It still is."

"Oh, thank you for saying so, Bill!" Charlotte whispered. "Thank you a thousand times for saying so." It wasn't until an instant after the words were out that she realized what had happened. She had called one man by another man's name. This wasn't Bill Andrews, her dear husband. This was Joe Hiestand, her pick-up. That big old silly Joe Hiestand, who always took so much for granted.

Joe had caught her slip; he grinned, but he said nothing. Charlotte would have liked to pass it over, but she could feel her color rising. She sailed past him, snatched the doorknob out of his hand, and said haughtily and a little too loud, "Good night, Mr. Hiestand. Mr. Joseph Hiestand."

"Good night, Lottie lady," he said and went off down the hall whistling. The tune was "Good Night, Sweetheart," and he whistled very well.

Charlotte banged the door and bolted it. She took the empty glasses out to the kitchen, poured herself a drink of ice water, turned out a few lights. Then she sat down and drew a long breath. A breath of satisfaction. A breath of fulfillment.

She belonged here. But she might just as well have belonged in Atlanta. Or in Des Moines. Or in San Francisco. Or in almost any fair city of our great and glorious country, if she had gone there to settle down and make new friends and begin life again on her own. It was not the city which mattered so much; all cities had their strong points. What mattered was the freedom of choice and the willingness to avail herself of that choice, the ability to start all over and work things out for herself and to make new friends who would like her for herself alone, not because she was Charlotte Emerson of the Saylesboro Emersons or Mrs. William Andrews of Andrews Motors.

And as for that Joe Hiestand—! Bill indeed! If her mind had run that way, there were as good fish in the sea as ever came out of it. But Charlotte wasn't thinking about a fishing expedition. At her age, and in her circumstances, the thing to do was stay on dry land, and if she really wanted fish, buy it at a proper market, and have her faithful handmaiden cook it, and see that just the right things were served with it.

She rose presently and set about her bedtime preparations. She was just pleasantly tired, and now that her party excitement was wearing off, she was beginning to feel sleepy. A curious thing, sleep. We all needed it. We devoted about a third of our lives to it. Some of us had partners and some of us slept alone. Yet nobody understood the exact nature of the phenomenon. Nobody needed to understand it, either. The experience was enough.

Behold Charlotte Andrews, then, ready for bed: clean, sleek, as properly turned out in a different way as she had been when she prepared to receive her guests Sunday at six. And now it was getting on toward one o'clock, and Monday morning was officially here, though for Charlotte it was never Monday morning until she had had her Sunday sleep. Here was her wide, comfortable bed, the bed which she had bought especially for this new home of hers. For a parting moment Charlotte stood and looked down at the night-time city. Then she established herself, and pulled the warm, light covers over her, and stretched out luxuriously.

An instant later she caught herself humming "Good Night, Sweetheart." As soon as she realized what she was doing, she stopped. But then she moved to the other side of the bed and began again. This time she kept it up to the end. After all, there was nobody here to tell her what she should or should not do. Nobody. Nobody whatever. What was more, there never would be. Never.

❧ 6 ❧

CHARLOTTE DIDN'T STIR out of the apartment Monday. A late rising, a hot tub followed by a cold shower and cold chicken were the order of the day. This was in a sense a letdown, but it did give her a chance to get her breath back. It was wonderful to have some time to oneself. Small children didn't feel that way about it; they even took favorite toys to bed with them to keep them company in the dark. Wild animals ran in packs. "The girls" lived together in the Gamma Delta house or congregated in some similar way. But when you were older you welcomed a chance to sit apart and think things over. Of course you did. Nobody with a particle of pride or common sense liked to live in somebody else's pocket. Charlotte might stand and look down at the darkening street and watch the crowds moving there. But it wasn't because she was lonesome. Certainly not! It was because she liked to stand apart, and watch, and think.

Her twilight meditation was interrupted by a phone call. It was Helene Coulter, to thank her for the lovely party. "Sometimes I bring work home with me; that's part of my job. Sometimes I bring worries home. Who doesn't? But last night I forgot everything except your wonderful home and your fine friends. Oh, and Mamie Lee's fried chicken! I thought I had tasted fried chicken before, but it was only hay and sawdust in comparison."

"Mamie Lee's fried chicken is special," Charlotte agreed. "I can fry chicken myself, but it's nothing like hers. Did your escorts go in with you?"

"Just long enough to be polite. A man always thinks he has to linger a minute inside the doorway, doesn't he?"

That was merely a random remark, of course, not intended as a hint or a dig, but Charlotte said with unnecessary sharpness, "I'm afraid you'll have to ask your friend Jean about that. She's the one who is acquainted with other people's psychology."

"I was just going to put her on the wire so she too can talk to you." There was the briefest possible pause; then Jean Cochran's voice took up, "That Sidney Miller of yours is quite an amiable drunk, isn't he? I offered him a hair of the dog that bit him, and he was all for taking it, but old prunes-and-prism Sam Groom reminded him that he had to be at the bank today."

"He hasn't such a hard job at the bank," Charlotte said. "I hope he made it all right."

Jean snickered. "He did. I looked in to make sure. He was right there sitting behind his big desk and looking very reserved and important."

"He slips behind that desk like an actor into his part," Charlotte observed. "He's quite a character in private life. Not a misunderstood husband, like so many others, but a misunderstood bachelor. Jean, how would it be if I put myself into his shoes and wrote an appeal to your column?"

"Do just that," urged Jean. "I'll answer it, and we can both wonder whether he will see that the shoe fits him."

Later in the evening it was Sam Groom who phoned Charlotte. His tone was a little chilly, like a high-school principal's who gets up to face a disorderly assembly room. "I gather that my esteemed housemate was very confidential with you last night. I hope he didn't say anything too far out of the way."

"He didn't give me any grounds to sue him for breach of promise, if that's what you mean," Charlotte said pertly. "Bachelors are handy people to have around, you know. They can always be counted on to fill in at a dinner party."

"Oh, your dinner party!" Sam branched out then into his little speech of thanks. Charlotte, listening politely and making suitable rejoinders, was thinking over the matrimonial status of the various people at her party. Quite a diversity, really. But she was the only genuine, unconverted widow among them. That was what she intended to remain. Of course nobody was inviting her to depart from that state. But it was just as well to know her own mind, in case anybody did.

So that was that. Mrs. Sanborn had made her little speech before she left. Everybody else was now accounted for. Everybody of any importance, that is. If silly old Joe Hiestand thought it mattered that he went down the hall whistling an old tune, well, she could just pretend she had never heard that tune before.

He hadn't called all evening, and she hadn't wanted him to call. Of course she hadn't. Maybe he had tried while someone else was on the line. Maybe he hadn't even tried. A fat lot she cared!

Then Tuesday afternoon he sent flowers. Her party flowers were beginning to look a little sad and needed rearranging; between the new and the not-so-new Charlotte spent a very happy half hour. It wasn't that she liked Joe

Hiestand all that much. But she liked flowers. And she liked gratitude.

Now the next move was hers. The motions in civilized society were like the movements in a minuet; everything must take its turn. She might sit down and write him a little note, though she had never done that before. She might call him, though she didn't much care about doing so. Or she might simply be ready with something to say the next time he called her. For she knew now that there would be a next time. He had simply "said it with flowers." But he was by no means tongue-tied, and the telephone company hadn't shut off his service for failure to pay the bills.

He called Wednesday afternoon and identified himself, "This is Joseph Hiestand, though people don't always call me that."

"Oh, I know, Joe! You have a name that abbreviates easily."

"Easy to remember, too, isn't it? Or isn't it?"

Charlotte ignored that, and proceeded to thank him for his flowers. "It's a very trivial acknowledgment," he assured her. "You went to all the trouble of entertaining me in your own home. I've seen you under many different circumstances. So often by shaded restaurant lights. Once as in a glass darkly—or was that the way you saw me?"

"I don't know what you're talking about, but go on anyhow. I'm listening."

"When a beautiful, gracious woman entertains in her own home, against her own chosen background, it makes a man grateful, and at the same time desirous. That is especially true when the woman is Lottie lady and the man is poor old Joe Hiestand."

"Thank you for the pretty speech, Joe. I still don't know what you're getting at."

"Won't you come out to dinner with me some night soon? When we are a little better acquainted, there is something very special I want to say to you."

"Better not, perhaps. Between a man and a woman, it's always safer to stick to generalities. Haven't you found it so?"

"It's a question of the particular woman, Lottie lady. Are you free for dinner Friday evening? Or perhaps dinner and the theater Saturday?"

They agreed on details, and made a date. Then he asked, "How good is your musical memory?"

"Good enough, I guess. I'm up to average in most things."

"Then would you recognize this tune?" He whistled the opening bars of "Good Night, Sweetheart."

"Why, of course!" Charlotte said promptly. "I've danced to it enough different times with enough different men; I ought to remember. It's 'The Beautiful Blue Danube.'"

Joe hung up.

Nevertheless, Charlotte looked forward to seeing him. It was flattering that he sought her out, and kept seeking her. He knew his way around the big city. He had money, and knew where and how to spend it. But he wasn't indispensable to her existence. He needn't think he was, just because she tolerated his existence—and had once made a silly slip of the tongue. She would show him just how far he could go, big old silly Joe Hiestand, who thought he was so smart.

She did like to argue with him. But that was no reason for tying herself down to a day-in, day-out—and perhaps night-long—argument. Charlotte didn't need a flesh-and-blood antagonist, anyhow; she could always sustain both sides of the dispute herself. Like this:

CHARLOTTE: It's better to let well enough alone.

ADVERSARY: But if I do let it alone, how can I tell whether it's well enough?

Or:

CHARLOTTE: Two it takes to make a quarrel, one can always end it.

ADVERSARY: Yes, but who is going to say which one will be that one?

It was like playing solitaire, in a way; you were out only to beat the game, and if you did succeed in beating the game, where did that get you? Still, there were worse pastimes than solitaire, and it was a game you could quit any time you wanted to.

They had a nice little dinner in still another place. This time Charlotte refrained from arguing and tried a new trick. Whenever Joe made a leading remark, she would roll her eyes at him and reply, "Really?" or "You don't say so!" Sometimes Joe ignored her words; sometimes he retorted, "Yes, really," or "Indeed I do say so." At least it was a new game, if not a particularly exciting one.

After dinner he asked, "Shall we continue our explorations?" When his companion again rolled her eyes at him, he elucidated, "Go out and cross a bridge? View little old Manhattan Island from still a different angle?"

Charlotte, still keeping in character, queried, "Is that what you would like to do?" It was, and they chose Manhattan Bridge this time. They rode for the most part in silence, and Charlotte stared out at the city scenery. Joe was similarly occupied, and their comments were few and brief. Twice when Charlotte glanced around at him she caught him gazing, not at the prospect, but at her. Once she smiled and jerked her thumb at the window. The other time she simply looked away again and moved farther into her own corner of the seat.

They returned through a city settling itself into that uneasy quiet which was the closest New York could ever come to repose. Charlotte turned to her escort to say in her sweetest tone, "That was so beautiful. All of it. I love the idea of a bridge anyhow: a bridge which you can cross, and then come back."

"Some other bridges are fine, too," Joe murmured back. "Once in a while there is a bridge which you cross, and go on from there."

"I'd rather not," Charlotte snapped. Then she remembered to get back into her act, and murmured, "Just as you say, not as I care."

When the taxi stopped in front of her building, Charlotte said, "It has been a lovely evening, *Joe*. I'll take all those beautiful sights to bed with me, and lie there wondering whether I am dreaming or remembering."

"There are lots of other places to go around New York," he reminded her. "For example, the Little Church Around the Corner, famous for weddings."

"I've been there, *alone*," Charlotte answered. For an instant her thoughts flew back to her own wedding day. It all seemed incredibly faint and far off, somehow. Almost as if it had happened to someone else.

"Thank you anyhow," she said as he helped her out of the cab. She didn't see what the silly fool was grinning about, but if he wanted to go around behaving like a Cheshire cat, that was his business.

Just inside the door of her apartment she turned to bid him good night. She drew off her gloves when she did so, of course. She still felt that a handshake through all that leather was no contact at all. But instead of grasping her extended right hand, Joe possessed himself of the other. "Do you want to lend me one of these as a gauge of size?" he asked. "Or would you rather come along when we pick out *ours?*"

"I don't know what you're talking about," Charlotte insisted. But her telltale color betrayed her.

"I've often wondered what happened to those discards," he went on. "Do they land in the safety deposit box in the bank? And how long do they stay there?"

"You have a lot more information on such subjects than I do," she reminded him.

"I've learned from bitter experience as well as from sweet. The point is, I *have* learned." He had both her hands now. He pressed them firmly; his enclosing hands were warm and strong. Then he raised them to his lips and kissed them. Still holding them, he leaned toward her face. Charlotte hastily turned a cheek. He kissed it obediently, but he laughed softly when he did so. Charlotte realized once more that he was getting the better of her. Or was she being defeated from within? She was behaving as awkwardly as a teen-ager at her first dance, she who had floated through so many dances with so many different men.

He was going now, making an effective exit, according to his wont. He was whistling, too, but he had changed his tune. This time the melody was "Annie Laurie." He had more than one tune in his repertory, more than one string to his bow. She would say this much for silly old Joe Hiestand: he might be a nuisance, but he was not a bore.

That night Charlotte undressed as slowly and carefully as ever. Perhaps even a little more slowly than usual, as if she didn't want the evening to end. Then at the very last moment, with her bed lying open and inviting, and her mind divided between satisfaction and a curious lingering unrest, she did a strange thing. She took off her engagement ring and laid it away in her jewel case. She didn't quite know why she did it. It didn't amount to anything anyhow. But she wasn't accountable to anybody for what she did. Perhaps it was just as well that she wasn't!

In the middle of the night it seemed to her that she was being driven onto a very long bridge. There was a man in the car beside her. He was humming "Love's Old Sweet Song." Charlotte did not turn to look at him, but it made her happy to have him there.

Then the bridge stretched on and on. At the other end of it was nothing but darkness. Frightened, Charlotte turned toward her companion. But she couldn't see him, either, in the spreading gloom. And he wasn't singing now; he was growling like an angry dog.

Charlotte woke suddenly, with the chill of nightmare still on her. At first she could not remember where she was, and when she switched on her bedside lamp, the room looked strange to her, and somehow forbidding. Then as recollection returned, she snuggled deeper in bed and smiled. Joe Hiestand might be flattered if he learned that she was dreaming about him, but less so if he learned the contents of the dream.

What was it that Old Pop Freud had said, back in the days when he was the one who laid down the law? "Every dream involves wish fulfillment." It couldn't be that she wished Joe Hiestand were right beside her, here and now. And that long, dark, uncertain future—surely that was a warning?

Sometimes her bedroom did seem a little lonesome—and the whole apartment, when she was here alone at night, awfully big and quiet. But there was nothing so terrible about that. She could always turn on her bedside radio, or read for an hour or two, or raid the refrigerator. She wouldn't have had all that range of choice if she had had someone with her at these odd hours. It was better to endure a little loneliness than to forfeit one's independence. Besides, a woman of Charlotte's years and experience must know that nectar and ambrosia come to us mortals only once, if they come at all. We were supremely lucky later on if we got Mamie Lee Jackson's fried chicken. A two-year-old child might cry for the moon. When you reached what were laughingly called the years of discretion, it behooved you to count your blessings.

Charlotte switched off her light and moved into the middle of the bed. She was dozing off when the thought occurred to her, *At least this wasn't the same bed. Not the same bed where she had slept with Bill.* She was too sleepy to figure out the meaning of the notion, but somehow she found it vaguely comforting.

Going about her daily affairs next morning, Charlotte felt the need of advice. So many times when people asked for advice, what they really wanted was approval. Still, it did help to formulate your problem. Jean Cochran had told Charlotte that in so many words. It was Jean's job to encourage people to do that.

But it was not to Jean that Charlotte turned. It was to Jean's housemate, Helene Coulter, who had had the experience which made her an authority on this one particular question. Charlotte managed to edge Helene aside over the neighborly popcorn, and inquired, "Do you mind if I ask you something?"

Helene smiled. "I'm not likely to resent anything you ask me. If I should, I can always invoke the Fifth Amendment."

"It's simply this: which is better, to do a thing and wish you hadn't done it, or to refrain from it and then wish you had gone ahead?"

"That's an easy question. Go ahead and do it. If you fail,

you fail. But at least you won't have to go on all the rest of your life haunted by a lingering doubt."

"Helene honey, you *have* helped. Thank you so very much."

"Always glad to be of service." This time Helene's smile broadened. "He really is a nice guy, Charlotte. Both Jean and I like him."

Charlotte soon accepted another date with Joe Hiestand. She again put on the engagement ring that Bill Andrews had given her. If she should decide to lay it away some day, it wouldn't be in a deposit box. She would send it and its companion to her daughter, Pauline, who seemed to be wedded to her career, but who was capable of making wise independent decisions. Let Pauline decide what was to be done in this case.

This time Charlotte and Joe covered the Triborough Bridge. Charlotte did not have any distressing dreams afterward. And this time she offered her cheek for his kiss as if it were already an established custom.

Then came one more dinner at a restaurant. When they had finished Joe said, "Another taxi ride tonight, Lottie lady? Or shall we just sit and talk a while?"

"There's no point in always enriching the taxi industry," Charlotte decided. "Let's just sit and talk—a few minutes."

"When we get married," Joe went on, "we might have the ceremony at the Little Church Around the Corner, and then breakfast at the Waldorf."

"The arrangements are usually left up to the bride," Charlotte reminded him a bit primly.

"Then you are going ahead—?" His face lighted up; there for a minute he looked strangely and touchingly young.

"That seems to be the only way to get rid of you," Charlotte said. "There, Joe honey, I didn't mean that the way it sounded. But you must be used to my saucy speeches by this time."

"I enjoy your quick answers, yes. And I always love the way you look when you turn up your nose at me."

"We can at least try being engaged for a while. And don't feel you have to bankrupt yourself at Tiffany's." Slowly and almost shyly, Charlotte drew off the diamond solitaire which another man had placed on her finger so many years ago.

Tonight their farewell in her apartment was tender and lingering. Toward the final moment he whispered, "It won't be long now until I can stay." He went down the hall whistling, and this time his theme was the Wedding March: "Here Comes the Bride."

So Charlotte turned back once more into an apartment empty of companionship but big with promise. She wandered around for a while, dazed, incredulous, happy as she had supposed she never could be happy again. Then she went to her bedroom, divested herself of her hat and shoes, and shook her hair loose about her ears. A glass of water, of course, and a final trip to make sure that the clocks were wound. One more look at herself in the bedroom mirror. Then slowly, inevitably, she turned to her clothes closet. From the remotest corner she produced Bill Andrews' old dressing gown.

She stood there caressing it. This was a moment of supreme understanding. If circumstances had been reversed and she had been the one to go, would she have wanted Bill to live on in a state of aching loneliness? Never! This way he belonged to her in a special sense, and always would. Her dear, dear Bill, who had never begrudged her anything. Her Bill, who would always be with her, even when she went on into the new love which was only a fulfillment and fruition of the old.

The city was so quiet now. And right here at the beating heart of it, she felt herself being soothed into peace. Peace, and happiness, and hope.

Corbett, Elizabeth
Sunday at six.

7-72